Previous volumes in the Spoon Knife series

The Spoon Knife Anthology: Thoughts on Compliance, Defiance, and Resistance
> Edited by N.I. Nicholson and Michael Scott Monje, Jr.

Spoon Knife 2: Test Chamber
> Edited by Dani Alexis Ryskamp and Sam Harvey

Spoon Knife 3: Incursions
> Edited by Nick Walker and Andrew M. Reichart

Spoon Knife 4: A Neurodivergent Guide to Spacetime
> Edited by B. Allen and Dora M. Raymaker with N.I. Nicholson

Spoon Knife 5:
Liminal

Edited by

Andrew M. Reichart, Dora M. Raymaker, and Nick Walker

Weird Books for Weird People

Contents

Foreword

The Spoon Knife anthology is a peculiar sort of animal. Most anthologies stay more or less within the bounds of some specific genre: sci-fi, horror, erotic supernatural western, whatever. Not so with Spoon Knife. The rules governing this series are loose and few:

- Each annual volume has a different combo of editors, who choose that volume's theme.
- We seek submissions that engage creatively with the volume's theme while in some way or another also touching on the themes of queerness or neurodivergence or both.
- Beyond that, anything goes, as long as the editors decide it works.

Within any given volume of Spoon Knife, one can find science fiction and dark magical realism side-by-side with poetry and memoir. Sometimes when one begins reading a piece it's nigh-impossible to determine what its genre will turn out to be, and sometimes when one reaches the end of the piece one still can't be sure.

The theme we chose this time around was a single word: *liminal.* In this fifth volume of Spoon Knife you'll find tales of thresholds and transitions, entry points and crossings-over, states of in-betweenness, things that lurk at the edges of memory or awareness or reality. We hope each reader will run across something or other in these pages that extends the edges of their own reality at least a little bit further.

Nick Walker

September 2020

Somewhere on the Border

Andrew M. Reichart

The Passenger

Beth appears on the other side of my desk. My troublemaker intern, who tries to dance with the catatonics. She says something about a dance therapist coming to see Miss Fechs.

"Dance therapist," I repeat. "Sounds like a wingnut."

"She's from Berkeley," she says.

"I rest my case."

She claims I have agreed to this some time ago. I have only a vague recollection of such a conversation. I remind her that she is only an intern. I tell her she needs to focus on mastering her understanding of legitimate therapies. For the hundredth time I voice my legal concerns over her attempts to dance with the patients. I remind her that Miss Fechs has an unidentified *chorea*, neither Huntington's nor Sydenham's, and the use of experimental therapies would be irresponsible, even for me. Finally, I remind Beth that she is just an intern.

Beth fumes at me. At noon, we stand at the door to the padded room of Christina Fechs with a woman who introduced herself as Ishtar, "Dance Therapist and Shamanic Counselor." Ishtar wears a necklace of huge turquoise stones, and around her hangs a cloud of what I thought was patchouli.

"No, sandalwood, of course," she replied. Of course.

We look in at Miss Fechs, the woman who never stops dancing. Who never speaks, who shows no recognition of her family. I hear Ishtar use the word "energy" and jot the word down on my note pad. Beneath it I write "soul retrieval," trying not to wince. Ishtar states that the patient's energy is "out of balance." I tick a hash mark next to the word "energy" every time she uses it. She offers the observation that the patient's movements are not harmful to her joints or spine, and therefore, "The spirit possessing her appears basically benevolent."

I catch Beth's eye and give her the fiercest reprimand I can without opening my mouth.

"It looks like the spirit is trying to communicate through movement," says Ishtar.

"Really?" I ask, struggling to keep my tone polite. "What is she saying?"

"It's not literal language," she replies.

I roll my eyes and glare at Beth again.

"But look at that pleading motion," Ishtar continues. "She's frustrated. She's asking us for help."

I thank Ishtar for her expertise, get rid of her as quickly as I can manage, and tell Beth to meet me in my office.

Beth is a nice girl. I did a soul retrieval for her after she was assaulted and her nightmares stopped. But I wish she'd warned me that her boss was such a stiff, Mother Mary. He means well, but look at those shoulders, boy, scrunching around your heart chakra. What are you so scared of? Tsk. What you need is a little fresh air and sunshine, my dear. Get out of this office, get out of this hospital.

I'm going to have to keep my speaking on a tight rein with this guy. He's the type that thinks you're a wingnut if you drop the word "energy" once.

Walking down the hall, aum, aum, try not to hate hospitals. Don't judge them for the money thing, don't judge them for the science thing. I find myself ogling the sickest aura zones like someone rubbernecking a car crash. Cold. So cold.

Christina's room is padded, but mercifully she is not restrained.

Oh Lords of Light, look at this poor creature. What a dancer! My heart sings to behold her. I turn to Beth and she's looking at me, smiling, knowing I understand. *Thank you* I mouth to her. She blinks and smiles and our eyes well up.

I watch the patient dance. She looks rapturous. But her aura is in torment. *Why?* I watch her pleading, opening her heart, opening her heart to us. What is she struggling with?

A twin aura!

From: b.ali@psych.berkeley.edu
To: r.weiser@psych.berkeley.edu
Subject: Re: duh, beth

Yea I knew Doc Smith would think Ishtar's a wingnut, but if he could just listen to her. Obviously there's no such thing as "spirit possession" or whatever, it's just a metaphor for a neurological imbalance we don't have scientific measurements for yet. But I know what she did for me.

I'm a scientist too dammit!! Just because I'm a student doesn't mean I can't think, and obviously Ishtar is able to see something he can't. All he does is write mean notes on his pad and show them to me.

He doesn't even dance, I have no idea why he's working with Tina. He has no intuition for her whatsoever. She would be freaking out and hurting herself like she used to if I wasn't dancing with her. Tina is so lonely! But Doc wants me to stop because there could be goddamn legal trouble with the goddamn patient's family if they find out. Legal trouble?? I'm the only f'n family that poor girl has, this whole system is FUCKED!! I'm not sure I can do this. Beth

I plead and again he ignores me. *Help me with this guilt!* I roll this body's head in frustration, around, around, what else can I do to show him? I roll the head and moan up from deep in the abyss in its chest: Oh. Oh. *Dance! Cleanse me of the guilt of killing my host's mind!* I plead. He stares at me, cold, clenched, brittle. Why will he not move? He tightens everything connected to his spine, coils his body down upon his fingertips, where he scratches, scratches, scratching jagged black lines. Why does he choose his jagged black lines over me? Am I worth less than a jagged black line?

He finishes his scribble and leaves me isolated in my cell, alone with my guilt. *How could I know your species have such fragile brains? I was the first of my people to come here!* Through the walls I sense faintly the malaise of troubled hearts.

The man returns, the man who does not know he has a body. *If only you knew what it was like to really not have a body,* I gesture at him. He does not even blink. I open the mouth wide and moan. I shake the head and turn away from him and turn, turn, spiraling inward with one finger, parodying his scratching, trying to smooth it from a nasty jagged line into a loving spiral. *Please love your body,* I think at him, casting glances out of the corners of each eye as I turn. *Please come join me in this world. Dance like you have a body!*

Oh, behind him comes the young woman who dances with me! But she stands behind the stiff man, hiding her heart from me, her limbs still. Here is another woman. Such a woman! Bedecked in blue rocks, blue like this world's sky! Sky woman, with your heart so wide, please come dance, please! I have been so lonely, I never imagined such loneliness! Please!

The sky woman stands in the doorway, shining at me with her heart. She stands still. I can see her longing to come dance, yet she stands still! Oh, wounded planet! I circle my head, I circle my head.

Andrew M. Reichart lives in California with his wife and a couple of dogs. He is author of the psychedelic science fiction novel *Wallflower Assassin*, now available from Argawarga Press in an illustrated second edition; and the *City of the Watcher* fantasy trilogy, coming in 2021 in a single volume edition illustrated by Tim Molloy. Andrew also co-writes with Nick Walker the webcomic *Weird Luck*, beautifully illustrated by Mike Bennewitz and serialized at weirdluck.net.

Brett Gaffney

In My Dreams I Find Them Dead

I always find them first.

Sometimes the reveal is a red ghost.

Sometimes they wait in their beds.

But it's not that Snow White sleep.

I know the way her mouth hangs open still,
I know there's something cold
in his skin already,
before I even touch him.

And then what?

How do I hold the phone
in my hands when I call for help?

Like a child?

Like a broken window?

Like a white rat, its tail curling

around my fingers until I choke it dead?

How do I make words out of this sunset?

Break Room Gossip

*I think Mark is fucking the zombie chick
from room four*, says the woman
with the knife buried in her chest.

Shit, really? her friend asks, long cigarette
balanced between her bloody fingers,
contacts the color of harvest moons.
*Sorry honey. How long you two been
together? A year or so, right?*

Three. She sighs, the weight of the blade
resting too near her heart. *Three years
and he just – oh baby your tit is coming off.*

Stabbing victim helps yellow eyes
with her rotten prosthetic breast, fastens
it back on with a safety pin, gentle as a mother.

Because that's what they do every night,
keep each other from falling to pieces.

At least until the show is over.

M. Brett Gaffney holds an MFA in Poetry from Southern Illinois University. Her poems have appeared in Exit 7, Rust+Moth, Permafrost, museum of americana, South Dakota Review, Moon City Review, Apex Magazine, Tahoma Literary Review, and Zone 3, among others, and her chapbook Feeding the Dead (Porkbelly Press) was nominated for a 2019 Elgin Award from the Science Fiction and Fantasy Poetry Association. She works as co-editor of Gingerbread House Literary Magazine.

Cody Goodfellow

Burning Names

When they needed to score and all their old marks were played out, Roshawn and Aida went shoulder-fishing at the County Clerk's. Aida was too tweaked to keep the numbers straight and stop picking at her face, today, so Roshawn fished alone. Aida was better with people, better at stealing, better at all of it, until she got like this.

An old man caught Roshawn looking on with her lips still moving as she read his social off his form request. She ducked out before he could alert the security guard, streaked across the lot and into the dent-resistant side of a brand-new Volvo wagon with kids and groceries in the back and a mom in a soccer coach outfit, and a fancy white leather purse, more expensive than all the things anyone had ever bought for her in her life, put together.

It was the purse that Roshawn studied as she jumped back from the coasting Swedish shuttle, not the screaming kids or the oblivious mom. It was the purse, which was sitting on the roof. She jogged after the car as it sped up and, to her delight, turned down the side street where she'd left Aida in her shit-box Fiero. She saw the driver's head turn and notice Roshawn in her mirror, dropped back so she wouldn't stop. *Go on, bitch, don't worry about me, go back to La Mesa.*

She broke into a run, rounded the corner and skidded to

a stop as twenties blew by her on the dank afternoon breeze.

Aida danced down the middle of the street, snatching bills out of the air and laughing. "D'you believe this? You say praying don't work, then what's this shit?" Swinging from one skinny claw, the purse.

Aida smoked cigarettes as she counted bills like she was sucking venom out of a snakebite, "Three C's and change," but she counted again. "Let's go see Hector."

Roshawn's nerves danced, sparks of autonomic joy sending the Fiero bouncing across the lanes on the eastbound 8. "The cards be trash by the time we get Hector out of bed," Roshawn said. "Use your head, that shit makes you so stupid. We max 'em out with a quickness and blow town. That was the plan if we got a fat one..."

"This bitch on the vapors. She lose her head, if it ain't tied on. We fry her now, she lock up the castle and call out the feds. She too hot now, but she on the vapors, like I said. She cancel these, get new ones in the mail. We don't need her cards. We've got *her*. We ghost her, and ride her to the next level."

Roshawn and Aida had burned more people than they could hope to count, but in short, sharp shocks. Card dips, picked pockets, mail shakedowns, small schemes Roshawn learned from Aida. They sold numbers and papers to the Trashman, who prowled the rich condo dumpsters. But Aida wanted to slow-burn this bitch herself, something they'd talked about, but never got the nerve to do.

"We could bleed her so long, we be livin' her life before she saw we took it."

Roshawn pouted, but she turned away from the mall.

Roshawn came from poor Tennessee Navy trash, stranded in San Diego by a dishonorable discharge, and grew up in the ghetto. She had to learn to pass for black, though she was abysmally white, with the close hazel eyes, ash-blond hair and awful dentition of the Scotch-Irish mountainfolk who paid for passage to America as indentured servants before slaves were imported from Africa. Mimicry was survival for as long as she could remember, but Aida showed her how to make a living at it.

As to where Aida came from, Roshawn had learned little that stayed the same from one telling to the next, and she was smart enough to see how Aida's lessons gave the lie to it all. *Know what your mark knows, let them see you're part of their world, and nothing more.*

When they first met, Aida's own stories of hardship as a military brat, of abuse at the hands of men, rang true, and bonded Roshawn to her. Overjoyed to find she didn't have to choose the lesser of masculine evils, thrilled to find someone who understood her, she didn't notice for a long time how much Aida had changed her.

In her more lucid moments, Roshawn guessed that the essential Aida must be whatever she was slowly changing Roshawn into, but she remained passive, fascinated. Becoming *anything* was better than what she'd been. She learned how to play men and women, straight, solid types who could draw cash on a credit card without getting the stink-eye from the manager. In between, she learned how to be hard and blank, to partake of the empty rituals of addiction without hope of pleasure, to endure the ugliest underside of life without pain or fear. It was a better life than she could have made, on her own.

They picked up three eight-balls of crank from Hector, but Aida swept into the bedroom, stripping off her clothes, and crashed on the waterbed. Roshawn sank in beside her, as close as she dared, wary of Aida's feverish glow. The arid heat redoubled and cooked the sweat out of her naked body. Roshawn longed to touch her, but feared waking her up. This wasn't normal, this kind of sleep, and she feared breaking it.

She lowered her head to the hollow between Aida's tiny breasts and lapped at the rivulets of sweat, tasting the smoke and ammonia and ether of crystal meth, and something else she had always figured was the true essence of Aida, because she could not guess what else it might be. For a minute, she thought she knew the real Aida, and was happy.

Roshawn didn't know how long Aida had been sleeping with the driver's license under her pillow. She changed the sheets whenever they stole new ones, because neither of them liked to do laundry.

It was no kind of betrayal that Roshawn could explain, but it derailed her cleaning binge and got her taking things apart, and that was how she found the books.

"What's all this shit?" she barked, when Aida breezed in from shopping.

Aida, confused, got defensive about the flock of gossamer shopping bags that seemed to float around her like balloons. Before Aida could stroke her, Roshawn charged her with the fattest of the books, something called the *Tibetan Book Of The Dead*. "What're you *reading* for? Why are you keeping shit from me?"

Aida took the book and pocketed the license. "Haven't you ever thought about your soul?"

Roshawn went slack. She hadn't even looked inside them. Books were for learning how to do things, and if the books were a secret, then what was she learning?

"These souls we got now, they pretty beat-up, Ro."

Roshawn looked into Aida's eyes, lost in the way the golden mandalas in her irises seemed to burn and turn when she operated. "We could stop..."

"We'd still be us, wouldn't we? Still damned, just starving, too."

Why did *she* feel like the one who was hiding something? "We could change..."

Aida smirked, mute shorthand for helpless recognition

of how dumb Roshawn was. "Ain't you heard of predestination? God knows everything, from the beginning to how it's all gonna turn out. So no matter what you do, if your name's not in the book, you never get saved. God made you, so He knows you can't change."

Roshawn tried the smirk, but only felt dumber. "Where'd you get all this shit?"

"Daddy was a righteous Calvinist. After a good Sunday-go-to-meetin' beatin', he used to tell me about the Elect––that's the saved ones. Since God knew how Daddy'd turn out in the end, he could do what he did to me, and still go to judgment with a clean conscience. This is *their* world, Ro. We just live here."

Roshawn snorted a line to keep from laughing. "So you're one of the Elect?"

"Hell no. Nothing in the Lord's big book about Daddy knocking up a whore in the Philippines who could track him down in the States. Daddy used to say I had no soul, anyhow. They do give you a lift, though, knowing you judged and damned, whatever you do. Everything's free, you know?"

"No judgment you need to fear, but mine, girl." Roshawn tried to look as brave as the words sounded.

Aida's long acrylic nails tickled the tender scalp of Roshawn's cornrow braids. "So *I* belong to *you*, now?"

Later, when Aida showed her the new ID with her picture and the mark's name, she was too stoned in love to care. Aida had only to look at her that way, that said she knew who and what Roshawn really was, and could bear to keep looking, though she would never, ever tell what she saw.

A week later, the cards came. A Titanium Visa, Platinum American Express and, just for laughs, a Discover. They moved into a decent one-bedroom condo and bought new furniture: solid modern black lacquered oak, not like the flimsy particle-board Ikea shit that fell apart every time they had a fight.

And fight they did, as soon as the furniture was delivered. Roshawn was edgy, tweaking for two days, and Aida, she suddenly realized, hadn't touched any in a week, hadn't even lit a cigarette. They had it out until Roshawn's anger, under Aida's careful husbandry, mutated into lust.

"Why'd you have to tear my clothes?" Aida asked, after.

"To get at you," Roshawn answered, but the lie had no legs. These clothes made her mad—frothy pastel floral prints, soccer-mom country club togs. Aida dressed like the mark, shopped in the same stores, cutting the game too close. She didn't care if Roshawn didn't like it, wanted her not to. Roshawn could steal, she could lie, and on a good day she could pass for a Wal-Martian credit-slave, but Aida could put on quality with or without the clothes. If Roshawn could get her hands on the thing that could enable Aida to leave her behind, she would gleefully rip it to shreds and eat it.

"D'you want to go out?"

"No," Roshawn moaned.

"Well, I do." Aida squirmed out from under her, skinned into fresh clothes and was gone.

Roshawn made herself look at the books. It wasn't even that they were hidden. Books, written words in any configuration, made her feel stupid and mean.

They were about souls, but not like Aida talked about. A couple of them were religious stuff, about good works and sin and prayer and salvation, but these were outnumbered and outweighed by the others––science books, the kind Roshawn hated most. A head-shrinker book said the soul was an illusion, but a very real one, while another book by a brain-mechanic said that the soul was an energy field made by the brain and DNA, and a third was full of poetry about the soul and its hiding places in the heart, the eyes and the brain.

Roshawn chopped out rails and snorted until her eyes teared up and she forgot most of what she'd read.

She thought Aida was going to clubs, or maybe to Hector's, because she hadn't dented her share of the crank. Whatever she was doing––and in their time, she had caught Aida doing *everything*––Roshawn could forgive, but what she saw when she followed her one night, she couldn't even comprehend.

Aida left her Fiero at the curb and walked down another block to a Volvo station wagon with Avis plate frames. Roshawn huddled behind a bush until the silver wagon's frosty high-beams died away, then ran back to the apartment for the spare keys to the Fiero.

She wasn't hard to catch. She drove so slow she might have been on the links, looking for a lost golf ball. Roshawn dropped back. The Volvo only went another few blocks to the outlet mall, where Aida parked in the front of the enormous, empty lot and just sat there. For an hour.

Roshawn shivered and scratched, sure Aida had spotted her, wondering why she didn't just come over and call her on it. *Because she can't,* came an unaccustomed rational judgment. *Because she's not Aida, right now––*

When the Volvo finally pulled out, Roshawn had almost fallen asleep. Her feet prickled with oxygen-starvation, the crank stealing all the blood from her extremities, but she made the little shitbox car go into gear and slipped in behind the crawling wagon.

She followed it to the park next, where it stopped beside the soccer field for another hour. Roshawn resisted charging the car and finding out what the fuck was going on, but she felt the old numbness washing over it all, every bad or inexplicable thing in her life getting cemented over so it seemed normal.

She loved Aida. She'd never told her, and never would, but Aida knew it, used it, wrung it dry. She'd never been this close to anyone, though, and wasn't about to fuck it up like everything else. When the Volvo started up again and pulled out into the street, Roshawn forced herself to turn around and go back to the apartment. Whenever she got home, they would figure out what was what.

Lying in wait in the dark, Roshawn snapped into action when the arc-sodium lamplight from outside spilled in the open door. She'd tossed the condo, found more books, more things she never knew Aida had bought. She took the book in her hand--on making mummies, of all fucking crazy things, not the heaviest, but slim and wide, lots of pictures--and pulled a muscle in her shoulder throwing it at the silhouette in the doorway.

The book met flesh with a pulpy crack and a scream that raised goosebumps of joy on Roshawn's skin before she realized she didn't recognize her victim's voice.

"What the fuck?" Aida shouted and flicked on the lights. She stood behind the woman Roshawn had hit--the mark. She wore sea-foam green silk pajamas and a matching wrap that looked like very expensive smoke. Her hands were tied behind her back with nylon rope, and duct tape covered her mouth. Her eyes were red and streaming, and her nose was crushed to the right and just starting to bleed.

"What's going on, Aida? What the fuck, girl--"

"Time to take it to the next level, Ro." Aida led the crying woman to the dining room and sat her on one of the new chrome and black leather barstools. "She can't help us any more, like she is."

"What do you want with her?"

Aida flanked Roshawn into a corner of the room so she couldn't see the woman, could see nothing but Aida's hungry eyes. "It's no good anymore, Ro. This life... it's all make-believe, you know? We keep using her cards, in a couple months, they going to catch on, and we have to run, and start all over.

And you and me both got bench warrants, fucking cops know us both from all fucking day, girl. I'm sick of this shitty deal, Ro. I want what she got."

Aida backed up to the bound woman, beckoning Roshawn closer. She ran her fingers through mark's sweat-plastered hair. Her tongue flicked out and lapped a bead of blood from the end of her broken nose, a tear from her rolling, popping eyes.

Roshawn wanted to vomit fire. "Too far, Aida, this is way fucking past too far…"

Aida jerked her back by her braids. Cranked as she was, Roshawn was fast, but Aida paralyzed her with a gaze, stopping just short of crushing her windpipe. In the air before her eyes hung that promise, that knowledge, that Roshawn hungered for. That look told her she might just be more than a throwaway drug casualty, more than a shitty little thief, and Roshawn knew, by now, that the look was its own reward, a tool and no more, but still she couldn't look away. "We can use her body," Aida whispered. "We burn this place up with her in it, and get gone, and they think she's me. We go on, like born again, and all that shit you been trying to forget, you just shed it like old skin. Just roll it off you and start over, and we can be together, baby…"

Roshawn gave this a moment. "Bitch, you so stupid. You watch them detective shows, same as me. They always get dumbfucks who try to play that. They got DNA, no matter how burned up she is, they still won't take her for me, and you? You a *mutt*, Aida. She a purebred."

"I can fix it," Aida said, beaming, so proud. "Been fixing it.

DNA is just records. Just shit on computers. It's fixed."

"And don't we need *two* bodies?"

"Yeah, we do." Aida went behind the bar and chopped out some rocks on the beveled, mirrored top. "We'll go back out and get yours, right after, I got it lined up..." Aida bent and snorted manfully of the fat rails at the bar. Roshawn came up behind her, and the rich bitch was watching, so she ran her hands over Aida, feeling electricity rushing through her, and she wanted to taste it, to go down on Aida right now and show the bitch who she belonged to. But Aida twisted away and slipped her the straw.

Roshawn knew this was not a time to ponder the situation. It was time to be a bullet from a gun, a kamikaze pilot, until it was all done. She sucked up a line and switched nostrils for the next, slaloming through the remaining six before sitting back to savor the burn.

Aida was tying the woman to the barstool with more rope, and getting books out and setting them on the bar, and opening a brand new toolbox full of shiny things. Aida moved so fast she blurred into a green shimmering comet, and Roshawn realized she must be wearing the same green pajamas as their hostage, the Volvo lady who'd forget her head if it wasn't tied on––

Roshawn tried to get up, but slopped bonelessly onto the burgundy Stainmaster carpet.

"Are we going out, or not?" she tried to ask, but the rug muffled her words as she blacked out.

She dreamed that she saw part of what happened next.

Aida sat down before the woman, but really, she just appeared, because she'd been a blur, and all the books before her, and so many tools for ingesting drugs she'd never imagined existed, for doing things to people that even she had never been subjected to.

Aida shouted in the woman's face, but Roshawn couldn't hear it. The woman screamed and sobbed back until Aida shrugged and rocked back on the barstool.

When Aida did the drugs and picked up the other tools, the woman in the chair suddenly came to life, her arms scissoring the rope, the tape slipping away, but she did not try to escape, nor did Aida restrain her. What she saw was not their physical bodies, which hung motionless behind them like shadows of candlelight.

Aida stormed the mark with her tools. She scooped out both eyes with a peculiar notched spoon, and swallowed them like oysters. She seemed to meditate on their digestion for a moment, then, finding something wanting, dug deeper.

The fluttering shadows of the rich bitch mirrored Aida's movements so that they seemed to eat each other in a dead heat, the clatter and scrape of their feasting competing with the slurp and pop of stolen morsels fitting into place in their new bodies, only to be torn away and eaten again.

Roshawn tried to say or do something to stop it, but it just went on and on until they were identical, and then Aida ordered her to be a dog, and the woman echoed her command, and Roshawn was a dog, and rolled over and thanked Aida for letting her go to sleep.

She woke up in the middle of the hands-down best visual trip she'd ever had in her whole life, because the whole room was wreathed in dancing flames.

She realized with a start that she was on the waterbed, and she called for Aida to see if she could see it too, but her voice was so small before the roar of the vision. Roshawn reached out and tried to grab one of the blue-gold snakes slithering across the headboard of their week-old bed. Her hand went right through it, but her hand jerked back and slapped her face and the pain had so much to tell her about how hot, how very real, the fire was, that she could only scream as it got closer.

The flames raced up the frilly canopy like spiders. Burning shreds of lace fell on her and sent her into fresh spasms of screaming, but now she leapt off the bed and bolted from the room, clawing the cobwebs off her face and trying to remember where the front door was.

The living room proved more than she could handle. The woman still sat on the barstool, still hog-tied, but she must have been splashed with gasoline, for all the fire pouring out of her. She sat upright like a martyr, with no face and the light pouring out from her hollowed skull and cracked ribcage. Roshawn could only conclude that Aida had been unable, as always, to decide what she wanted or needed, and so took it all.

Now, the novelty value of the fire had completely worn

off, and Roshawn dove out the window and into the tasteful decorative landscaping.

The sad honk of the fire alarm brought sleepwalking adults and excited children out into the common area, but Roshawn was already gone, palming Aida's spare key to the Fiero under the bumper and peeling out for the suburbs.

She got three blocks away before the shock of it hit her, before what happened and what it meant blinded her with tears. She pulled over and gathered herself, slotting the new developments into her life. Then she started the car.

She almost didn't find it. The cul-de-sacs and twisting, junior-high poetry street names lulled her into a blind, slow-motion panic. The identical buff-stucco ranch tract houses rolled by on both sides like teeth in a jaw, only the colors and makes of the SUVs and European sedans in the driveways to tell them apart. Roshawn was sure she was going in circles, mistrusting the hazy memory of the address, and then she saw it. The silver Volvo out front, but it might have been any Volvo, but for the fancy white leather purse on the roof.

Roshawn sat and looked at the purse, and suddenly had no idea what to do. Maybe if she had a line, if someone smarter was there to tell her what to do. If Aida was there—

The front door opened and they came out in their Sunday best. Twin towheaded boys chased each other around the Volvo until their older sister collared them, and Dad, sandy-haired and tanned like a movie star, with an expensive sweater on even though it was summer, told them to quit it or no brunch after church. Roshawn started to get out. Maybe she should tell them what happened, and go, before the cops came. Maybe she should just go––

And then she came out. She wore a smart, fashionably pious blue dress that Roshawn had seen her buy at Nordstrom's. The children fell silent and got in the car as their mother smiled at the beauty of the morning, took her purse off the roof, and then fixed her gaze on Roshawn.

Roshawn's hand went numb on the latch, slipped away. The woman's eyes skewered her, though she couldn't meet them for more than an instant. When only the two of them could see each other, the woman's face went away, and she could see the real Aida. The mark had given Aida as good as she'd gotten, and what was growing back in its place was anything but flesh. It only took that long for those eyes to tell her exactly what she was, and send her on her way.

Roshawn followed the smoke back. The alley behind the condo was choked with fire trucks and ambulances, but they were already packing up. Nobody noticed her as she stumbled over the hoses and cables and the odd knot of die-hard fire-watchers to stand in the carport across from her condo unit.

The fire gutted their place, and ate most of the upstairs neighbor's before they put it out. The firemen tramped around the upper floor, chopping down smoldering furniture, but there was nothing left to save. Not that any of it had belonged to her, anyway.

Something rustled in the shadowy carport behind her. The plastic tarp over a car crumpled and something breathed charcoal and cremated bacon on her neck.

"All she had to do, was ask," said the woman.

Roshawn jumped and bit her lip. Policemen across the alley stood with the manager, who pointed at the burned-out ruin and mouthed, *junkies*.

"Your stupid friend hurt me so, and still almost fucked it up... All she had to do was ask."

The police said there were no bodies, or maybe they said *nobodies*.

"What are you...?" Roshawn whispered. She turned and looked, and the more she looked, the more she saw Aida, and not an eyeless apparition of glowing bone embers and melted spandex dripping on the concrete. She looked no worse, now, than plastic surgery disasters Roshawn had seen in tabloids, and she kept changing. She didn't have to work at it like Aida had, because her kind just got whatever they wanted. *The Elect--*

"I'm myself, ain't I?" said the mark. "And I guess you belong to me, now."

Roshawn bit back a scream that would have brought all the police for miles. Empty sockets worked and blew bubbles that clouded and became gold-flecked, turning, burning eyes. "Come on, Ro," she said. "Let's go shopping."

Cody Goodfellow has written eight novels and five collections of short stories. His collections *Silent Weapons For Quiet Wars* and *All-Monster Action* both received the Wonderland Book Award. He wrote, co-produced and scored the notorious Lovecraftian hygiene film *Stay At Home Dad*, which can be viewed on YouTube, and presides over several Cthulhu Prayer Breakfasts each year. He "lives" in Portland, Oregon.

Athena "Tina" Monday

I Am a Garden

lush
poised
perfectly groomed
bright
colorful

A collage of
fruit
petals
growth
light

Gaze upon me
when I show myself

I will feed you

but

Leave me untended
and
I
will
fade

I am a garden
once prized
now
brown lawn
weeds
dandelion
violet in the back yard
leaves
vines
thorns

I still grow
untamed

My thorns don't
stop you taking
my fruit
as it appears
wild
between
unsuccessful
siblings
starved

for
light

I will feed you

but

untamed
untended
I plot your undoing

I am a garden
and there is power
in being forgotten

Unseen
I move
against you

Foundation
roof
façade
growth

Now
I consume
the pieces
of what you were
that you

preferred

to

wild

beauty

I will feed you

but

I will also

bring

your house

down

upon your head

Athena "Tina" Monday: I'm a woman and a faggot and I am not going to stop writing mlm erotica just because I got my name changed and went on estrogen. Fuck you if you don't like it, I did my time sucking dick while I was on testosterone and I'll write about it if I like. I used to be Michael Scott Monje, Jr.

Alyssa Gonzalez

Light Was Her Burden

"Deep breaths, children." The instructor kept her eyes closed, sitting in a chair while eleven high school students knelt at her feet. "Seek inside yourselves this aberrant intruder. Find it and seize it."

The students clenched and concentrated, a few stealing glances at the posters around the room, square linework ribcage designs captioned "Normalcy Belongs to All of Us" and "Aberration is Optional" and the announcements for Trevor Jiang's next guest lecture on the subject of the aberrant menace. The young doctor had made a name for himself when he invented Suppression and started the preeminent aberration research program. He made a point to visit at least once a year to promote his work, so there were many grinning advertisements on the walls. Some of the students shook, the churning under their voluminous sweaters showcasing what they were failing to restrain. Some of them darkened the very air around them with their exertions. One, in an oversized T-shirt and knee-length shorts, stayed almost perfectly still, fists tightly clenched, a faint white glow emanating from her skin.

"The same force that filled our lakes with monsters left its mark on you, and you can defeat it." The instructor stood, walking around and between the students. "The water may call you, but with Dr. Jiang's guidance you will answer to the light. Find the unnatural taint that was imposed upon you," she commanded. "Seize it and drag it inward. Bury it with the full weight of all your strength. Claim your normalcy."

The churning sweaters calmed a bit, even as their wearers looked exhausted. The glow from the one flashed once, illuminating tendril shadows in the dark, and then dimmed. The teacher stood and walked beside her.

"Excellent work, Lucero," the instructor said, putting a hand on her shoulder that made her flinch. "Your progress continues to be an example to your fellow students." She raised her voice, getting the class's attention: "See here the true power of suppressing the aberration within."

The others didn't look at her, only down at themselves. The bell rang, and they hurriedly shuffled out of the room. Lucero took a bit longer to collect her things and exit, taking a pensive look at her classmates as they nearly ran down the adjoining hallway.

Does it always feel so bad, for them? she wondered, as a long flexible eyestalk slipped out of the neck of her T-shirt. With a clenched fist, she drew the tendril back into herself, her hand glowing until she felt the eyestalk retreat under her skin. A tap on the arm startled her, and her best friend Sarina waved at her as she turned around.

"How are you holding up?" Sarina asked, putting a hand on Lucero's shoulder. Carefully manicured, it contrasted strongly with the general unkemptness of Lucero's presentation.

"Good, Sarina," Lucero exhaled, smiling. "Really, really good. I feel like I'm making real progress. Things are starting to make sense."

Sarina took her into a hug, tight enough to feel the tentacles hiding under Lucero's skin. She whispered, "I worry about you, Lucero. It's not healthy to bury so much of yourself."

"I think I need to," Lucero whispered back, holding Sarina tightly. "I'm scared of what might happen if I don't." The eyestalk peeked out of Lucero's neckline again, keeping covert watch behind her.

"Just...take care of yourself, okay," Sarina implored, separating from the hug. "All of yourself." As she walked away, Lucero felt the bristly caress of a translucent limb, gone in a moment.

Lucero made it most of the way home before the eyestalk she'd forgotten to suppress sent an electric jolt of terror through her body. She turned around in time to be pushed backward instead of forward. Three large schoolmates sauntered toward her, one carrying a baseball bat.

"Looks like the *freak* knew we were coming," the one that had pushed her announced.

"We'll have to do something about that, won't we?" the one with the bat continued.

Green tendrils began to peek out of the edges of Lucero's clothing, and she concentrated hard. As she started to glow, they retreated, restoring her human shape. The three boys lunged at her, and she put a glowing fist deep in the first's stomach, knocking him several meters away, where he stayed. The second one attacked her with his bat, which shattered against her crossed, incandescent arms above her. The third lunged at her midsection, knocking her to the ground. Discarding the remains of his bat, the second one kicked her in the side, but she caught his foot as he withdrew. She crushed it with her glowing hand and pulled him to the ground as she pushed the other off of herself. Looking at the one partner writhing in breathless agony and the other with an apparently pulverized heel, he fled.

*The true power...*Lucero thought to herself as she resumed walking home, looking at her hands, eyestalk restrained inside, ebullient. The mood lasted until she passed by the creek near her street.

Every day, she felt compelled to approach the water, and every day, she fulfilled that compulsion. In ages past, she was told, people would cast lines into this creek and pull up the occasional sunfish or catfish, but there were no anglers now. The Chiasmal Shudder drove them off. Ever since that wan, green-tinged day, a few years before she was born, the fish were changed, their bodies unfamiliar, their behavior unmistakably intelligent. They did not acknowledge baits or traps, and they congregated in strange intervals, seeming to watch people nearby. Those few that fishers did manage to catch were musky and foul, often evaporating on stoves instead of cooking, and no natural predator would touch them.

It wasn't long after this that the first human aberrations entered the world.

Lucero sat next to the water, stands of arrowhead plants dotting the shore. Several aberrant fish came close to her, so close that they nearly stuck out of the water. They looked at her, and with a few shudders of their long bodies and an excess of fins, returned to the water. It was hard for Lucero to shake the sense that they found her...pleasant, fascinating, even beautiful. She dangled fingers at them, and they responded with a dance of fins, flaring and waving.

No matter what happened on her way home from school, these moments by the creek brought her to peace. The wind rustled the arrowhead plants, gentle and sweet. But this place also filled her with doubt. Suppression gave her a sense of power, and she'd had ample time to see that power demonstrated, much like today's encounter. It seemed natural that creatures like her should bury themselves, becoming strong by the sheer exertion required to hold it all inside. But the aberrant fish felt no need to hide. People hated them, shot at them, and more, but they did not fear, and they still came to shore to visit people like Lucero who stopped by long enough to say hello. In some strange way, she felt a kinship with these creatures, and she feared what that meant. The longer she stayed, the more her Suppression practice slipped, her skin taking on a greenish hue, tentacles emerging around her body.

When the peace gave way to her nerves, she got up, refocused her mind until her strange anatomy retracted, and finished walking home, hesitantly waving goodbye to her piscine hosts. Once there, she had a quick supper and went to sleep.

A lurid red-orange sky, the ground beneath lightly swirling yellow-gray sand. Dull black shapes hovered slowly toward her, too far to be distinct.

I've had this dream before, *Lucero thought. She dusted off her red T-shirt, and the particles wafted away cleanly, feeling like nothing. The sand gave a few inches beneath her as she stood, some buoyant surface beneath holding her weight. The dull shapes continued their approach. She stepped back, and they sped up.*

That's new.

As the three closest shapes came into view, she saw their bright blue scales, spiny fins, and unblinking eyes. Now they dove into the sand, fins cresting through it. She turned around, and they lunged from the surface to face her, close enough to punch. The three leapt on her and pulled her through the sand, claws tearing at her dream-flesh, the only view a kaleidoscope of colors and lights.

When she wrestled herself free, she was on the shore of the lake just past school grounds, and the fishmen stood a meter away, snarling. Their piscine faces slowly shifted, taking on the shapes of her three assailants from that afternoon.

"Looks like the freak saw us coming," one announced.

"Better make sure it regrets that," another answered, drawing out of nothing a hideous, spiked club.

Lucero clenched her fist and concentrated, but no light came.

"There's no hiding here, freak," the third one intoned. The three advanced, and Lucero stepped back, toward the water. The

sudden warmth gave her a shiver. "Here, the only thing you can be is what you are."

The fishman raised his club and struck down at her. She put up a panicked arm, but a filmy green wave stopped the blow. The leading edge sprouted a few eyes, some looking at her, some at her attackers. She thrashed, sprouting a second wing as the first knocked the fishman across the shore in a clattering heap. Her skin took on a greenish hue, and further tentacles, some with eyes, burst from the torn openings in her clothing. She snared one fishman's limbs in tentacles, holding him still, and swatted the third into the lake with a single wingbeat. The first tried to attack her again, but she spewed something acidic from an eyestalk, reducing him to a tarry stain on the sand. The one in her grasp began laughing.

"Yes. Good. Show us. Show us all the monster within. Show us all how dangerous an aberration can be. Every moment makes us more right."

Lucero watched in horror as the fishman's too-human face shifted again, this time becoming that of the suppression instructor.

"Find it. Seize it. Bury it. Just like we'll bury you." She cackled even as Lucero raised her wings and slashed her to ribbons with their sharp edges.

Lucero woke screaming and huddled tearfully in her green-fleshed secret limbs until dreamless sleep took her.

Lucero couldn't focus at school. It was everything she could do to keep her Suppression practice, and her hands ached from focused clenching. When she could take notes, they devolved every few minutes into swarms of penciled eyestalks and sandy vistas. The students seated beside her looked at her paper and her seething efforts and made faces at one another, expressions she knew her fellows faced routinely: disdain, amusement, contempt. She had learned a long time ago that these were what everyone else heard when Trevor Jiang told the world that the most important thing creatures like her could ever want was normalcy. One threw a wadded paper at her, and in her lapsed concentration she felt a tentacle emerge near her waist, mercifully still within her shirt. Despite her better judgement, she flattened the paper and found a drawing inside: a large hammer smashing a tangle of segmented limbs. Her wings writhed inside her as she put the drawing away, and she fought back tears. Finally, the class bell ended her torment. The one who threw the drawing body-checked her into the lockers in the hall on his way out of the room.

Lucero was about to head to her next class, but at the next set of lockers she saw someone huddled on the floor, mostly hidden behind a trash bin. She recognized him from Suppression class.

"Felix?" she asked him as she knelt down beside him. He jumped in surprise and landed on his seat. The air around him darkened, and Lucero felt the oily touch of his shadowy being.

"It's too much," he gasped out, the shadows coalescing into shapes like jointed limbs. "I can't hold it in anymore."

Lucero put a hand on one of Felix's limbs, its touch like insubstantial velvet. He shivered, and his breathing steadied.

"Focus," Lucero intoned, gently grasping the limb. "You're stronger than you think you are."

Felix's breathing steadied. The limbs again became shadow, and Lucero put her hand on his shoulder instead. As he concentrated and breathed, the shadow fitfully withdrew into his body, leaving a slightly shiny film on the surfaces it had touched.

"It takes strength just to *be* us," Lucero explained, "and we can do *anything*."

"But we shouldn't have to," Felix replied, his clothing darkening with renewed shadow.

Lucero tried to find one of the explanations she had memorized, but no words came. Her mind saw only the fish in the creek, and the fishmen by the lake.

"Why do we *do* all of this, Lucero?" Felix asked plaintively. "All of this reaching in and grasping and seizing? All of this hiding?" He looked out the nearest window. "They all know exactly who we are either way. They all still hate us. What do we get, besides nightmares and self-loathing?"

Lucero thought back to her assailant's bat shattering against her glowing arms. "Strength and resilience," she thought out loud. "The effort...it's training, in a way. It makes us stronger."

Felix was silent for a minute. "I should have guessed you wouldn't get it." He sneered, "It's *easy* for you. You fit right in. Not like the rest of us."

"Felix, that's not—"

Lucero's objection landed nowhere, as Felix released his limbs and propelled himself bodily through the open window, scuttling out of sight.

"That's not true at all," Lucero muttered, collapsing in defeat, three tentacles emerging under her clothes to provide a hug.

The next morning, Lucero and the other Suppression students took turns making furtive glances in the direction of Felix's empty chair. The irregular schedule was disorienting enough even without their collective unease and fear. Lucero concentrated harder than ever, but her light stayed dim, her clothing in visible motion, and the others' luck was no better.

"Seize it," the instructor commanded, warmth gone from her voice. "Seize it and do not yield." She stood, looking down her nose at each student and sniffing as she walked around the room, her low growl adding to all of their anxiety. "Take hold of it and bury it with the weight of your convictions." When she walked past Lucero, she offered only a disappointed sneer. Lucero swore she saw her teacher smile slightly at Felix's empty seat.

When the class ended, Lucero's classmates filed out as quickly as usual, but past the door, she overheard one muttering to another, "Felix didn't come home last night. No one's heard anything since he skipped class yesterday." She followed them, listening.

"That's four this month, between the three schools."

"You think he's not coming back?"

"I watched his parents send his younger brother to pre-school. They didn't look worried. They looked relieved."

Lucero's eavesdropping came to an end when Sarina appeared next to her, and the two took their lunches by the lake. There was a spot near all of the "No Swimming" and "Keep Out" signs where they could sit undisturbed, looking out at the murky water and the aberrant fish within. Sarina ate at a natural pace from her bento, but Lucero couldn't so much as lift her empanada.

"Felix never went home last night," Lucero announced, nerves finally compelling her to grasp the fried dumpling. Sarina looked worried and put down her chopsticks. Some of the fish congregated at the shore, watching them, seeming to listen.

"If it were anyone else, the school and the news would be in an uproar, and they'd at least be asking around to see if his friends know where he is. But it's 'only' us." Lucero took a tiny bite, chewing slowly. "No one misses an aberration. Not even his parents."

Sarina looked at Lucero, deep in horror at her friend's too-accurate observation, saying nothing. In silence, she took Lucero's hand. Lucero extruded some of her tentacles, which met and clasped a few of Sarina's. At her touch, Sarina's extra limbs blushed red, no longer transparent, their segments gleaming softly in the noonday sun.

"Whatever happens, we'll always have each other," Sarina insisted, moving over to Lucero's side and putting her head on her shoulder. Lucero put an arm around her, holding her close. They finished their lunches. When the class bell rang again, Sarina kissed Lucero on the cheek before getting up. "No matter what," she finished.

Lucero smiled. "No matter what."

Lucero turned to face the water before following Sarina back to class. She glanced over at the distant island in the lake and saw the unmistakable sheen of windows in a wooden structure before clouds blocked the sun. Even more oddly, it seemed like the aberrant fish in the lake were gesturing toward it. Lucero nodded assent, and they dispersed.

Lucero kept her ears open the rest of the day, to the detriment of her studies. Teachers seemed to refuse to acknowledge that Felix had ever existed, to the point of silently erasing him from ongoing group projects. Fellow aberrations repeated what she'd heard before in hushed tones, and Lucero tried not to think about why they weren't having those whispered conversations with *her*. It wasn't until the end of the school day that she walked past the person who had pushed her into the lockers yesterday and overheard, "I'm glad he's gone. It's about time someone cleaned up the slime. I wonder which one is next."

Sarina found her on the way off of school grounds and joined her for her walk home. Lucero stopped at the creek, and Sarina followed her to the water's edge. The pair sat on the ground, and the creatures within took notice, coming close.

"It's been too long since I joined you at your spot," Sarina began.

"End of term is always the worst. So many projects," Lucero answered.

"Do you ever wonder why they call us?" Sarina stretched her legs out toward the water, and the fish responded by crowding close to her shoes, each taking its turn at being the closest. "Or even how?"

"People like us started being born a little after they did," Lucero remembered. "In some way...I think we're the same. Whatever made us, made them, too. And even if we couldn't feel that...people hate them just like they hate us. Maybe they can feel *that*."

"We see ourselves in them, even when we don't see ourselves." Sarina leaned on her friend, and Lucero put her arm around her. They stayed that way for a few minutes, as the fish continued to swarm at their feet.

"What's it like, not being assigned Suppression?" Lucero asked. Sarina curled in on herself, voice sad.

"My parents accept that this is what I am. Most of the world doesn't see it, doesn't see me. I think that's why they haven't talked to the school to get me assigned. Because I'm invisible. Because they can pretend I'm not one of us." Her eyes welled. "There's a reason we never meet at my house. Because me even knowing you ruins the illusion for them." She grasped Lucero's hand more tightly, and her welter of tentacles blushed deep red, curling around them both. "Part of me knows that this life comes to an end the moment they think I don't hide it well enough, and part of me almost *wants* that, because then at least I wouldn't have to pretend anymore, and could just acknowledge that this is what I am.

But Suppression...we can all see what it does to us. None of us deserve that. I wish they'd never found you."

Lucero sighed heavily, and held Sarina more tightly, her own tentacles emerging to join the embrace. "I've had to fight for everything," she announced. "They would attack me in the street, even when I was small. Everything I am, it's because I had to defend myself since I was tall enough to reach doorknobs." She looked at her fist, calloused, powerful. "But I wasn't good at it until they put me in Suppression classes. It takes such strength to hide...I could put that into my fight, and suddenly, I started winning. Whatever kind of fear they felt before, after that, it was *real*." She opened her hand, feeling the motion slowly, each muscle and tendon relaxing in its sequence, a medley of tension and ease. "But I keep thinking...It didn't have to be this way. *I* shouldn't have to be this way. And I envy you."

The pair sat that way for a few minutes, each filled with words they couldn't quite say, each half of a story the other needed to tell. Eventually, Sarina let go of Lucero with all of her limbs, and her tentacles resumed their invisibility.

"We should go," she announced. "We still have time to finish that group project tonight."

Enmeshed in each other's emotions, the two girls got up and started walking again. Neither noticed that things other than the aberrant fish had been watching.

The next morning, Lucero got an early start on her walk to school, too on edge from nightmares to bother with more time at home. She continued her breathing practice, trying to get her mind under control, fighting her green limbs back into her body with her glow. About halfway to the school, she felt herself becoming heavier. The sensation grew more intense, and then she felt elephantine footsteps coming closer. With a heaving breath like her chest was being crushed, she turned to face it, arms glowing up to the elbow. The massive, leathery beast continued its plodding approach, and Lucero felt herself continue to become heavier, even as her strength rose to meet it. It came within arm's reach of her and tried to grab her. With a roar of effort, she punched it in the stomach, sending glowing ripples through its flesh, enough to throw off its aim. Its second reach latched onto her arm, and it lifted her into the air. Once it had raised her to eye level, she punched it in the face, and it dropped her. It was disoriented enough that its gravity field seemed to weaken, and she ran. Her path took her to the creek, and the fish within kept pace with her, waiting when she lagged and prodding her to keep running around to the back of the school instead of the entrance. She heard sounds of struggle, a familiar voice crying out. *Sarina!*

Behind the school, she saw a hideous orb covered in tentacles paddling across the lake's surface. Below the water, the tentacles emitted periodic sparks, keeping the fish at bay, and above, they restrained Sarina tightly. She flexed and fought to no avail. Sarina scraped against her captor with her bristled limbs, flashing red, leaving scratches that it didn't seem to notice. In a panic, Lucero searched for a way across, spotting a rowboat on the far side of the lake, but by the time she got to it, the monster and Sarina had vanished onto the central island. When she boarded the boat, the strange fish in the lake hefted it into the water for her and pulled it toward the island faster than she could row. *You're helping me,* she thought. *Thank you.* At the shore, she nodded at them, and they nodded back. They remained, apparently waiting for something, and Lucero ventured farther into the island.

It didn't take long for her to find the cabin, only partially concealed behind a thin row of trees. She climbed in through the first window she found, making little noise. The sight of all of the tables lined with belts and cuffs, hand-drawn diagrams of aberrant anatomy, sleek modern laboratory devices, and tools and sinks caked with blood and strange, shiny oil slowed her from her frantic rush, horror mingling with urgency. With a few more steps, she started to overhear a male voice, increasingly familiar. It took her a moment to connect his voice to too many school assemblies, and she gasped almost audibly when she did: Trevor Jiang.

"I suppose what I find most fascinating about your kind," he intoned over the muffled sounds of preparing blades and gloves, "is the *variety.* Some of you are full of slime, amorphous and flowing. Others are like you, full of segments, insects and worms in human guise. Some of you have many tendrils, others just a few. Most of you have a whole suite of aberrant limbs, and others live out your taint through the standard four. There are ways in which you lot are all the same, and others in which each of you is an entirely unique tragedy. And you, Sarina Miramishi...you're something special." Trevor paused, making Sarina's sounds of struggle the loudest noises in the cabin. "None of the rage I so often see, none of the conflict, none of the pain...just, life. Your parents don't even see you as an aberration, do they?"

"What kind of a question is that?" Sarina demanded. "How could I hide from them?"

"But you do," Trevor continued. "These limbs of yours... how often does anyone at school see them? How often do they see...you? The others, the Suppression instructor could flag for me, but you avoided an assignment in Suppression. You could already hide, not just from them, but from *us*. And that makes you just the one I've been seeking. You could cure them all, Sarina, and I am going to help you."

As Lucero followed the voices to where Trevor was holding Sarina, she saw him climb into the grotesque limbs of the tentacle-beast that had taken Sarina. He took a seat, holding his scalpel and a marker. The monster lifted him to face Sarina, who was trussed up in a vertical restraint, the clothing on her back cut raggedly away and leather belts and cuffs holding her tentacles. The creature brought other tentacles toward Sarina, sparks flaring from the ends, as Sarina tried to pull away. In a glowing fury, Lucero lifted a metal tray from a nearby table and flung it at the monster, knocking an electrified tentacle into a nearby laboratory instrument. The machine jolted and caught fire, and the monster extracted a bloodied, burned tentacle full of glass shards as Trevor and Sarina turned toward Lucero.

"I see Orthon met with some resistance," Trevor snarled.

Lucero seethed, her glow reaching her shoulders. "Let her go."

Trevor's voice remained smooth and unwavering. "I'm impressed. Orthon never leaves a job unfinished, so you must be...truly strong. Perhaps even more so than Sarina. I'm going to like exploring your possibilities."

"What does that even mean?" Lucero asked incredulously, before a meaty arm slammed her through the wall to her left, onto the shore.

"It means that I've got work to do, Lucero Sarapó. But you're next."

Lucero shook her head, dusted herself off, and stood, her shoulders rising and falling with her rage. She ran back into the cabin, ignoring the splinters and scratches, and jumped to deliver her fist directly into Orthon's face. The elephantine beast was soaking wet and covered in tooth marks, presumably from wading across the lake after her. The monster reeled backward, and she pressed her advance, delivering another glowing fist to the creature's chin before it could right itself. She punched its stomach, forcing Orthon backward once more, but it seized her by the waist in a single hand and lifted her off the ground. She kept attacking its arm, but no amount of bruising seemed to weaken its grip this time. The world began to seem heavier and heavier. Trevor busied himself with tracing out paths on Sarina's back in marker, the other monster's tentacles raised threateningly around them and emitting sparks. Orthon slowly raised its other fist.

"Suppression is what he *wants*, Lucero!" Sarina shouted. You can't fight it while holding back!"

Lucero dropped a two-handed glowing fist into Orthon's forearm, feeling the bones break under her, yet the monster's grip did not weaken. *Holding back*, she thought, meeting the creature's empty gaze.

Sarina shouted again: "Stop fighting yourself!"

Lucero's glow flickered. *I'm wasting strength on holding everything in.* She looked back at Sarina, at Trevor's smirking face, and let it go. Her skin turned greenish and from her back emerged two green wings, forcing Orthon's hand open. Eyestalks and tentacles appeared across various places on her wings and body, and one of them spewed acid on Orthon's hand. As it dropped her, she flapped upward and drove her bladed wings through both of Orthon's arms. The beast's hands thundered to the floor, and she flapped across the room, seizing Trevor from his perch and thrashing him into a wall. Orthon plodded forward, the sounds of its footsteps partially drowned out by the torrent of blood from its two arm-stumps. Lucero held Trevor there, a foot above the ground, with a wing, glaring into his eyes. She saw no fear.

"Go ahead," Trevor goaded. "Be the monster they know you to be."

Lucero glared harder, pulling in closer, keeping him off the ground.

"I'm going to cure you," Trevor continued, still unfazed.

"Don't you like that? Don't you want that? No more Suppression, no more stares, no more fights in the halls, no more strangeness deep in yourself that you hate. You'll be normal, just like the rest. Doesn't that sound beautiful?"

Lucero let him drop, and he fell to his feet. "What I am isn't ugly, and what *we* are isn't a disease."

"How unimaginative," Trevor continued, a sinister smile crossing his lips.

Behind Lucero, the other monster had gotten close and raised four electrified tentacles to attack position. Just as quietly, Lucero's eyestalks drenched those limbs in acid, and the creature screeched in pain, electricity bleeding from its corroded, disintegrating tentacle-ends. It lurched back past the restrained Sarina and into Orthon's gravity well. When the two collided, the tentacle creature's leaking electricity jolted through the still-bleeding Orthon. It tried and failed to regain its feet, the gravity and blood keeping it slipping until Orthon fell to its knees and then its side, dead.

Trevor was unamused. "Do you know how long it's going to take me to collect enough aberrant fish to make another one?"

Lucero turned around, keeping her rear eyes on Trevor, and hacked Sarina out of half of her restraints. She stared down the tentacle beast, who continued to stagger back as Sarina finished freeing herself. Some of her limbs felt the oily stains on the nearby wall, sensing something.

"Seek out that intrusive feeling, and crush it," Lucero cursed back. She watched the creature get to its feet and Sarina riddle it with holes in a flurry of translucent red limb-stabs until it, too, expired. Trevor lunged at Lucero's back with his scalpel and a syringe, and she swatted him across the room into another wall, next to a stinking vat. The wall splintered, showing the sunlight outside and casting a few lurid beams on the vat, highlighting the heap of aberrant student remains within. Lucero strode toward him, acidic eyes and wing-blades trained on him, resolute.

"How many was it? Five? Ten? A hundred?" She wedged a wing on one side of him, missing him by a centimeter, damaging the wall even more. "You invented Suppression, made teaching us to hate ourselves part of every school, and that wasn't enough for you. It wasn't enough to tear us down until most of us wanted to die and a lot of us did?" The other wing, on Trevor's other side. "You had to start killing us, too?"

Trevor looked around frantically, walled in every direction. One of Lucero's tentacles stroked the oily shadow-stain on the rim of the vat, and she seethed with renewed rage when she recognized that sensation: *Felix*.

"I'm so close to a breakthrough, Lucero." Trevor scrambled up the crumbling cabin wall. "You have to understand, I'm trying to help you."

"Help us with *what?*" Sarina demanded, appearing behind Lucero. Her tentacles all pointed forward, pulsing angry red. "Everything you've ever done has made our lives worse."

"You know what's *really* going to help aberrations, Trevor?" Lucero pulled her wings out of the walls and floor, raising them high. "Making sure you never kill any more of us."

Trevor pushed his way through the crumbling wall and ran down the shore. Lucero crashed through the wall behind him, shaking shards of wood from her wing, Sarina following. He ran into the lake, trying to swim across, but the aberrant fish found him. A few minutes after they pulled him under, his dismembered remains began to float to the surface, only to be snatched back down again. Across the lake, the Suppression instructor looked on in terror, and ran.

Lucero and Sarina walked down the hall to class together. Lucero's skin was green and her eyestalks and tentacles emerged from holes in her clothing. Only her wings were retracted, for their sharp edges and sheer size. Sarina's limbs coiled around her, blushing red when she looked at Lucero. Around them, other aberrant students also let themselves be visible, a medley of additional limbs, eyes, and scales. The other students gave them a wide berth, which made moving through the halls easier. There were enough witnesses to Trevor Jiang's demise that the story was already circulating by the time the news broke out, and with it, investigation of his cabin. Aberrations all over decided, then and there, to stop hiding, daring the ordinary to stop them. Few Suppression instructors kept their jobs after that, and many were hauled in for questioning, or as Trevor's accomplices, over the following days. Lucero and Sarina had given their share of testimony, enough that the names Miramishi and Sarapó were part of almost every conversation that week. It was only when those immediate calls went quiet that the two had returned to school, and even now, they faced stares, class-mates in awe and gratitude, others trying to confirm if they were looking at *the* Lucero and Sarina who had killed the monsters hunting them. Most kept a respectful distance.

The two girls walked past the room where this school's Suppression classes had been held. The instructor's belongings were in a box on her desk, and custodians were removing the posters from the wall and dumping them in the trash. Outside, other aberrant students tossed bits of fruit and ham into the lake, to the aberrant fishes' delight. Sarina sighed in satisfaction at the view, but Lucero was pensive.

"I wasn't born this strong," she said, stopping at that door and watching the cleanup. Lucero looked at the ground and then at her hands, still rough and calloused, fighter's hands. "They did that...to me. Them, and my parents, and Suppression, and this whole awful place."

Sarina put an arm around her, and Lucero returned the gesture.

"That's why we have to keep fighting," Sarina responded. "To finish making a world where we don't need to be that strong."

Lucero kept looking at her hands. They were her natural green, showing none of the light in which she once took such pride, only the aberrant hue that was her secret, comfortable release until so recently.

Sarina looked up at her. "It's your strength now, Lucero." She blushed across her entire body. "You get to decide what you're going to do with it."

Lucero took Sarina's hand, and a few of their tentacles

intertwined. The two girls looked into each other's eyes, smiling. There would be no bright burden of shame between them any longer. "We'll get there. First, we're about to be late for class."

Alyssa Gonzalez is a biology Ph.D., public speaker, and writer. Her fiction uses science-fiction and fantasy elements to explore social isolation, autism, gender, trauma, and the relationships between all of these things. She writes at The Perfumed Void (the-orbit.net/alyssa), on the subjects of about biology, history, sociology, and her experiences as an autistic ex-Catholic Hispanic transgender immigrant to Canada. She lives in Ottawa, Canada with a menagerie of pets.

Brianna Bullen

Awakening

in the morning
an eye,
i,
blinks, opens
its blinds
shutters
shuddering
with breath
both mine
and his
against
my neck.
i duck
duck
goose
under
gander feather
touches, down
as a pillow
stuffed. casing
unstitched, i
unstitch my
mouth, lips

of multiple

pouring

words

words

words

water

myself

so used

to saying

nothing

my voice

comes

as a surprise.

The diagnosis

When I was eleven, I was autistic,

finally formally fitted

into the right box. Previously I was just abnormal

freakish, fickle, friendless

taking joy in soft sound, rhythm, facts, order, animals.

I never knew the word before being it.

Teachers softened terms: 'smart,' 'quiet,' 'obsessed with
    rules.'

A classmate called me 'Dodo,' my wrists flapping

in excited-terror-anxiety at the world, overwhelmed by
    sensation, letting it out

through conduit hands, bird-branch veins flowing with
    energy.

I quipped if I were to be a flightless bird, I would rather be a
    kakapo, dying out

but not dead. Just a very odd parrot. I spent my lunchtimes
    collecting fallen feathers,

rocks, flight patterns

and facts, avoiding conversation unbound by logical rules.
    Watching

swallow chicks learn to fly

outside the toilet block. Shit, piss, and smoke repugnant but
    barely registering

enraptured by their yellow-starburst mouths: chirping
    chasms for caterpillars

express-delivered by overworked parents.
But I digress, tangent lines easier to follow than memory,
innocent past pre-knowledge.
Pre-word, I assumed everyone was equally obsessed
with the geographical distribution of Canadian Geese.
Post-word, I spent days unlearning everything I knew, facts
    unravelling away
like mum's sewing. My interests and behaviour made me
    'other,'
I wanted to be 'them.' Recovery is in rejecting this. Mum
    cried
over the phone, the teacher's aide of another autistic boy at
    school reporting symptoms:
moral rigidity, repetitions, shakings, rockings,
sitting off to the side, pretend group member
never quite getting there, existing in impressions of social
    life.
A formal diagnosis was advised.
Happiness, laughter, words came at awkward intervals,
flowing like champagne at funerals
making everything chaotic and indistinct,
painful and numb. Mum's tears
the soundless bullets to my brain-pan.
'What's the retard done now,' my brother hissed, hisses still
    in memory
not quite photographic, embellished to link with other
    moments
to make reality more linear, less trustworthy.
The heater stuttered dust.

The word reverberates through every future moment,
     self-awareness
censoring me simultaneously as I try to break through my
     own self-stigma.
It reverberates
with the words of my older brother, younger in mental past
     time travel.
After learning I was autistic, he'd call me:
Spastic, Schizo. Retard. Special. Fuck-up. Freak—love from
     my brother
over the following weeks, months, years. 'Different.' My
     sister chasing me
around the house with knives and scissors and sticks and
     fists. Terror
made me unable to use a knife for the longest time
without cringe-small-making. May have saved my life
at several knife-points, unable to go further, or
may have damaged me to that point. Hair cuts
left me a reduced mess with stranger's scissors
near my head. Younger me
turns back to her birds
before developing her weaknesses, hoping one day they'll
     invert
along with her introversion. She waits. And waits. And
waits. And—

Brianna Bullen is an autistic bisexual woman and Deakin University PhD creative writing candidate writing about memory in science fiction. She won the 2017 Apollo Bay short story competition and placed second in the 2017 Newcastle Short story competition. Her manuscript was previously a finalist in the 2018 Subbed In Poetry Chapbook competition but is currently unpublished. In 2018, she was part of Nexus, an Arts Access Victoria collective for artists with mental health recovery lived experience.

Noley Reid

Sick Days

When mom is out sick from work, she bakes trays of brownies for Sean and me. And a whole one for herself. She plans the night before and comes home with a party size bag of Cheetos, a pack of Twizzlers, and a box of Entenmann's donuts. She'll give us money, say, "Order two pizzas. You know what I like."

She does her eating in her room, in her bed. She doesn't want to be seen. When the pizzas come, we knock and leave hers outside her door. No plate, nothing. A minute later, the box is gone. Sean says she goes feral on her eating days. I don't disagree. Once I caught sight of her leaving the empty pizza box outside her door. She wasn't dressed, just rolled in a fitted sheet, one of its corners wrapped over her forehead, the elastic biting a jagged pink moon into her skin.

All the rest of the days in the year, she diets. Eats just 750 calories a day. And I know you won't believe that number. But her metabolism is messed up, okay? She's been little and huge and little and huge a billion different times in her life and if she eats more than 750 calories a day, she gains weight. So that's what she eats and she weighs every gram of food, usually. And she gets these pills, Adderall and Topamax, from her psychiatrist to push her weight loss along because she's still 240 pounds. And it's working, last year she was 337. But the sick days.

They scare us.

Today is Saturday and she's supposed to be at her drive-up teller window with the pneumatic tube sending people's deposits and withdrawal slips back and forth all day but she's in her room and we're in the living room, lying on the carpet with Foster, our dog. He's white and brown because he's mostly a Jack Russell but also kind of a pit bull, so he's bigger and taller for a Jack Russell or smaller and shorter for a pit. Whatever you think he is, basically, he's wrong.

"We should do something," says Sean, rubbing Foster's belly.

"Like what?"

He sits up. "Maybe if we curled her hair." He touches his own short hair between two straight fingers like to curl it.

"She doesn't want her hair curled," I tell him.

"Maybe she does. You don't know everything, Amelia." He's back to stroking Foster again and again in the same spot so that a collection of shed white fur piles up. I watch him to see what he's going to do with it.

"Let's go out," I tell him.

Sean shakes his head. "We could brush her hair." He picks a bit of the pile of loose fur off of Foster and sprinkles it down to the carpet.

"Don't do that," I say.

He shrugs. "That's where it all goes anyway."

"You could put it in the trash," I say.

He lies back down and Foster goes over to his bed and curls up, his little tail wagging as he lies down. Sean is nine and I'm twelve.

"Do you hear that?" says Sean.

It's Mom.

We go sit in the hallway outside her door. Foster follows us, though we have to pull him back because he's panting and trying to sit against her door and we don't want her to hear him. She's talking to her computer men. All giddy now because that's how she gets. She just talks on sick days then never talks to them again.

We hear her laugh. We can't make out the words she says. Just laughing and her voice is higher with them. Sometimes she says *No* but she doesn't say it the same as when she says it to us. It's like a *Yes*. It's a *Yes-No*. She moves around the room, walking while she talks, I guess. I picture her still in the fitted sheet, the elastic biting her forehead and I shove my fist in my mouth to stop the giggle. Sean gives me a death glare and Foster starts to lick my cheek. I turn away from his slobber. Mom's saying *No* and laughing some more but then she must hang up because the house goes silent except our breathing and Foster now licking my knees.

Sean and I don't move. We side-glance our eyes to each other but we do not move. She won't come out, right? She wouldn't come out. Not until tomorrow.

"Hel-lo," we hear.

Thank the baby Jesus. Oh my God. I thought we were going to die.

And she's laughing and there are *Nos* and *Yes-Nos* and more laughing. Foster lies down. Sean lies down. My knees are slimy. I get up and go to my room, grab my jacket and head outside.

It's November and the air is cold on my wet knees. I walk to Chrissy's building, go to her door.

"Want to come out?" I ask.

"Where's Sean?" she says.

"He's too young for you."

"Oh my God, Amelia!"

"Kidding!" I say. "He's back at home, staking out my mom's door."

"Why?"

"She's sick."

"Oh." She runs a cherry Chapstick over her lips and holds it out to me.

I shake my head. "Come on," I say.

We walk to the playground equipment by the parking lot. Chrissy sits on a swing so I sit on one next to her.

"What were you doing?" I ask.

"Nothing," she says. "YouTube."

I walk my swing back to push off but just stand there for a minute, waiting.

"You?" she says, she walks her swing back, too, then pushes off and is in the air.

"Nothing." I let myself go and I'm in the air now, too. Both of us pumping to stay up, go higher.

"Exciting lives we lead," shouts Chrissy, laughing into the wind we're making.

"Totally."

Chrissy is a tad bit pudgy. I don't know if she knows. She doesn't act like my mom. She doesn't go nuts with restricting calories and she doesn't go nuts with indulging in calories.

Mostly, she doesn't go nuts. But in school, she doesn't get called on for dodge ball teams until it's the special needs kids. And she didn't get a role in the class play when everyone got a role in the class play; instead, she was made stage manager. At the end of a school year, teachers and parents always say get ready for the next year, it's a big step up in maturity. But sixth grade is when everyone decided to care about superficiality so now there's a boy, Wayne Moten, that calls Chrissy Lane, Chubby Lane. In fifth grade, he was her boyfriend and she was just as pudgy. And on Meet the Teacher Night, when my mom signed up to bring cookies for a bake sale, Gordon Riley saw her name is Marjorie and now asks me every day, "How's Marge the Barge?"

Sean and Foster come running up now. "She came out!" he yells. I pump my legs and he backs up out of the way of my swing.

"What?"

He's breathless. "She came out!"

I stop pumping. I reverse pump. "She's out?"

Sean nods.

Chrissy stops pumping. She slows down.

I jump off in mid-air. I walk away from the swings because I don't want Chrissy to hear. "What did she say? What did she do? Was she in the sheet?"

Sean says, "She had a dress on and said she was going out."

"Going out," I repeat.

"On a date," he says.

"A date?" It's Chrissy. She's come up behind me now and is scratching Foster behind his ears.

"How can she go on a date?" I ask. "I mean, she doesn't even know any of these men. They could be axe murderers."

Sean says, "They could follow her home, tie us all up and make us watch *Wheel of Fortune* while they force feed us cubes of green jello."

"You are so weird, Sean," says Chrissy.

He smiles and Foster wanders over to the slide.

"We should go home," I say. "See you later, Chrissy."

Foster's pooping by the slide now. We're supposed to pick it up but I don't have any bags so we pretend we don't see him.

When we get home, Mom is playing her old Depeche Mode and Yaz and getting ready for her date. Going down the hall to her room, we can smell the curling iron heating up and Sean says, "See? She did want it." He runs in her bathroom and offers to curl her hair and she sits on the toilet and lets him. He's actually really good at it. Mom has long, light brown hair like mine but hers will hold a curl, mine won't. I got my dad's fine, straight hair.

Foster uses the stairs to get up on Mom's super high bed and I sit on the bed, too. I listen to Mom and Sean. They don't talk much but they make soft sounds particular to each of them—Sean's are high-pitched oohs and Mom's are low thrums—and all of a sudden I feel homesick for each of them and both of them together, even though they're right there. I know it doesn't make any sense but my heart aches like I'm a million miles away.

"Ta-da!" says Mom, stepping out of the bathroom and spinning around to show off her hair. "What do you think?"

"Really nice," I say. "Beautiful."

"Are you okay?" She touches my cheek and looks in my eyes.

I blink a few times.

"What is it, Melie?" she says.

"I don't know."

She hugs me and holds me and that feels right. But now Sean has to come get in between us because he likes to be the peanut butter.

"How about Amelia helps me pick what to wear tonight," Mom says.

"Okay," I say.

"But I'm better at that," says Sean.

"Be nice," she tells him. "Besides, you got to do my hair." Mom goes to her closet and starts moving hangers from right to left one by one.

Sean lies down on the bed next to Foster, says, "Fine, we'll just be over here not helping you look your best, right Foster?"

"Don't be a butthead, Sean," I say. I go stand with Mom. "Do you know where you're going?"

"To an Italian restaurant for dinner."

"Okay, so something a little bit nice but not *too* dressy." I pull out a white collared shirt, some skinny jeans, a wide black belt, and her black suede boots. "Good?"

"Great job. What do you think, Seany?"

He lazily lifts his head from the bed and sighs. "It will have to do."

I go to her jewelry box and pick out an amethyst geode necklace and some amethyst threader earrings while Mom gets dressed.

We go out to the living room and wait. Sean rolls around on the carpet with Foster. I sit on the sofa. Mom stands.

"When is he coming?" I ask.

"Forty minutes." She checks her watch for the millionth time.

"Well, you may as well sit down."

"Sit down here with me," says Sean. "Foster wants you." Foster wags his stumpy tail.

"She doesn't want to get dog fur all over her date clothes," I say.

"That's true," says Mom. "Sorry, Sean." She goes to the windows like maybe she'll see him walking up the path right now.

"Do you even know what this guy looks like?" says Sean.

Mom doesn't turn around. "Yes, from his picture."

"If that's really him," Sean says.

"True," she says.

"What picture did you use?" I ask.

"Uh, well—"

"I mean, is it a current picture or, like, an out of date picture?"

She turns back to me now and I feel accused. "You mean do I have this body or a slimmer body in it? Am I dishonest about my current physique?"

I feel bad for asking now. What does it matter? She's still the same person, isn't she? Well, except that now she eats obsessively little most of the time, except for sick days. So maybe she's not the same person now but not in the way those men will think.

"Are you nervous?" I ask.

She nods.

Finally she sits on the couch and we watch some of a Jim Gaffigan comedy special. There are too many self-deprecating fat jokes and Mom laughs at them but they aren't funny, they're just mean. I think about Chrissy and text her not to watch it. She answers "Why?" and I don't know what to say so I don't answer.

The doorbell rings and Foster goes crazy barking. He runs to the door. Mom jumps up and tells Sean to get the dog. I get up, too. So we're all standing there in the entryway when she opens the door to the guy.

Mom says, "You must be Kirk. Come in and meet everybody."

"Hi. Hey," he says. He's all right looking. He has wavy hair and he's kind of short, shorter than Mom, but his face is cute like a baby's with a really good smile.

"This is Amelia," says Mom.

"Hi," I say.

"Hello," he says and shakes my hand.

"And this is Sean," she says.

"Hi," says Kirk and shakes Sean's hand.

"And this is Foster," says Sean.

Foster's quiet now and sitting between Sean's feet.

"He's a real cutie," Kirk says, "will he mind if I pet him?"

Sean says, "Go on."

So Kirk strokes the top of Foster's head and scratches his neck. Foster gets that far-off look in his eyes.

Mom takes me aside. "The instructions for the lasagna

are on the counter. I'll be home by 10, 10:30 at the latest."
She looks at Kirk.

"Scout's honor," he says.

"She should have worn a dress," says Sean.

"You should wear a dress," I say.

He disappears. A few minutes later, here he comes in my old summer dress he loves to wear.

We eat the lasagna and Sean feeds some to Foster. We watch the rest of Jim Gaffigan and wonder what happened because he used to be so funny. We roll around on the carpet with Foster. We watch stupid TV and then Sean falls asleep and I get my book and I must fall asleep reading because the next thing I know, Mom is here and Kirk is here, too, and Mom is telling Kirk Sean's dress is for practicing a role in a play and then she is carrying Sean to bed. Then they come back for me and I get up and go to bed and Mom follows me and leans over me and whispers, "You had to let him wear the dress tonight?" and I feel sick.

In the morning, Mom is whistling and mopping the kitchen.
She calls out to me, "Good morning, Sunshine."

"Morning," I say.

"Sleep well?"

"Yeah."

"Seany's still sleeping."

"Oh," I say. I sit just outside the wet floor on the carpet. Foster noses under my arm so I'll pet him. He lies down beside me. "Did you have a good time on your date?" I ask.

"Yes, ma'am," she says, running the mop over the same patch of linoleum over and over again.

"Your hair is still curly."

She reaches up and lightly squeezes a couple of the curls. "Your brother does such a good job on it, doesn't he?"

"When will the floor be dry?" I ask.

"A half hour."

"I'm hungry."

"Sorry, Sugar."

"Do you have anything in your room?"

She turns fast to me. "I don't hoard anymore."

"Oh. Okay." Foster is starting to snore so I focus on him. "I guess it's good you went out on a sick day. So you could eat."

"I'm done with sick days and 750-calorie days," she says.

"What are you going to do?"

She stops mopping and smiles at me. "I'm just going to be happy. Kirk says I'm beautiful."

I go crawl in bed with Sean. He's still in my dress. I curl up behind him and Foster jumps up with us, too. He curls up at our feet under the covers.

When I wake it's to the sound of water. The splash and spray of Mom in the shower so I get out of Sean's bed and go to the kitchen for something to eat. But she's there. Cutting up strawberries and mixing up batter for pancakes. Sean is still in bed.

"Who's in the shower?" I ask but then I don't need to ask and feel dumb for saying the words.

"Kirk's apartment had the water shut off this morning," she says, "so I told him he could come back over here and use ours." She stirs the batter more vigorously, which you're not supposed to do. You're supposed to leave some lumps. She stops stirring and looks up at me and smiles.

"Foster didn't bark."

"I guess he's used to Kirk now, plus wasn't Foster in sleeping with you?"

"He would have heard the door. He would have barked," I say.

Mom picks up her stirring spoon and starts waving it at me. "I don't know what you think you know but that's not what's happening here, so stay in your own lane, Missy."

I go get changed and get my jacket and leave for Chrissy's apartment. By the time I get there, I'm seething. "Come out," I say and I pull on her sleeve to yank her out the door.

"Let me get proper dressed," she says so I go in and sit on her bed while she changes. "What's going on?"

"She had the date."

"Was he cute?" says Chrissy.

"Who cares. Not the point," I say. "He's in my apartment right now."

"Oh my God! Go, Marjorie."

"Gross!"

"When do you think is the last time she had sex?"

"I don't."

"But really, I mean, she's a human being. Your dad left when she was pregnant with Sean, right? So has there been anyone since him?"

"Why are you being all realistic and humanistic and kind to her? You're supposed to be grossed out and want to call CPS that some guy she just met last night is in my house right now and, apparently, was the whole night." I go to Chrissy where she's standing at her dresser and put my hands on either side of her head and give her a good shake. "I could have been raped or murdered or raped and murdered!"

"Were you?" she says.

 I roll my eyes.

"So maybe he's nice." She sits down on the bed, so I sit next to her.

"Maybe he's pretending to be nice."

"Maybe but why?" she says.

"To kill us all in our sleep."

"He could have done that last night but didn't so that's probably off the table."

"I guess."

"What are you really worried about?" Chrissy pops her knuckles.

"I don't know, what does he want from her? Can he really like her?"

"Because she's so big?"

"I'm sorry, Chrissy, it's just that most people don't want someone my mom's size."

"I know."

"You're nowhere near that big, anyway," I tell her, but it doesn't matter. She won't look at me now.

We sit quietly on the bed for a while.

Finally, I say, "Let's go outside."

"I don't really feel like it today," she says.

"Chrissy, I'm sorry."

"It's okay. It's how you feel. Whatever."

"It's not how *I* feel. I love you. You're my best friend."

"But you wouldn't marry me."

"I'm not gay."

"That's not what I mean!"

"I know."

At home, Kirk and Mom are giggling over pancakes at the dining table. Foster lies waiting between them, hopeful.

"Get over here, Amelia," she says. She's got real syrup on the table and a big puddle of it on her plate. "Where've you been?" Then to him, she says, "Probably went to see her best friend Chrissy who lives a couple of buildings over that way." She points behind his head.

He nods.

I stand beside her. "Want me to get you the diet syrup?" I ask.

She lays down her fork and looks up at me. "I'm doing just fine, but I thank you."

"Just trying to help," I say.

"Why don't you go wake up Sean and make sure he gets

dressed in a shirt and pants today."

"Oh Mom," I say, "is today the day for small minds?"

Kirk looks between us and back to his plate.

"Go, Amelia. Now."

Foster follows me to Sean's room. We both get on the bed. I give Sean a shake that gets progressively more violent until he finally opens his eyes.

"I knew it was you," he says. "I just wanted to see how far you would take it. You took it really far."

"All the way to shaken baby syndrome?" I say.

"All the way."

"Mom wants you up," I say. "And dressed."

He pops up. "Ta-da!" He does a little curtsy with the dress on top of the bed. Foster sighs and moves down to the end of the bed.

"She said 'shirt and pants,'" I mock her voice and squeeze my nonexistent curls.

Sean doesn't laugh. "But it's the weekend," he says.

"You don't understand. The guy is still here."

"Still?" Sean sticks his finger in his mouth like to puke.

I nod. "They're eating pancakes and—get this: she's eating regular syrup!"

"No way!"

I nod.

"He just stayed all night?"

"She had some line about the shower blah, blah, blah. He definitely was here all night."

"Gross!"

"What's going on in here?" It's her, it's Mom standing in

Sean's doorway. Who knows how much she heard?

"Nothing," we say and Sean sits back down on the bed with me.

Mom comes in. She walks to the bed and puts a hand on each of our heads, like we're still babies. She says, "I know you probably have some questions about Kirk and me and what all this means for us but I really, really like him and I'm asking—no, I'm begging you to please show him kindness and exert a little self-control. Amelia, please no snarking comments or judging. And Sean, please no dress until he knows you better."

"So we can't be ourselves," I say.

She removes her hands. "Just be your best selves for a little while."

"What does a dress have to do with whether Sean is his best self or not?" I say.

"You know what I mean," says Mom. "It can make people," and now she lowers her voice, "especially men, uncomfortable."

So I speak loudly: "That sounds like their problem."

"Amelia, God damn it," she says, cutting her eyes at me hard. "This isn't up for debate. No dress." She turns around and leaves.

Sean hugs his legs to his chest and we sit here quietly until we hear Mom back in the room with Kirk, laughing hysterically. That's when Sean loses it. He rolls over in a ball and sobs without a sound and Foster and I wrap ourselves around him and his dress.

For weeks Mom and Kirk are inseparable outside of her work hours. He sleeps here most every night and they stop making up pretenses for his early morning presence. They go out at night to restaurants and bars and bowling and movies. Once they took us with them but we were more uncomfortable then than they were—we spent the night talking in Muppet voices—so we doubt they'll ever repeat that.

Tonight is their two month anniversary. Mom even bought Kirk a pair of cufflinks, which is stupid because he sells cars at a place where everyone wears red polo shirts with the S. Smeltzer logo on the shirt so he can't wear the cufflinks to work and maybe he'll wear a button-down shirt on a date with her, but one with cufflink holes? No way. Anyway, they're monogrammed with his initials, KRK, and if you look too fast it kind of looks like KKK so what was she thinking and what were his parents thinking?

Mom is standing at her closet, trying to figure out what to wear tonight. She's had to go backward in her sizes because she's been eating so much and going out so much. She won't tell us how much she's gained but she's gone up three whole sizes. I guess Kirk doesn't care. There's a big difference between size 28 and size 22. There's a big difference in her face now. In the fullness of her cheeks and the invisibility of her chin. Other kids have moms who change their hair color, maybe, the cut, but that's it—the rest of her stays the same. Our mom changes everything about her: her face, her skin, her size, her shape, her movement when she walks, how she sounds when she talks, how she eats, how she thinks about food, what she says to us, how she loves.

She pulls a long black skirt and a black vee-neck sweater from the far end of the closet and she dresses inside the bathroom. She chooses her own jewelry, just like she's been curling her own hair all this time. We don't offer to help and she doesn't ask. When she's finished readying herself, she turns to us where we are on her bed and asks, "Good enough?"

"Good enough," we say, and we all file out of her room.

She's at the dining room table now, moving some of the contents of her regular purse into a smaller purse for tonight.

Sean goes to her. "Mom," he says softly, "Two months is a long time."

"I know it is," she says, stopping what she's doing and getting giddy. "I'm so excited."

"So does he know me now?"

"Of course he knows you." She strokes his cheek.

He whispers, "So I can wear my dress now?"

"Oh," she says. "Let's just give it a while longer. Two months isn't all that long for something like that. We'll just give it a while longer."

"Oh," he says.

Sean disappears into his room and I go to follow him.

"Wait, Amelia," says Mom. "I need you to grab Foster when Kirk gets here."

"Can't you?"

"It's easier with two people."

So I wait and I hold Foster when Kirk arrives with his bouquet of pink roses that Mom hands to me. So now I'm holding a dog and a bouquet. And with her at the door, I see there's a flat spot on the back of her head where she didn't curl some of her hair. Sean would never have let that go. I smile at that, then feel bad.

"Sean, come say goodnight!" she calls but he doesn't come and she gets impatient so they leave.

I leave her flowers out of water and I go to him. "They're gone," I say.

He nods.

"Do you want to watch something?"

He shrugs.

I go in his dresser drawer and get the dress. "I think you should wear this."

"You heard her."

"Who cares?"

"I can't."

"Sure you can."

He shakes his head.

"Do you know, if you wanted, you could wear this dress everywhere you went? Everywhere. I mean, you could go outside in this dress. You could go to school in this dress. You could go to the grocery store in this dress. You could have a job one day in this dress. You could get married in this dress. You could do anything and everything in this dress."

Sean picks at his cuticles. "I don't think it would still fit me then."

I give him a little shove. "You know what I mean."

"But she says I can't."

"She's a person. You're a person. I'm a person. But you are the person in charge of you. She's not. You get to decide what's right for you. And if it's wearing this dress, then you get to do that."

"But what will she do to me?"

"I don't know, be mad?" I say. "Ground you. You don't go anywhere anyway."

"Hey."

"Will she stop loving me?"

"It's not possible. If she did, if she possibly could, then she didn't really love you in the first place."

He takes off his T-shirt and slips the dress over his head. Now he runs and spins in the living room with Foster, singing, "*I feel pretty. Oh, so pretty. I feel pretty and witty and bright! And I pity anyone who isn't me tonight.*" He spins and spins, the skirt of the dress, flaring out around him like a tutu. Sean is the happiest I have seen him in months, maybe ever. I take a video and some pictures on my phone. He spins and sings until his legs give out and he collapses in a heap with Foster licking his face and then I take pictures of that, too.

We make the freezer pizza Mom left for us and eat it, watching *Tin Star*. Sean eats his cheese off first, then scrapes the sauce off with his teeth. Then eats the crust. "You know that's weird, right?" I say.

"I know it's delicious," he says.

"Weird."

"Melie." He pauses the show. "Don't let me fall asleep in the dress tonight, okay?"

"How else will they see the real you?"

He takes hold of my arm and shakes it. "Please," he says. "Swear it."

"Okay."

"Swear it," he says.

"I swear."

He tries to look me in the eye.

"Start the show," I say.

I don't purposefully fall asleep.

Or maybe I do. Maybe I've become a liar and a terrible human being no one should trust anymore. So we are asleep in the living room when they walk in and there's no time to strip Sean out of the dress and, let's face it, would I even if I had enough time? I keep my eyes shut.

Mom steps over to us quietly, then sees what he's wearing. "God damn it," she whispers. Now I hear Kirk, the jingle of his keys, come closer.

Mom says, "Oh Kirk, he must have been practicing that play again."

"They still haven't finished that yet?" says Kirk.

"I wish they wouldn't have boys dressing like girls," Mom says. "It's so confusing to young kids." She must be giving Sean a little shake to get him walking to bed. "Seany. Sea-ny."

For a while the room is quiet, only it's not completely quiet. Mom is gone and Sean. But without their noise, I start to make out something else: Kirk's breathing. So he's sitting somewhere, not too close, probably the dining room, and just breathing. And it's an intimate sound and an intimate thing to be hearing and I don't want to be shut in a soundscape with just him but Foster must have gone with Mom and Sean so it's just the two of us. I try to focus on my own breathing and the sound of my heart beating and pumping blood through my ears. It isn't enough.

"Amelia, I need to see you in your room. Now."

My eyes pop open. Could she tell I wasn't asleep? I go sit on my bed and Mom follows. She shuts the door and sits beside me.

"Your brother is heartbroken." There is something green in her teeth.

"Sean, why?"

"Because you told him to wear the dress when he was forbidden from wearing it and because you *swore* you wouldn't let him fall asleep in it."

"Aren't you glad your son has character?"

"My son is nine years old. I don't think he knows what he has yet."

"You're blind," I say.

"Don't talk to me like that." She shakes when she says it.

"Since when do you not want to see who he is? You used to love all his little differences. Now you shut him down and say he doesn't know who he is? That's crap and you know it."

Her cheeks are red, either from wine or from me. "I said,

don't talk to me like that. Show me respect."

"Then deserve it."

She stands up and the bed creaks.

"Why are you changing for some guy? Your son isn't a cis boy, don't make him be one."

She leaves. I walk the back hallway and go to Sean. He's not in the dress. I tell him I'm sorry but he's asleep, tears dried across his cheeks, Foster curled up against Sean's belly. I tell him I'm sorry again and again. I squeeze in bed around Foster and fall asleep there, too.

In the morning, I wake alone in Sean's bed. I go get dressed and can hear their voices, the three of them. When I come out, I see they're playing Candy Land and Kirk just fell all the way back to Cookie Commons. Sean is up near Candy Castle so he's happy. Mom is in Lollipop Woods, neither ahead nor behind.

Kirk pats the chair next to him, says, "Come on over. I think next up is Farkle, right Sean?"

I stay standing. "I hate Farkle," I say.

"That's too bad," he says. "Maybe we can vote on Farkle."

"No, I think the lineup's all set," says Mom. "Maybe you can make a suggestion after Farkle."

"It's fine," I say. Sean won't look at me. I go to the kitchen, get a bowl of Crispix and there are her roses, their heads bent and petals mushy.

"Don't make a mess," Mom says. "I just finished cleaning up after our breakfast."

"No problem." I dump the cereal into the trash and put the bowl back into the cupboard. "I don't need any breakfast."

"Amelia, quit it with the attitude, thank you." Mom draws her card and advances to a purple square. "Your turn, Hon."

Kirk takes a card and it must be something good because he whoops and says, "Thank you, thank you, thank you!"

"Um, you're still in last place," says Sean.

"That is true," says Kirk. "But I'm on the move now, I can feel it."

I go stand at their table again and try to get Sean to look at me and he just won't so then I shoot daggers into Mom's eyes and into the side of Kirk's head. Now I go to my room. I pull all of my old clothes, all my old dresses out of my closet and heap them onto the carpet. I go back to the kitchen.

"What are you doing rummaging around in there?" says Mom.

"Spring cleaning," I say, pulling out a garbage bag from under the sink.

I go back to my room and Foster has made a nest out of the clothing. I pull at each hemline and sleeve to get him off and put each dress in the bag and then I start to cinch it up. But it's not finished. I go to Sean's room. I get my old dress from his dresser, take it back to my room, put it in the bag, and tie up the bag.

I drag the garbage bag to the front hall. Everyone turns to look at what I'm doing.

"What is that?" Mom asks.

"Spring cleaning, I told you," I say.

"No, really, what is it."

"Old clothes to donate." I put my hands on my waist.

"Don't do anything with that before I get a chance to go

through it," she says.

"They're my old clothes and they don't fit anymore," I say. "Surely I can dispose of them how I wish."

"Well I bought them, so no, I get to say how we dispose of them."

"God!" I scream and run to my room and slam the door. I feel like I want to throw up, listening to them roll the dice and yell *Farkle!* I do a crossword on my phone for a while but get stumped so then I just start writing in angry words everywhere, crossing hatred with fury and wrath, revulsion with murder and loathing, and so on. I fall asleep, I guess, and when I wake up I hear Sean crying just outside my door and then going down our hall to his room. Mom's voice trails after him.

I stick my head out and see the garbage bag open. He found the dress. Kirk is alone at the dining table. I go and sit at the other end of the table.

"Hey," he says. "You feeling any better?" He's dealing himself a Solitaire game.

I shrug.

We don't say anything for a while. The game boxes are stacked in front of me. Candy Land, Farkle, Sushi Go!, Exploding Kittens, Blokus, and decks of cards.

He moves a King stack to an empty spot. Then he says, "Your mom said you and Sean used to get along so well and with her, too. I kind of wonder if it's my fault for being here that's messed things up for the three of you."

I shrug again.

"Well if you can think of anything I'm doing wrong, please

tell me, okay?" He deals an Ace of hearts from his hand and plays its two from his board.

I pull out my phone. I pull up the video. "You really want to know what it is?" I say.

"Of course." He lays down his hand.

I give him my phone, say, "This is who Sean really is. This is what makes him happy. Hit play."

Sean comes to life on the screen, spinning and singing, "*I feel pretty. Oh, so pretty. I feel pretty and witty and bright! And I pity anyone who isn't me tonight.*"

He hands the phone back to me. "Does Marjorie know?"

I nod.

"I don't know what to say." He runs his hands through his hair and lets out a deep breath. "It's different."

"No it's not," I say. "If he were a girl, you wouldn't find it 'different.'"

"But he's a boy. Just give me a sec, okay?"

I look at the first picture after the video, of Sean's elated face.

I go to the kitchen. Kirk packs up his Solitaire game. I make cereal again and take it to the living room.

Eventually, Mom follows Kirk to the door and Sean follows Mom, watching from the open hallway. Mom's crying, saying, "Please don't go."

"I'll call you tomorrow," says Kirk, one hand on the open door. "I just need a little time to think it through, is all."

"We can think it through together," she says, her hand holding his other wrist he's twisting to free. "We can make a plan for the family."

"Marjorie, I love you, but we aren't a family just yet. You three are, I'm just an onlooker at this point and it's important for you to be firm with that distinction."

"Please," she says. "Please don't go. I'll throw away the dress."

I look at Sean's face and, this time, it's stone.

"I won't ever let him wear another dress ever again," she says.

"I don't think that's probably the right thing to do," says Kirk. He removes her hand and gently places it at her side. "I'm sorry."

Kirk doesn't call the next day or the next or ever again. Sean puts the dress back in his dresser but he doesn't wear it anymore and one day I go to check on it and it's not there. I've stopped asking Chrissy to come out with me because she never will. So it's just Sean and me on the swings with Foster anymore. But there is something gone between us. Something spun out of the way we talk and move and are with each other. Mom calls us *sullen* these days and I guess that's about as good a word as any for us now. But I think maybe *sad* is what Sean is instead.

Today is a sick day so we want to be anywhere but at home where she's gorging on hoarded forbidden foods in her bedroom. We're sitting in the swings but not swinging. We kick our toes at the rocky dugout beneath each swing. I reach out a hand to my brother and it takes a minute for him to notice or to want to hold mine but he does. He reaches back and holds my hand so maybe there is that little bit of something left in a whole lot of nothing.

Noley Reid is author of the recent novel *Pretend We Are Lovely* (Tin House Books), which O, The Oprah Magazine called "scrumptious." Her previous books are the short story collection *So There!* and the novel *In the Breeze of Passing Things*. Her fiction and nonfiction have appeared in The Rumpus, The Lily, Bustle, Los Angeles Review of Books, the Southern Review, Meridian, and Other Voices. www.NoleyReid.com

Lucas Scheelk

Maternal Death-iary

Dedicated to Susan Scheelk (1960-2019)

ONE

I never got to tell you how much your anger hurt me.

From 12 years old, when you threw the telephone against the kitchen wall after I said I wanted to live with my dad. You yelled at me through my closed bedroom door that I didn't love you anymore. I only stayed because of fear.

From 18 years old, when we had a misunderstanding over graduation cards and you threatened to kill me.

From 26 years old, when you gave me vague instructions on how to wash your clothes and you yelled at me afterwards. I had a flashback to the telephone incident. I lied about why I suddenly had to go see a friend. She wasn't the one in a crisis.

From an indeterminable age, when I had to apologize to anyone you lost your temper to.

From an indeterminable age, when I learned to read your mood from the way you walked through the door, from the tone of your words, and from your breathing.

From an indeterminable age, when my anger became internal.

TWO

I wish I told you more how much I appreciated you.

Riding in the car with you, and Elton John would play on the radio; this became our routine.

Como Elementary did not like the idea of mainstreaming an autistic child in the 90s – you believed in my education and fought the school.

You took me to a live showing of the Rocky Horror Picture Show for my 23rd birthday. You noticed, way before I did, that the guy sitting ahead of us was trying to flirt with me.

You took me to Priscilla: Queen of the Desert at the Orpheum.

You took me to see Joan Jett at my first time at a casino.

You took me to a local production of Sunday in the Park with George. Afterwards, you told me you could see why it was my favorite musical.

You were the first to see me as your son.

You were the first relative to acknowledge my conversion to Judaism.

THREE

I can't wear grief like accessories
They don't complement my outfit

I lost my manual, an inheritance from
Mother down to mother down to son

Wine on my tongue
Mount St. Helen's on my left
MIKA's "Stay High" made
30 minutes to Portland faster
I can't wear grief like accessories
They don't complement my outfit
I lost my manual, an inheritance from
Mother down to mother down to son
At my first séance, your arrival was announced
Of course the gay man has Mom Energy
The medium said you apologized for being hard on me
But the dog mention brought me Houdini levels of wary

I can't wear grief like accessories
They don't complement my outfit
I lost my manual, an inheritance from
Mother down to mother down to son

50mg edibles in and quickly back out
Turns out they don't mix well with vodka
Between an inaccessible convention, and driving to Powell's,
My promise to be sober was the biggest disappointment

FOUR

You're signaling me to stay alive

A message from mother to son
Though states away, I hear Elton's tunes and
Remember where we used to haunt

If I press your ashes to my eyelids
Will my pupils stop dilating in slithers?

Your obituary saved on my phone
This is how I keep you with me

Smoke appears at each alarm
My hologram calls it medicine

Your ashes rest atop my dresser
This is how I keep you with me
I've become the ghost from the day you died
Sobriety is reset daily

Every 18 days I reach for prayers inside pomegranate seeds

Not changing my last name
This is how I keep you with me

Every 18 days I reach for prayers inside pomegranate seeds

I see you in Pepé Le Pew
This is how I keep you with me

I see you in Vikings' purple and gold

This is how I keep you with me

I see you in miniature wood elephants
This is how I keep you with me

I see you in a well-worn book cover
This is how I keep you with me

You're signaling me to stay alive
A message from mother to son
I've become the ghost from the day you died
Sobriety is reset daily
My pupils dilate in slithers
Thursday is actually Tuesday
If I press your ashes to my eyelids
Will it stop the alarm?

Will it stop my hologram stealing pomegranate seeds and let
me wear grief sober?

Darling

(can be read or sung)

No phase describes your love

        darling

Gender expression blended

        darling

You can look up to you

        darling

Your love is expanded

        darling

He, she, they, ze call you

        darling

Arm-in-arm down the street

        darling

Each violet a gift to you

        darling

Each carnation a gift to you

        darling

Ease trauma your own way

        darling

Fabulousness incarnate

        darling

Don't despair for those gone

        darling

They left that path for you

Word Association Quiz

Pick one of the following from each question

You have enough time as the void will allow

The void does not keep score; you know you

Queer is to mourn as mourn is to

1. words spoken

2. silence

3. disconnection

4. conditional love

5. other (please specify): _______________________

Queer is to time as time is to

6. refreshing for likes, hearts, reblogs, retweets, swipe rights, signal boosts

7. planning escape routes

8. becoming anew

9. mourn

10. other (please specify): _______________________

Queer is to live as live is to

11. others determining worth on mathematical symbols

12. eggshells as insidious as U.S. politics

13. the moment your narrative shifts

14. mourn
15. other (please specify): ________________________

Queer is to love as love is to
16. whispers of affirmation to counteract past whispers of scorn
17. armor
18. self-taught or poorly taught comprehensive sex education
19. mourn
20. other (please specify): ________________________

Queer is to birth as birth is to
21. accessories not included
22. deadnames equaling to, "that's actually my cousin"
23. purple in a pink-or-blue country
24. mourn
25. other (please specify): ________________________

Queer is to milestones as milestones is to
26. surpassing the average life expectancy catered to your identity/identities
27. victory in one community but suppression in another
28. "first of" popping in news reports
29. mourn
30. other (please specify): ________________________

Queer is to humor as humor is to
31. reclamation

32. therapy
33. community
34. mourn
35. other (please specify): _______________________

Queer is to rebirth as rebirth is to
36. mourn
37. mourn
38. mourn
39. mourn
40. other (please specify): _______________________

Emotion regulation is a fucking PhD program

When you eliminate the impossible bullshit that autistic people don't have feelings, whatever remains, though illogical, is our truth

Emotion regulation is a fucking PhD program

I NEED TO SHARE THIS RIGHT NOW OR I WILL FIGURATIVELY EXPLODE

Sorry, I was never a fan of the alien comparison, but then Spock came into my life

Spock is a descendant of Sherlock Holmes from the Conan Doyle canon and what if Star Trek existed in the Elementary universe and Sherlock related to Spock as a sproutling the timeline would align more for Sherlock encountering reruns than the original airdates since Sherlock was born at least five years after the original series ended but anyway staying on point when non-disabled people make the Spock and Holmes connection my brain goes ABLEISM AHEAD CAPTAIN but when disabled people do so it is HEALING and my thoughts keep on this loop like my own fucking merry-go-round and I'm physically vibrating until

I FALL ASLEEP or SPIN AROUND or WALK ON MY
TOES or DANCE or DO CARTWHEELS or EXPEL THE
EXCESS ENERGY

That keeps me physically vibrating on this thought loop like
my own fucking merry-go-round it is HEALING when dis-
abled people make the Spock and Holmes comparison but
when non-disabled people do so my brain goes ABLEISM
AHEAD CAPTAIN the timeline would align more for Sher-
lock encountering reruns than the original airdates since
Sherlock was born at least five years after the original series
ended but anyway staying on point what if Star Trek existed
in the Elementary universe and Sherlock related to Spock
as a sproutling did he perceive himself as an alien then like
Spock half-human but not quite the Conan Doyle canon
could never have predicted this but a creator of Elementary
in the past alluded to Sherlock being alien-like so Spock is a
descendant of Sherlock Holmes full stop

I was never a fan of the alien comparison but then Spock
came into my life sorry

I NEED TO FINISH THIS AND I'M FEELING LIKE I'M
BEING INTERRUPTED UNLESS YOU'D RATHER I WALK
ON MY TOES TO EXPEL THE EXCESS ENERGY I NEED
TO FINISH THIS

I was never a fan of the alien comparison but then Spock
came into my life

A creator in Elementary in the past alluded to Sherlock being alien-like the Conan Doyle canon could have never predicted this but Spock is a descendant of Sherlock Holmes full stop sorry did Sherlock as a sproutling relate to Spock as if he too were an alien half-human but not quite if Star Trek existed in the Elementary universe the timeline would align more for Sherlock encountering reruns than the original airdates since Sherlock was born at least five years after the original series ended but anyway staying on point when non-disabled people make the Spock and Holmes connection my brain goes ABLEISM AHEAD CAPTAIN but when disabled people do so it is HEALING and my thoughts keep on this loop like my own fucking merry-go-round and I'm physically vibrating until

Full stop.
I no longer feel like I'm going to figuratively explode.
Emotion regulation is a fucking PhD program
When you eliminate the impossible bullshit that autistic people don't have feelings, whatever remains, though illogical, is our truth

Lucas Scheelk is a white, autistic, trans, queer-identified poet originally from the Twin Cities, now living in Washington state. Lucas uses they/them pronouns. Their work has been featured in Barking Sycamores, Assaracus, QDA: A Queer Disability Anthology, and the 2017 Saint Paul Almanac IMPRESSIONS Project, among others. You can find Lucas on Facebook (lucasscheelk), Twitter (TC221Bee), and Instagram (lucasscheelk).

Alyssa Hillary

The Bridge

I *am* a researcher.
I *am* a participant.
I *am* the subject of research, and this makes me a bridge.

A committee member tells me researchers can forget:
There are no disembodied abstract conditions.
Their work applies to *people*.

I am a person now.
My so-called optimal outcome would be to cease,
I hit the wall in protest.

I am a person now.
Introduce the class to my neurotype and my work,
Sneak social-relational disability into neuroscience.

I *am* a student.
I *am* a teacher.
I *am* the curriculum, and this makes me a bridge.

Nita Callahan told me about bridges between worlds,
Born to one, living largely on another.
"Took a wrong turn," is the colloquial phrase.

Did I take a wrong turn?
I can't call who I *am* a wrong turn,
My brain is not a mistake.

Did I take a wrong turn?
Biomedical engineering is not my home,
But it is where I'm working today.

I *am* a student.
I *am* a teacher.
I *am* the curriculum, and this makes me a bridge.

Professionals pay lip service to disabled expertise,
Our individual perspectives are enlightening.
They're also all we get.

I have expertise.
Your questions apply to professionals, not users.
In truth, you need my data.

I have expertise.
All research shows the researcher's perspective.
Your field is a bias, too.

I *am* a researcher.
I *am* a participant.
I *am* the subject of research, and this makes me a bridge.

Alyssa Hillary is an Autistic math teacher, part time AAC user, and PhD student in neuroscience with a tendency towards poetry and/or well-cited rants when Emotions happen. Sometimes the well cited rants become journal articles. Their work appears in several previous Autonomous Press anthologies, on Disability in Kidlit, in Autism in Adulthood, and on their blog, yesthattoo.blogspot.com.

R. M. Conrad

The True Art of Medicine

I wake under a bright light in a dark room encased in feminine tissues. Plumes and sprays of silks descend around a copper loop that rings a bejeweled central organ on the ceiling. Beyond this lustrous film lingers leather furniture the color of flesh and fresh blood. The functional inner boning of these chairs and couches is suggestive, but supports nothing more provocative than the tattered remains of my concierge's coat. An altar sits to one side where mute, eyeless plaster faces of alleged beauties offer their unrepentant countenances from behind the fingerprint-smeared glass of wooden shadowboxes. Stacked nine high in the shape of a pyramid, anyone can gaze upon them all they want without fear — they are only masks.

"Hold still," the man says, but I have no idea why. His tone is enough to pull my attention from the furniture haunting beyond the veils toward the brilliant halo of light that surrounds him.

"That's good. You've lost a lot of blood, but we're getting it back in you with some nutrients to boot. You're gonna make it, so just stay awake with me. How you doing? You having any pain?" The voice is muffled by a mask of a different kind.

A pink, surgical face-cover patterned with rose petals swaddles chin and nose below a deeply lined forehead. Swarthy skin and a jet black beard. A set of brown eyes with dilated pupils peer out at me between the mask and a tangled mass of wiry, black hair.

"I don't feel and it feels...great," I murmur. I'm not sure if I actually said it out loud or if I just thought it.

There is a slow knock, as if from within some distant fish tank, and the artificial sun sets behind his shoulder. It begins to fade like some god is slowly closing the aperture of the sky. All around me, the plaster beauties close their empty eyes to sleep.

There is a burning on my solar plexus, bone on bone. It rouses me.

"Hey, stay with me," the man says, low and quiet. I try to take a deep breath but my chest won't rise; the space where the air should go is missing. I turn my head to my left, and an IV stand rises an impossible distance with a bag attached. It is filled with a sticky, reddish-brown sludge that slowly drains down the length of a fine polymer tube into a stent in my arm. Below the IV, the tatters of my bloodstained shirt half cover three airtight, portable transport coolers sweating in a neat pile between the feet of the stand. I turn my head to the right and study the shredded remains of my coat hugging the warped cursive 'm' contours of a chaise lounge. Bourbon laughter and hushed and heavy footsteps pass by the door, causing a gilt playbill from the Miku Theater to shake loose from the breast pocket and whisper to the floor.

"Quite a scrape you got here. Care to tell me how you got it?" he says. His voice has the kind of conviviality that veils concern.

The answer is there, on the tip of my tongue, but I struggle to remember well enough for my voice to reply. I have left the answer, or my voice, somewhere else: downstairs wrapped in chiffon in the hive of cubbies behind the reception desk; on the low table beside the digital clock next my bed; hidden in a lock box in the upper terminal at the Marin International Seaport; in my blue locker at the Night School training gym; or in a grey duffle bag with the interlocking rings logo of the Taltas Interplanetary Spaceport. All related, somehow, but none of these has what I'm looking for. It must be somewhere in one of my pockets, but I can't remember which one. I rifle through those pockets, turn them inside out, make an inventory of what is there. In one pocket, the wooden booth at Sheep Eaters Bistro where a client pushed a purse of money to me next to an icy Sazerac in a perspiring rocks glass; in another, the heavy flap and the rippling rush of a velvet theater curtain on a hard wooden stage; in another, the snap-crackle hiss of applause, and the zip-ripping crack of a stiletto splitting a seam; still another, blood running down manicured fingers from a scrap of black fabric torn from a concierge's coat. That is it. Now I remember the job. That is why the man is telling me to hold still. I swallow and my voice appears from nowhere to croak an answer his question: "The theater...you can almost make a killing....but never a living."

"Usually I'm the funny one," the man chuckles. He is doing

something with his hands that I can't see, and there is a draft on my left side as if someone left the door open. His eyes slide up from the work he's doing to look at me sideways, and he asks: "Did you know the true art of medicine is amusing the patient long enough for nature to take its course?" His gloved hands rise and then fall, a circular needle catching and threading something with black surgical floss, and I realize I'm not wearing a shirt. I feel the disgusting, distant pressure of the needle going in and out, but my flesh is as insensate as the fabric of my coat.

"That sounds terrible, Doc."

"Sorry, I usually tell it better."

"But doctor...will I dance again?"

"Sure."

"Really? I wasn't able to before."

"Two left feet?"

"Will that cost me extra?"

"Are all concierges this funny? I don't remember them being funny."

"Only the ones that want to live."

"Your dancing partner give you that bruise on your jaw?"

"Could say that. Could also say it was self-inflicted."

"What was that all about?"

"Money."

"How much?"

"Not enough to pay for all this."

"Another concierge?"

"How'd you guess."

"You have it coming?"

"More like should have *seen* it coming."

"How'd he get the better of you?"

"She. Sucker punch. Rounded a wrong corner."

"Well she got you good. Wore a ring or a brass knuckle from the looks of your jaw. Collapsed your lung. Tore a nice gash in your side here."

"The heart..." I say. It was what Skully was going for when she socked me in the jaw and stabbed me in the side, backstage at the Miku, over that stolen grey duffle bag brimming with coins. I start to tell him all of it. Turning that corner, distracted by a glossy pin-up with a thick graffiti mustache; then walking into that sucker punch, and the stiletto clawing its way through a seam to my flesh; the crisp crackle of applause as the curtain fell, but I'm too short of breath to explain. The volley of words has caused my breath to vanish into another pocket beyond my reach. I try to take a breath, but my chest still won't rise. My pulse rises to meet me in panic. Beyond the pink and lavender veils, the empty eyes of the whores' death masks flicker in the candlelight of the altar; but I forget about them until someone shaking my shoulders makes me remember.

"Hey, hey, hey!" he insists. The light returns to the eyes of the masks as he sits and resumes his tailor-fine work with the needle and thread. "That's right. Stay with me. Don't want to die in a whorehouse, do you?

"Who...?" I finally manage to wheeze. My finger weakly points towards him.

"Might as well tell you who I am. You'll just ferret it out, eventually." He breathes out a sigh through his nose, briefly inflating the front of the mask. "Ms. Kiss-Chase always did. Couldn't hide anything from her growing up."

I know that name...

"Ms. Kiss... house Rooking...?"

"See? Can't hide anything from you. They call me Doctor Rook here, but you'd know me by my given name, Nestor. Careful who you go whispering that too, though. What's your name, brother?"

"Quickban...Rookings aren't..."

"In the theater? I know. Terrible actors, we Rookings. We auditioned after the war for our own program on the vids, but House Telemon passed. We were lucky old Ambrose Rooking had a fallback, yeah? Can't act, but yes, sir, can we pave streets and build highway overpasses!"

Not just house Rooking...I know him from somewhere...

"But you..." I point at him, an illustrator of vague recognition.

"Wanted something more? I suppose we aren't so different, you and I. Is that what you were about to say?" He pulls the slick thread tight, shortened from his efforts, and grimaces as he deftly bites off the end of the floss with a snap of his teeth. "As you were about to point out, we Rookings don't act, and as sure as the Underworld is dim, don't practice medicine. We're engineers. Builders. Much like Appaloosans don't concierge. They're laborers and hirelings. Why is that, anyway, when all that separates you from me is a genetic skin abnormality?"

"How did I..." but I can't finish. My voice escapes me on half a wisp of a breath.

"Easy...your left lung is collapsed. Here, let me do the talking for a spell. The actors brought you here." He pulls out a thin, flat, oblong tub full of some jelly that smells strong and stinging, like camphor or menthol.

The light brightens and my heartbeat rises. My sinuses clear but my eyes water. I wipe away the excess moisture with the back of my hand and manage to ask why.

"Because I pay them to." He collects a dollop of the jelly with two gloved fingers. "Gonna apply the wound sealant now. It might feel a little strange, then again, you might not feel anything at all." His large fingers apply the jelly in a jagged, chilly line across my ribcage. My whole body breaks out in nauseating gooseflesh.

"They thought you were dead. Sold you for spare parts."

"Who...?" It is all I can manage.

He snaps the cap back on the tub, crosses his legs, and leans an elbow against the table, looking me in the eye. He pulls the mask from his face, letting it dangle at his left ear. He is probably in his late thirties, but with the gentle, boyish features of a ladies' man between two ears that protrude like the handles of teacups.

"The way I see it, Quickban, is I can either pass boldly into the Underworld in the full glory of a passion, or fade like a seagull in the fog. See, I prefer the former, so when I was old enough to run away and join the circus, I did. Oh sure, my parents tolerated me playing doctor among the work crews, so long as I knew the right balance of calcium, silicon, aluminum and iron in a bucket of cement; and I did know it. But I wasn't interested in pouring cement just because that's what my family's done since the founding of the Dominion Providence."

He snaps off the bloody pair of purple medical gloves, and fumbles a smoke from the breast pocket of his shirt beneath his surgical apron. Once the cigarette is lit and well in hand, he regards me in a heavy-lidded fashion, for just a moment, like a lover or confidant.

"See, I have this thing with the word 'no,'" he continues, exhaling smoke. "I just don't do no. And I also have this thing for medicine, which I like very much, but if I'm being honest, the better part of it is just that I was told no. 'A glaring deviation' my mother said when I told her I wanted to study medicine, as if the mixture of a man's composition could be likened to the right mix of cement. So I defied my family's well-laid plans for me, and hired myself a concierge to find me a new identity and secure a medical apprenticeship - the Red Rover, I believe his name was. I'd already done the basic medical training, so he pulled some strings and the next thing I know, he's smuggling me out with a new name on the night train to Baltimore. Says I have an apprenticeship as a med-tech patching up the Arvanians in Baltimore. Says I can finish my training there and live the rest of my days in Atlanta or wherever I please. Sometimes getting that 'yes' doesn't turn out quite like you expect it to, does it? All I had to do, besides pay the Red Rover of course, was renounce my family and homeland." He passes the palms of his hands across one another twice as if shaking some dust from them. "At least that is what I thought.

"He wasn't funny, either, Red Rover. Not like you. You think that's why he disappeared on me earlier this year?" He puts a finger over my lips as I go to speak. "Don't answer that. I'm sure you've done the math already, but I like to hear myself tell it. Well, Red Rover and I became *very* chummy over the next few years. He'd call on me when he was in town, take me to some Orangeville restaurant, ply me with booze, and ask me peculiar, very specific questions about letters we had exchanged. Gossip mostly about the top brass at the hospital, who I'd seen at the clubs on my nights off, or which ladies of the night were popular with the officers. I never understood the rhyme or reason of the questions, and the one time I asked he said he was just looking out for me. Figured it fit into some arcane puzzle you concierges are always putting together, and I'm not one to kick a gift horse in the tires; figured it didn't matter. That's what I told myself, anyway, but at the time, Baltimore was neither ours or Arvania's; it was somewhere in between. She had remained somewhat independent, Baltimore. Kept herself out of the fighting, and got a little too fat in the process. Oh, sure, the Dominions cut out that fat when they took control of her, but they'll never capture her spirit. She has a hybrid soul, and because she sits on the border of our two nations, the lives and stories of both sides flow into one another like nowhere else. It was, and is, a hotbed of intelligence. Spies everywhere, me least among them, and I didn't even realize it.

"Anyway, as only a concierge knows better than me, a man makes plans, but luck always has the last laugh - funny or not. When you wade out into the waters of fortune, you don't know you're in too deep till you hear luck's laughter behind you on the shore. Lucky as I was, luck has a territory, and fortune has a tide; that which comes in, must go out. Ms. Kiss-Chase saw to it that the tide went all the way out in Dominion territory at the behest of house Rooking, thank you very, very much. I'm sure you saw my face in the feeds a few years back, minor scandal that it was. Turncoat, they say in the salons, now. Dissident, they call me in the feeds, if they speak of me at all; which they don't. Not that I'm watching, mind you. Seems to me the Arvanians bleed red like you and me, brother; and they didn't start that war, but you can never go home again. Not after all that. Not that I'd want to after all that I've seen." He sticks his tongue out and goes cross eyed running it across his teeth in an effort to chase a stray bit of tobacco from his tongue.

I say something breathless and vague, but even I can't understand it.

"How'd you guess?!" he replies. "I did spend the better part of the war unwittingly spying for the Dominion, all the while thinking I was just getting my hands dirty learning medicine the hard way at Galen General Hospital in Baltimore. The plan was to stay on there and practice, right? Get established. Let that new name and identification Rover had cooked up for me wash away that recipe for cement with the tide of good fortune. Maybe find a way to make up with the family somehow. Then Intendant General Rastus Tyr marched through Baltimore on his way to Atlanta, and of course that means MercyCorp marched into Galen to commandeer it for the Dominion, waving their notices of clientage in the air. With the wave of those papers we went from being students and employees of Galen General to indentured servants of MercyCorp; and where MercyCorp goes, you know House Khat is pulling the strings. Meanwhile, everyone is going bananas, all up in arms about having their contracts bought out, and I'm up to my elbows in blood and gore from a massive influx of wounded. Could say they caught me red handed. So I'm just trying to puzzle out how this poor bastard's mess of a thigh is connected to the rest of his leg with the help of a rather surly surgical AI, but as soon as those MercyCorp clowns walk in and order us to stop working, well you didn't have to tell me twice. It was only a matter of time before they figured out who I really was. Think those papers Rover cooked up for me would hold up? I don't think so either. So I put down my clamps and suction and ran first chance I got. I knew she had me, though. By the balls, no less. The short hairs, you know what I mean? In too deep and luck laughing on the shore behind me."

He bends over to pull out a long, thin tube from a stiff plastic wrapper.

"So, if luck was gonna have at me I wasn't going to go quietly. The choices were either run, serve out a life sentence for offering aid and comfort to the enemy, or come clean to MercyCorp and try to cut a deal. I called the Red Rover again, and said: 'Get me a deal with MercyCorp.' He did. I took the deal and ran with it as far as I could go, which isn't very far, as you can see here." He gestures to the gossamer room that serves as our clinic for the evening. "Now it's going on a year ago that fortune's tide dragged me back here. I could have fled deeper into Arvania, I suppose. Disappeared, maybe, but the writing was on the wall for that war, and I was there as a student, not for my conscience; not that the war was justified, mind you. I'm a doctor. I don't take sides, but a man's gotta eat; so, being a fugitive on the tides of fortune, blackmailed into ripping organs in the demimonde of Boston to keep House Khat's organ banks full, beats the piss out of being locked up as a traitor — or building bridges, or being told no. Not that I have much of a choice."

There is a crisp crackle as he opens of the plastic wrapper and uncoils the long, thin tube.

"That's a good question," he says, as if I had said something. "'You're a Rooking. Why not just make nice with mother and father, and go finish your apprenticeship at the famous Khat Clinic,' you ask? Rise through the ranks and become an intendant physician to some minor house? Well, even if Ms. Kiss-Chase hadn't salted the earth of the house that raised me, well, that is a needle even the best concierge can't thread. I said I was a doctor, but really, I'm as close to being a doctor as you can get without actually being one. Never finished my apprenticeship. I was good enough to assist the Arvanians during the war, but war is chaos. It's 'Triage this' and 'Run that IV, now!' and 'Wheel the surgical AI over here, med-tech!' or 'Give that one the Morphum she's too far gone!' I learned everything you need to know to be a doctor, and then some; but medicine, the elevated art of it practiced here in the Dominion Providence, is a far cry from the mongrel beast we strut and fret in the theater of war. First, it's not funny; not at all. No sense of humor, which is perhaps my biggest obstacle to the lofty medical career to which I aspire. Second, you need to complete your medical training; but not just that, you also need to be the best at what you do. I can do the second part, I'm already the best. But the third and last part is all about reputation. That is something I surely don't have. As you concierges are so fond of saying, reputation is everything; and I burned mine when I sat my ass down in that coach class seat in a night train to Baltimore. You need a sterling character and references. Lots of fine, well-established references, and yes sir, you'd better believe they check every single one of those! In their eyes, I am just a defector from a minor house, a duped spy who couldn't play the game, and a dilettante of medicine being blackmailed into ripping organs in the finest establishments of ill repute in the Circuit - punishment for a lesser being stealing knowledge from his betters. Sound like a paragon of ethics to you? An exceptional candidate for the Hauto School of Medicine? Yeah, you're right. It just sounds like that guy's luck's run out for good. Like maybe that 'no' he was running away from finally caught up with him. Like his only choices are ripping organs in whorehouses, or rotting in a cell for the rest of his days. Future sounded pretty dim until some actors dumped a punch-drunk concierge suffocating from a popped lung into the whorehouse he, that being me, just happened to be working in - and I *do* work here, so don't get it twisted, brother." He swirls the cigarette, and punctuates the last few words with a stiff finger to my solar plexus.

I cough.

"Why didn't I just hire another concierge, then, you ask? Mr. Alphabet, or maybe Ms. Jumpskip? Just any concierge won't do for problems like I got." He wags his finger twice. "Luck turns anything she smiles at to gold, but luck's a lady. You can't just wait for her to smile at you. You gotta earn it. So I'm waiting on the barren shore of fortune's sea until I see that smile, and Quickban, I think she smiled when they dumped you all blue in the face on my table tonight."

He rubs his hands together three times rapidly.

"Seems to me luck is having her way with both of us both. Conspiring we be lovers or brothers of a kind. Lucky for you I was here instead of supervising road construction in Northlands, yeah? Lucky for me the actors brought you here rather than just dumping you to feed the rats in some alley. Lucky for all of us, though perhaps not so much for the gal with the steel right hook. I know how you concierges get with your vendettas. Reputation and all that."

"Like a dog with a bone," I gasp.

"More a surgeon with a scalpel. Very...precise, youse." He pokes the cigarette towards. He plops the cigarette between his lips, hunkers down, and goes about fitting the tube into something in my side. I can't see it, but I can feel the bland, rhythmic motion of the fitting. "I think you'd better let that one go. Take a small loss to that reputation for a long-term gain. I was thinking we can help each other."

"Are you proposing, Nestor?"

"If you'll have me, Quickban."

"You don't waste any time, do you doctor?"

"Don't make me sound cheap, now. The way I see it, a concierge's work is dangerous, if you and ol' Red Rover are examples. So, I figure this isn't the first time someone has managed to flay the flesh from your ribs, and it won't be the last. You'll be needing my services sooner rather than later. The kinds of wounds and conditions you'll need treatment for are the kinds I specialize in."

"Ones from the theater?"

"I might not be an actor, but I spent plenty of time in the theater. War is vicious art form, brother. You could say I'm something of an expert in theatrical wounds at this point. I also run a small compounding pharmacy out of my apartment, which you will want access to now and again, I imagine."

"And in exchange you want..." I start to reply, but I've run out of breath before I can finish.

"...Out of the slippery clientage I've got with House Khat. Yes, sir! Listen, I know it is a lot to ask, and I realize it won't happen overnight, but you've also lost quite a bit of blood, so I figure you'll be grateful enough to work the long game steady, yeah?"

I nod with a wheeze.

"We can settle the exact terms later, because I've got a more pressing question for you, Quickban. I need to re-inflate your lung, but first, I want to smoke some of this *very* delicious Milk of Valhalla I mixed up for Melia." He reaches into his bag and pulls forth a flask with a long and a short arm, cradling it as if it were a pet. "Do you know Melia? Works here in room 203?"

I nod again, carefully regulating my breathing so as not to pass out again.

"Well, then you know it is *very* delicious."

I gasp something thing thin and airless in agreement.

"What is that? I can't hear you. Shouldn't we wait till after, you say?" A deadpan expression on his face as if I've said something obvious and stupid. "And risk deflating your lung again? What kind of physician do you think I am?" He shakes his head disapprovingly and mutters, "Do they teach you nothing in concierge school?"

He opens a surgical tin, pulls out the white, gauzy webs of the Milk of Valhalla, and stuffs them through the short arm of the flask. "This will go nicely with the anesthetic I gave you earlier. We used to call this particular mix 'Arms of the Angels' during the war. We'd get juiced up on it and re-program the surgical AIs to perform sex shows for us. Helps with the boredom. Sometimes."

The webs turn oily and then iridescent under the pop and hiss of the flame of a butane lighter applied to the bottom of the flask. The smell of burnt sugar and the tang of brass rises as the glistening sludge transforms to pure white smoke. He expertly caps the short arm with his thumb before the smoke can escape, and then releases his thumb to suck the entire contents through the long arm in one practiced inhalation. Holding his breath, he holds up a finger, and begins to count by nodding his head. By the time he gets to ten he's slid a glass pipette into the tube in my side and leans toward me as if to kiss me; but instead, he places his lips to the pipette, counts to three on his fingers, exhales sharply into the tube. There is a single, distant, dull point of pain center left within my chest, and then the world comes into sharp focus. I bolt upright, a circulating pressure in my chest, put my hand on his shoulder, and then exhale an exclamation point of thin grey smoke.

Nestor belches out a used-up candy-flavored laugh. "One more question, Quickban," he says, draping his arm around me in return. He lays his head on my shoulder. The heat of his skin and the prickle of his beard against my bare shoulder sing a song of a thousand nerve endings dancing.

"Yes?" I reply, breathy from the smoke, but suddenly sure of my voice.

"Have I...amused you?" He giggles behind his hand like a girl with a fan, pie eyed, pupils the size of saucers.

I don't have to answer. I'm in the arms of the angels.

R. M. Conrad is a public health professional by day, and a literary science fiction writer by night. While they have worked in a variety of disciplines, writing has always been central to their practice touching on themes of queerness, liminality, subculture, gender, sexuality, and the hybrid paradoxes of being incarnate. They are currently working on a literary science fiction novel about those themes.

Allyson Shaw

7/7

You can ride the Circle line forever, or at least until 00:29, which in that case would be the next day. You have ridden the train into the future, so is the Circle Line not a kind of time machine? It just goes round and round, both clockwise and widdershins. At 8:49, 15:47, and 21:00, it pauses briefly right before you get to Bayswater, or after it, if you are going the other way. Behind a facade of a house at number 23 Leinster Gardens, the train pauses. From the street this house looks like a white Victorian terrace, a twin to number 22, except the windows are painted over. From your seat in the train car, you see it from behind, and it's as flat as a stage set. Presumably someone lives in 22, as people will live anywhere in London, even beside a fake house on a tube line, but does anyone live in 23?

The first time I saw you, you were wearing a tailored skirt suit. Your blonde hair fell in layered curtains over your shoulders, and diamonds glinted from a ring on your index finger as you clutched the stanchion. Your sunglasses reflected the fluorescent lights of the train car. Our shifting fortunes revealed themselves slowly. You lowered your glasses to get a good look, or to show me something. Your eyes, ringed with bruises and watering, met mine. You showed me a rictus of perfect teeth, as if you were gathering breath against a terrible task, or maybe it was a smile.

Say we were born in a cave, never seeing the sun. Everything before us was a dumb show. Stop me if you have heard this one before. One of us might turn and look at the fire burning in the corner of the cave and go blind. The blind one might be freed from the chains and stumble into daylight. Pale chthonic dweller, she would only be able to take in the night at first, but gradually she would see the sun, look right into it. Her faith, built on shadows, would be shattered by this ball of fire. She returns to the cave to tell the others, who of course can't bear it.

I was riding on the starboard side of the tube carriage, a pile of groceries in my lap. It was late, and the car was filled with a few people nodding off. We paused behind the facade at number 23, and in the darkness it was hard to see anything but one's reflection, until the other car pulled up. The interior lights were on, illuminating a crush of passengers drinking and laughing. Someone was pole dancing in a sequined bikini. You were there, kneeling on the seats, one hand braced against the window. You looked back at me through the silence, your hair pulled back, the dark circles under your eyes deepened by the harsh lights. I stood as if at attention, the groceries spilling across the floor, one swede tumbling against the polished shoe of a suited man. As I reached my own hand out to your reflection, you and the revelers had gone.

I ride the train again and again. Some days it seems I am stopped for an eternity behind number 23, other journeys are a blur, as if the train is going too fast and there are no stops. It's 7th of July, and I'm on the port side to get a good look at you. According to the Birthday Paradox, if you have for instance a tube carriage full of twenty three people, there is a 50% probability that two will have the same birthday. Twice that and it's inevitable that you will find someone born on the same day. Taken in the multitudes riding the Circle line at 8:30am, isn't it possible you would find yourself? I would have been riding the train since 05:08, boarding at High Street Kensington. I watched through the thick window of the car, conspicuously turned away from the other passengers, staring at my own dark reflection through the tunnel. This cipher in the dark glass was my ghost: singed hair, a fire-blackened summer dress. This moment, at number 23, is where I doss down.

The rupture might be any of the strange noises the cars make, the hissing, barking language of the brakes and engines. Then the boom, like an ice shelf breaking, precedes the ball of flame. I return, in perpetuity, to this final sun to find you.

Things are walking through the tunnels all the time. Foxes nesting in tunnel fluff—balls of clothing fibre and human hair.

Bats. Half a million mice live in the Underground. We've seen one scampering across the rails and hoped it would survive, despite the habitual loathing we'd feel if it ran over our foot, or was in the carriage itself. In the heat haze of the tunnel, through the churn of black smoke, I wouldn't see you—me—walking barefoot, covering our face and stumbling. We have no witness at the last, no self portrait from the window of the Circle Line at rest, in the darkness of number 23. We have nothing to take back to the cave.

Allyson Shaw hails from California and London. She now lives in northeast Scotland. A poet by vocation and metalsmith by trade, her work has appeared in the *Monster Verse* anthology in the Everyman's Pocket Poet series and is forthcoming in Fiddler's Green, The Bottle Imp, Liminality and Sycorax. You can find her field notes from witches monuments across Scotland at http://www.patreon.com/Allysonshaw

Alice Beecher

Rafter

Rafter cracks the rapids,
Takes off his white helmet
And pinches the granite,
A worm revolving through his temples,
A stutter in the lungs.

The river smells like
A long sea
Grieving her skeleton.

The mountains map
Our nervous circling,
Our dirty masks and dollar coffee,
Our cars collecting the dusk.

The dead have no army.
The living march on,
Their feet full of raspberry blisters,
Their eyes wet with the sweat
Of an aging empire.

The rafter buckles
Collapses his flat kayak

And the current mutters and froths,
Like sugar in the maw
Of a hungry dog.

Our gardens fill up with flood,
The slick mud stealing the turnips,
The wash constant and clamoring,
A dance that won't undo herself.

Another man is dead
In the cities of the midwest.
Our hearts leak into the pavement
We braid our stinging eyes with holy water,
Wait to be combed free of this wicked world,
To be washed through of it,
Lost plastic in the thick of a river,
Finished and full of everywhere.

Fog

it was three days after the last snow

of the past her welcome winter

and the fog felt up the shoulders of peters mountain,

stood between the pawing of our threadbare hands

like a cottony ocean,

like the glistening insides of the milky oats

just opening their long mouths

on the crooked elbow of the trail

crisp slipping beneath us,

the slow click of your

long bootprints against the mud,

the forest scratching

the wet second skin of our plastic parkas,

the pipe ringing close like a dull scream,

the fog breathing closer, gathering the crease of her damp
   dress,

your hand unraveling,

the white pines roaring under sheets of limestone,

how quickly the legs can forget

which direction they are going,

the mountain threatening to swallow

the bitter and cold and half clutched hook of our bodies

whole as a morning swallows a dream.

June

See the ants, crawling up the cooler like young punks,
   dumpstering the yellow kale and the pickles you scolded
   us into keeping, because you never know, you said, when
   you might have nothing left to throw away.

See the busted front panel of the 2000 Saturn SL1, the one
   that you didn't bust but no one believes you (what with
   the loose change rattle of your hands, what with the
   slack and slip of your weak eyes), the one that matches
   drove all the way down, all the way from Ohio, deep into
   the belly of the cumberlands, right after that shit man
   totaled the first car in a snowstorm, right before another
   shit man would buy you junkyard gold, how that would
   be enough to love him, forever, for now.

See the hand painted trump signs and the hack healers and
   the moon shedding her dress on some other mountain
   where your end ended up, where you boiled sticky water
   from the ragged creek, watched the rabbits eat the Swiss
   chard, watched the dragonflies fucking, watch the virus
   whittle the want from all of us.

See the dead slump on, merciless, bickering, buying fidget
   sticks and orange koolaid at the dollar general, still out,
   still eyeing, us and our expired inspections and hot hand

sanitizer, us and our lovely illusions (that we might stay
a little longer, that we might outlast this earth).

See the best ice cream in the universe at the only gas sta-
tion in Hillsboro, West Virginia, how it makes your teeth
cold just thinking of it, how the honeysuckle dripped
from the hills like a sugary sweat, how if you would you
would return and let that be enough, the redneck hills
and the milkweed seeds, let the want want on, let it
sleep in the throats of the holler dogs like a long swallow.

The Bear

The bear and the butter in the eggs I burned, the bear and
   your hard jaw, stiff and screaming dry as the screech
   owl, the bear and the blood in the bedsheets, the bear
   and the hornet's nest in the blade of the window, the
   bear and her body a sweet bomb walking, the bear and
   the black of the rotted leftovers, the bear and the butt of
   your palm on the steering wheel, winding, the bear and
   the bottle unopened but humming, the bear who never
   chose to be a breathing gun, who never chose to be a
   witch woven to the oak tree, slow slumberer, stumbling
   sycorax, the bear and her blackberry breath, her honey-
   suckle hands

All those years I lived in west virginia and I never saw a bear
   like you,
You and your highway-colored hair,
You and your juniper jaw
You and the milk you made of the chickweed.

(the dog stiffened, you were hum-lumbering, the day sud-
   denly sharp as a whip in the stomach)

All those years lifting my hips to hard men, kissing in the
   scratch of oak and poplar
Sitting in the lack by the kitchen table

And I never met a bear like you,
You and your long weight sinking,
You and your night-torn body,
Your quiet temper,
Your teeth sharp even as you sleep.

All those years and now you come running
Through the city's sweet trash, honeyjunk and heart medi-
	cine,
Sweet baby-rays and bags of bug dust,
Now you come sudden, as the virus did, as the bad men do,
A bone in the splint of my bed, half-monster, half-baby,
An old bark buried in your belly, you broke boy, you hot
	constellation,
Ursa major & minor, a growling in the gutter, a howling in
	the heart.

(I walk by, will not be tempted by your heavy-step, by the
	fumble of your breast,
By the fruiting of your haunches like a set of strong man-
	hands, will not walk
Into the death that rests between us like a woman weary
	and worn.)

Alice Beecher is an organizer, social worker, popular educator and occasional poet currently living on occupied Cherokee land in Western North Carolina. Originally from New England, she has been working and living and fighting capitalism in Appalachia for the past 7 years. Sometimes she tries to grow things and they usually get eaten by rabbits, sometimes she plays songs on her banjo which is usually cranky and out of tune. She was the 2016 winner of the West Virginia Emerging Writers contest and has had work published in Still: The Journal, Heartwood Literary magazine and a handful of weird anarchist zines. You can find more of her work at alicebeecherpoetry.org.

Dora M. Raymaker

Gender-Monsters at the Edge of the World

It's 1988.

It's the edge of the world.

Really.

It's one of the last islands--*really*--of civilization on the north-western edge of the Atlantic. It's where the sun first touches North America in the morning and the salty sea-dragon corrodes everything it breathes on. The sun has long since set, autumn's gold melted to purple twilight and blinked to black night. The wind mumbles about the sub-zero temperatures lurking past October's bend.

Here there be monsters.

K and I leave my apartment and enter the Mount Desert Island night. We'd gone to my place straight from high school on the bus, enduring yet another episode of spitballs to the back of the head. But it was warm inside my apartment, and safe.

Outside now, the moonlight exposes our New Wave angles, our black eyeliner, our androgyny clear as David Bowie's voice. I like an oversized men's sweater and jacket over a long skirt and bad-ass boots that say shit-kicker in any gender. K likes patterned shirts with big jewelry and the collar turned up. Our hair is short in back and long in front.

The streets of Bar Harbor are deserted. We walk them, alert like mice to owls. Nine million people come through here between June and September, but year-round it's just shy of four thousand--and that's only that because of Jackson Laboratory. No one wants to actually live at the edge of the world. The windows of the Olde Tyme Shoppes are boarded up against winter's fangs.

This is the plan: We take the bus from school to my apartment. I walk K home. K drives me back to my apartment in Mom's car. K drives Mom's car back home. It's our daily routine. It's dangerous for us together, but moreso for us alone.

"I overheard the rednecks in the hall," K says, "talking about how they're 'gonna shoot them there cat-killahs.'"

"Guess that explains it." I respond quietly, so the night can't overhear. "Creep-o in the baseball hat in homeroom kept muttering 'gonna getcha' to me."

"I guess they're gathering on Cadillac Mountain Saturday with their guns. I think it's for real this time."

"Good day to stay inside then." I swallow. Then with a bite of delayed anger, "Bet they're the ones killing the cats."

We start up the hill to K's house. The black trees won't tell me if they're providing cover for us or for an ambush.

There's no dispute over whether or not cats are getting killed. The Bar Harbor Police Department believes cats are getting killed (and maybe skinned--the details vary) and left in mailboxes, so that makes it true. The cops are questioning our friends. They'll come for us next. They're not on our side and they never will be. The cops won't help us if the rednecks gather on Cadillac Mountain with their guns. We're alone on the road between safe houses. We're alone at the edge of the world.

We're almost at the parking lot, almost at the safety of the car, we just have to cross the street.

Snarling light from a ten-eyed tank crests the hill. A jacked-up pickup, armored in running lights, stabbing out our eyes. This could be it, it could be it, it could be guns, or glass bottles, or, if we're lucky just eggs or piss, or maybe they'll plow us down and leave us dead or dying in the ditch, roadkill, oops--

K pulls me into the bushes to wait out the passing, our breath camouflaged in the rasping of autumn's last leaves.

We park ourselves there a good long time after the truck has passed.

We park ourselves until my toes start to go numb with cold.

Sometimes the truck'll turn around and come back with the running lights off, death on hate-pumped tires.

No need to discuss how long to wait; we know how long we need to wait. No need to discuss how fast to run the rest of the way to K's house, either. We've been prey for sixteen-seventeen years now and predator evasion's a reflex act. Fear keeps us alive. We can't release it from our ribs until we're in K's mom's car.

The heat blasts on.

The music too: SOMETIMES I FEEL I'VE GOT TO--

It's safe inside

RUN AWAY I'VE GOT TO--

the Soft Celled dance hall of the

GET AWAY FROM THE PAIN YOU DRIVE INTO THE HEART OF ME--

big old car's steel belly.

Rinse. Repeat.

Senior year of high school.

High points of fall term: The rednecks don't shoot us dead.

Fall gives way to winter. The roads are deadly with ice. The air is deadly with cold. Spend more than a few minutes exposed and it's a one-way trip to *To Build A Fire* City. I don't know who's driving. Someone's driving. In the big old car's steel belly. I don't know whose car. I'm a little high and the smoke from this cigarette makes cool curls through the crack in the back car window. A snowstorm's coming and maybe there's school tomorrow or maybe it's a weekend or a snow day. I don't know what day it is now or tomorrow just that I'm always full of holes colder than the icy road and the kill-you air and I never know what day it is even when I'm not a little high. There are no boundaries between things. No *beats* to tap out the time. If we break down out here, on this big ice parking lot, we die.

But we arrive somewhere, someone's house. It's warm and safe, full of people in New-Wave Punk-Rock Hippie-Shit angles who've got each other's backs. We crowd around the fizzling TV, the antenna blowing on-and-off-signal in the seaward wind. The signal catches on Friday Night Videos, providing a frame-of-reference.

Providing a beat.

Something to mark time to.

Something to mark ourselves to.

DIG IF YOU WILL THE PICTURE

(Prince is us)

I'M A SLAVE TO THE RHYTHM

(Grace Jones is us)

YOU SPIN ME RIGHT ROUND BABY

(Pete Burns is us)

SWEET DREAMS ARE MADE OF THIS

(Annie Lennox is us)

The music is us, the beat is us, we spin right-round-record in sweet, rhythmic picture-dreams of in-betweens.

Someone arrives with a bootleg copy of *Akira* on VHS. There are no subtitles. We get fucked-up on weed and sticky-sweet wine coolers and watch it in a woozy-warm tumble of awe. We are *that* too, mutant monsters, hot and powerful and reviled on our red motor bikes.

We've got no subtitles, either.

In Times Square, the ball drops. The year turns 1989.

Still no fucking subtitles. But I've got my own car now—a gold Subaru that's beat to shit but Bowie-level glam too. No more spitball bus hooray! We can take a short step back from the edge of the world--though what constitutes the "edge" is relative to one's scale.

I pick up K in the gold Disco-ru and drive thirty miles inland to the Queer Dance in Bangor.

The parking lot is the shark-infested waters we need to swim through to reach Paradise Island.

Everyone knows about the monthly Queer Dance. Everyone. Including the shits who murdered Charlie Howard in 1984, and they've been out of jail two years now. They got less than two years in, because who cares if you kill a faggot. Murder gets downgraded to manslaughter if you kill a faggot. I'm sure two years in jail is worth it to some of them for the chance to get us. Even if Charlie's murderers don't come for us, it's not like there isn't a long, eager line behind them. It's not like the cops are suddenly on our side.

We sit in the car and breathe.

Yeah, sure, we've been pushed, slapped, punched, emotionally battered suicidal-senseless, had hard, sharp objects hurled at us--yeah, sure, there's been some kind of assault every day for most of our so-far-short lives.

But this is different. This isn't getting up after being shoved down. This is kill-you-dead. Creep-o in his baseball hat in homeroom and his gun-toting posse call the State Street Bridge "Chuck-a-Homo Bridge" and we're parked right next door to it. One of us was killed right by this parking lot, just four years ago.

We step out of the car.

The wind has an edge of warmth to it. We ignore it. It's early spring's cruelty. All these slushy puddles in the parking lot will freeze over in crackling real-time like a horror movie effect as the night progresses. Never lose awareness of the cold.

I pick up my step with a few skip-hops get closer to K, and we reach for each other's hands.

Behind us, tires grind on half-frozen asphalt. Breaks squeal.

"Faggot-ass faggot," we hear, with the snickers.

A sound of breaking glass.

Don't turn around.

Shitfuck don't turn around. Don't run. Don't do anything, just keep walking. Head high. Eyes narrowed. Don't let them see a crack. Like Orpheus through Hades, if you turn around you die.

My pulse is overwhelming. K's hand sweats into mine.

Squealing tires, keep going, keep going, keep--

OHSHIT I CAN'T KEEP MY SHIT TOGETHER

Our panicked sprint starts at the same time, some psychic connection of fight-or-flight tripping over OH PLEASE DON'T SLIP ON THIS ICE

We make it to the building and pull open the doors.

Heat floofs out like the puff of a feather boa.

Inside--streamers and disco lights and--Oh-SNAP-SNAP-sweetie, it's motherfucking RAINING MEN!

We spot M and N by the DJ stage, tall, thin, vampire boy/girls with tiny rat-tail braids and cheekbones cut like glaciers. K goes to join them. I consider going to the table to say hi to C, butch-cut hair, black-and-white crisp-cut perfection, but hit the dance floor instead. There's a hole that needs filling with the beat. There's a touch stone, a reference frame, a look, a feel, the sound--

WHY CAN'T I GET JUST ONE FUCK yeah, sing it, sing it, grind it, dance it, Violent Femmes-it

ADD IT UP

fill the hole with light and sound

ADD IT UP

on this dance floor, no one will ever hurt me.

The year churns to 1990.

I graduate from high school; K has one year left to go. I move down the coast to Portland, Maine with my partner H trying to back away from the edge of the world. K comes down every weekend, break, and designated class-skip-day to stay with us. Friends go to college. Friends return from college. Friends take friends dancing. S--who graduated the year before me and has been going to Hampshire College where there are no grades, you make your own curriculum, and queer studies is a thing--showed us the post card from the queer bookstore in Boston:

"He/she was the man/woman of his/her dreams."

It captions two people in a mishmash of drag gazing into each other's eyes. We laugh and laugh. It's a good joke because it's true. Not a one of us has a gender that fits the symbols on a restroom door. Pronouns come and go with how we *perform*. I'm he in a tuxedo, she in a skirt; S is she in knee-length blonde curls, and he in tight jeans.

K and I do our best Divine imitation:

"Divine, does the smell of blood turn you on?"

"It does more than turn me on. It. Makes. Me. Cum."

H and I kiss and accidentally knock off each other's top hats.

M asks me, "Hey, D, can you write your name in the snow?"

"Well, duh, can't everyone?" So confused.

"OH. Oh!" M laughs, "I forgot you're a girl."

"What's that got to do with--oh!" I get it, laughing, "Well, it's easy to forget, what with my fucking huge-ass dick-and-balls and all." Nah, I never feel the need to pack because my dick-and-balls are motherfucking *real*.

"Girlfriend," I wave at M, "pass me that nail polish."

M finishes off a glitter-pinky and hands the bottle over.

Sometimes he, sometimes she, sometimes both, sometimes the slash between them: she/he is always us.

It is always danger-us.

We are making frames of reference.

We are finding bigger dance floors.

The moonlight makes silver crescents of our jawlines while we wait to enter the club. White neon letters cast movie-light on ice-slicked sidewalk, spelling out:

ZOOTZ

the name of the dance hall

hissing behind fogged glass

hissing from the radiator promising heat

hissing from the vibration of the sub-woof

beneath our feet.

The tails of my tux touch the backs of my knees below the hem of my leather miniskirt. The white dress shirt's too thin and the tie and cummerbund are no help at all. Fuck this twenty-degree chill. Fuck this cold, dry night, and parking lot of a cover-queue. Waiting in this line is not going to kill me. Nuclear holocaust, sure that might still kill me, who knows, but not this godsdamned non-nuclear-winter cold. I'll be hot enough once I start dancing. Hot with the pulse-beat rattling the neon-fogged window, coming up from the dance floor beneath.

boom-boom-boom-boom-boom-boom----

boom-boom-boom-boom-boom-boom----

K casts behind us toward Forest Avenue. "Why isn't the

line moving? It's just a five-dollar cover. It's all ages; they don't even need to card anyone."

They'll get us every time: roadways and parking lots. They come packed with as much hate in Portland as they do in Bar Harbor and Bangor. We're still too close, I guess, to the edge of the world.

"Faggot!" Portland's version of creep-o from homeroom passes by and yells. Spits out the window. "Fucking lesbo. Fucking disgusting! Fucking queers."

Here's hoping no glass bottle.

Here's hoping no barrel of a shotgun.

BUT IF THERE IS BRING IT THE FUCK ON

We're snarling piss-mad now.

We are the gender-monsters of their worst nightmares, scarier than Akira on a red motor bike. I turn around, stare them straight in the eye on their next pass, and scream, "FUCKING DISGUSTING FAGGOT-ASS-FAGGOT," right-the-fuck-back at them.

K gives them the finger and H and S snarl on-beat with my scream.

They don't come back around the block again.

We've been through this shit long enough we're done with being prey. We have *numbers*. We're HERE we're QUEER get USED TO IT motherfuckers. We'll tear them apart with our bare hands if we have to.

Or die trying.

Yeah, we'll probably die trying.

boom-boom-boom-boom-boom-boom----

But let's dance first, yeah.

The queue to enter finally moves in the direction of safety. All of us fucking faggot-ass-lesbo-faggots cannot WAIT to be fucking inside dancing.

This is our sound rattling the drenched window pane. Our industrial shape-shifting gender-bending monster groove. Our self-exploding nihilistic beat to die by because if we're going to die it's going to be on the holy-ground of the dance floor.

The four she/he of us--S, K, H, and I--reach the door of the club and push inside. Air the consistency of sweat coats my glasses.

Klang-pound! Ding-ding-ding-ding-ding-ding. Klang-pound! "LET ME SIT ON YOUR FACE / LET ME SIT ON YOUR FACE--"

The landing we stand on shakes with Lords of Acid and I can't get my cover-cash for the bouncer out fast enough because I don't want to miss the whole song, I don't want to miss--

Klang-pound! Ding-ding-ding-ding-ding-ding.

Hand over a bill blind hope it's the right one run downstairs to where the music lives. Can never figure out how this place is built; it's pitch-fucking black except for the light show. But I know how the music's built, shit-fucking-hot as a red motor bike YEAH

I can't

can't even

can't even WAIT

Pressing through the crowd exploding outward dancing outward dancing dancing

HEY POOR! HEY POOR! YOU DON'T HAVE TO BE POOR ANYMORE!

"JESUS IS HERE!" I shout the lyrics along with the crowd and smash my black boots into the concrete hard enough to feel the shock shoot straight my shin bones FUCK YEAH

We do Front 242 for a while and then the DJ mixes it back-to-back with REACH OUT AND TOUCH FAITH

Depeche Mode, music is my faith, music and dancing until I break the fuck apart and it's the only time I'm ever whole.

EVERY TIME I SEE YOU FALLING I GET DOWN ON MY KNEES AND PRAY

Yes, yes, yes, give me New Order, give me Bizarre Love Triangle, give to me the Holy Queer-Fucked Church of Sound.

My feet are smoldering coals by the time I've burned off enough stress to notice the rest of the room.

When I do, everyone around me is the man/woman of her/his dreams.

In the Last Dance Club before the edge of the world gender-expression doesn't have "male" and "female" for its endpoints but feathers-and-sequins and leather-and-chains-- and even then, everyone is free to mix-and-match.

Skip-trip: 1998. Ten years from start.

It's a post-internet world. The world wide web networks the reference points we made from music videos, bootleg anime, fear, and hope. They *distribute worldwide*. It's a trip-hop, future-pop, gender-fucked cyber-rave world. I'm in the "other" Portland, the left-coast one, about as far away from the edge of the world as a gender-monster can get. R and I put on special outfits because that's clearly the only way to go grocery shopping.

"We're from the future," R announces after giving us a good look-over. "In the future there is no gender."

I tilt my top hat just so. "But there are very tall boots. And scarves. Lots, and lots of scarves."

and dancing

All <3s to K. Sennett for reviewing this piece for accuracy of memory, and for being the reason I have memories at all.

Dora M Raymaker, PhD, is an Autistic/queer/genderqueer scientist, author, multi-media artist, and troublemaker whose work across disciplines focuses on social justice, critical systems thinking, and the dance between hope and fear. Dora is the author of the novels Hoshi and the Red City Circuit, available from Argawarga Press, and Resonance, coming soon; and of the short stories "Heat Producing Entities" and "Hearts and Tails," which can be found in previous volumes of Spoon Knife.

Margaret Killjoy

A Pale Thing, A Bright Thing

The air is full of leaves like snow

Caught up in the wind coming down off the mountains

And last night under the full moon

Some creature galloped across the field

A pale thing, a bright thing

It stopped to look at me

There are ghost dogs in the mountains, everyone knows
    that

I can't say a word

Because I will open my mouth and

The gale will break my teeth and fear will break my teeth

Because I will open my mouth and fog will sink into the
    valley

Out from my throat across the creek into the willows

bright fog

Because I will open my mouth and

Nothing and nothing

It stared at me bright and pale
I clapped
And it ran

I Haven't Been Sleeping Well

I haven't been sleeping well and
I wish it were somebody's fault

I wish it were my fault
For stumbling strangely into the night
Shouting at fireflies
Shouting at the same trees
At the steel bars of the forest

I wish it were her fault
Like I could claim she were my keeper
Come up the path to bring me salt
And mead

I wish it were her fault
I wish she were keeping me up
Scratching at my skin instead of sleeping
Both of us forgetting to dream

I haven't been sleeping well
Because the same sun sets behind the same mountain.

One day it must fall off course

It must burn the air and flood my veins with light
Making a map of my skin
For her to follow, as she wants

I haven't been sleeping well and
I wish it were so simple

It should be so simple.

Maine

The lake was still
but for ten punks
in various states of undress
floating in the water
or crouching on rocks.

Birch crowded into us,
and wild blueberries,
and those ones you shouldn't eat,
the ones that look
like wild blueberries.

The distant middle of the lake
was a single rock,
almost an island,
two strangers.

I put myself on my back
and tried to forget what I was doing
and swam
and I couldn't touch bottom
and I've never been a swimmer
and I've always known myself
to be craven.

And when I made it there
we were like mermaids—
or maybe just barnacles--
with birthmarks and
big bellies
and an overcast sky
and lily pads.
Even I was smiling.
And I was shaking.
I was a quarter-mile in
and I wasn't tired or cold but
I was afraid
maybe of drowning
but mostly of panic.

"I'll come with you,"
she told me
and I didn't argue
and I wore myself out
trying to swim with my head up
so we could talk about bullshit and Russia
and maybe I wanted to impress her
and she could have done laps around me
but she stayed abreast.

And I was happy
as much as I'm ever happy.

Who are the ghosts in this forest?

Sometimes railroads sing long, slow notes that move slowly through pitches. It's music. No one who has ever heard it doubts that it's music. But it's not human. Rail song is not ours.

The first time I heard it—the first time I really heard it, without the background noise of cars and brakes and the rest of a city or the rest of a rail yard—was in the forest, in Oregon. I was a ten mile hike from the nearest paved road. It was two AM or later, and I was hidden behind a fallen tree below a logging road. I was reading *Lord of the Rings* by the light of a red headlamp, and my friend—who was supposed to be on watch with me—was sound asleep.

The song crept across the forest, like ent-song. It has to do with the curves in the tracks, I suppose, but I haven't looked much into it because I don't need to, because I know what it is. It's song. I put down the book, enchanted, and for minutes or hours I listened.

Rail song reminds us that the world is alive, that the world is moving. That we can move with it.

The first time I met forest defenders was at an anticapitalist convergence in Washington DC called The People's Strike. That was a bit grandiose of a name, if I'm being honest. It wasn't the residents of DC on strike that day, it was a large but motley assortment of labor activists, crusty anarchists, radical pagans, and organizers who fought for immigrant communities. I was one of the crusty anarchists—and let's be honest I wasn't that far off from being a radical pagan. We were there to try to stop some vestige of neoliberal globalization or another, some gathering of politicians carving up the developing world for corporate profit.

I met forest defenders in a construction dumpster in the middle of the night, where we plotted to disrupt the meeting of world leaders. I spent the night after that hogtied on the floor of a police training facility with around seven hundred other people. The night after that, I was released without charges and without having ever given my name to the police—sometimes stubbornness is a suitable replacement for courage.

Then we made our way down to the swamps of North Carolina, the same swamps that were once home to the famed maroon communities. At that regional Earth First! Rendezvous I got to actually meet the forest defenders properly. They were so fucking cool. I mean that both positively and disparagingly. They'd hitchhiked or hopped trains or something across the entire country, leaving behind their beloved Cascadian forests to join us in the strike and to teach us forest skills in the swamp. They were young, they were cocky, they were queer, they were beautiful. The forest defenders didn't have time for anyone who wasn't part of their crew. I was nineteen. I hated them and I wanted to be one of them.

Scant months later, I made my way west to join them.

I don't know if I believe in magic. I'm reasonably certain I'll die one day, still uncertain if I believe in it. I've seen it, I've felt it, but my mind filters it out. A witch once cured me of nightmares. I'd been dreaming about police chasing me, every night, for months. In an old growth forest, a witch next to a creek picked at my aura for five seconds, and I've never had that dream again. I still don't know if I believe in magic.

The timber sale I went to first was named Straw Devil. There's nothing to a name, of course.

The National Forest timber sale program is a scam. I don't know if there's any other way to put it. The National Forests are publicly owned, but huge swathes of them are sold at a loss to private timber companies who patchwork them with clearcuts. They funnel some portion of their profits to lobby lawmakers to make sure that the scam stays available, and the forests themselves—as well as those of us who enjoy access to nature whether professionally or personally—pay the cost. It's a net loss in almost every possible way. Even if your goal was a healthy economy—rather than a healthy ecosystem—a healthy forest offers more revenue through recreation, and a clearcut does no one any good.

A motley crew of anarchists and activists and hippies and punks, the forest defenders went up against the might of these government-backed timber companies. Their motto was "full-time direct action." Their lives and their subculture were entirely devoted to saving forests and fighting oppression. It was intoxicating. There is nothing quite like being in the company of passionate people, and the forest defenders were nothing if not passionate.

They've fought for countless forests. They win sometimes. They lose most of the time. Sometimes, in the process of fighting ecocidal logging, they catch felonies. Sometimes they die.

A man named Sparrow died at Straw Devil. He was the agent of his own death. I knew him. Not well, but us goth anarchists were rare enough that we stuck together when we could. A third goth anarchist, a medic, was the first responder on the scene. Sparrow didn't die a simple death. His death was a ritual. For what purpose, no one will ever know. No one saw him die. They only saw what he left behind.

I'm not afraid of ghosts. I'm afraid of everything, but I'm not afraid of ghosts. If they're real, they're real in this... this abstract way where reality is something we collectively create but all of us are capable of stepping outside the collective reality into a reality shared by fewer people. If ghosts are real, they don't hurt us. If they're real, they watch over us. They can't help us. They can't hurt us. They can help us make ourselves brave, or they can help us make ourselves afraid, and courage and fear are powerful. But they're abstract.

I'm sure Sparrow wasn't the only person who died in that forest.

The forest is afraid of people, and you don't see most of what lives there because everything hides. At night it's worse. Things move at night. Subtle things. Flitting, flickering bits of shadow. Reflective eyes. Sometimes at night, while I was busy breaking this or that law, the moon would cast shadows through the trees that danced in the wind and my heart collapsed into my gut and fear rose to take its place.

I'm not afraid of ghosts, but I am afraid of cops. When grizzled forest defenders sit around the fire, trying to scare newcomers, the boogieman they conjure up is the super freddie.

Fifteen years later and I don't know how to parse the stories I heard, but the idea is this:

First of all, a "freddie" is a federal agent. All forest rangers are technically federal agents, though the worst of our vitriol was saved for the Law Enforcement Officers of the Forest Service. A super freddie though... I believe in them, more than I believe in ghosts, but they serve the same purpose. A super freddie is every bump in the night. And in the forest, everything bumps. A super freddie is a fed in camouflage, living in the woods alongside us even less seen than the wildlife. They didn't seem to make arrests. They didn't seem to interfere. They just fucked with our heads. The best guess was that they were special forces, training their stalking on soft targets... on us. I have friends who've stumbled across them, or have had terrible things whispered in their ears from just outside the firelight.

There might have been super freddies at Straw Devil. I don't know.

I wasn't there long. I lived at Straw Devil for a few weeks a few times, and I wasn't good for much, so I volunteered to do road security. I volunteered to crouch behind a log at night, making sure cops didn't come up on us unannounced. It's a good role for me, because it was low-key. Because I got to sit around and read books (tree sitters mostly sit around and read books too, and I tried that a couple of times, but my fear of heights and mediocre rope skills left me ill-suited to the task).

Headlights cut through the dark and heavy tires rolled over gravel. You can't drive quietly on a forest road. An SUV went past our position. I followed, keeping to the trees and hopefully out of illumination of the taillights. It was almost impossible for it to be a coincidence that an SUV was driving through those woods at two AM. We were expecting the police to raid, because we'd lost a lawsuit or something and logging was set to resume and we were set to interfere with that logging and the police were set to interfere with our interference.

A quarter mile up the road, the car stopped. I stopped too.

I heard a car door open and close, and the car three-point turned and left the way it came. They'd dropped someone off.

It was another half a mile to our tree sits, and I walked silently under the moon. Determination is a good replacement for bravery too.

"Hey Tree," I shouted up the base of a sit, because every treesitter's name is "tree" while they're aloft for security reasons.

"Yeah Ground?" I heard in response.

I told the sitters what I'd seen.

Then I had to turn around and walk back to position. Alone. With a super freddie in the woods. I clutched my knife, and I walked in the middle of the road so no one could jump out from the trees. That's when I was afraid. No determination, no stubbornness were available to me. I had no choice, though. Lack of choice will cover for courage in a pinch.

The next day, a new recruit was in camp. Her father had driven her in his SUV. They'd gotten lost and didn't find the place until two AM. No super freddie after all. The next night, I was back to position, reading *Lord of the Rings* while the other person on watch slept soundly. The rails still sang their inorganic song of freedom.

Sparrow was a ghost in the forest, the cops were ghosts in the forest. The rails were ghosts in the forest. The wildlife were ghosts in that forest. We tried to be ghosts ourselves. Wherever we went, if we heard a car, we took off into the trees. Our camps were well off the road, hidden from view. Our food caches were camouflaged. Some of us—not me, but some of us—had years of experience living in the woods illegally.

Super freddies, if they're real, exhibit no bravery when they stalk us. They have homes to return to. They have tens of thousands of dollars of equipment. They have the entire weight of the legal system behind them. They risk nothing. They're doing nothing special.

Ghost stories of super freddies only scared the newcomers, and it took me a long time to figure out why: because super freddies weren't the real power in those forests. We were. We climbed the highest trees. We literally fought off the bears who tried to get into our food. We wrote our own playbook. Forest defenders earn their cocky attitudes. They deserve their confidence. They took real risks. They put everything on the line. They lived real lives. Passionate lives.

Some passionate lives are longer than others.

I live in the woods now, alone a lot of the time. If something happened, there would be no one in shouting distance.

I'm not much afraid of the forest anymore, or at least I try not to be. I tell myself that I am the creature worth fearing. I have fangs and claws enough for whatever might try to fuck with me.

I don't know if there are ghosts. One day I'll die not knowing if there are ghosts.

Margaret Killjoy is a transfeminine author and editor currently living in a self-built cabin in the Appalachian mountains. She is the author of the Danielle Cain series of novellas, published by Tor.com. She can be found complaining about things on twitter @magpiekilljoy and on her blog at www.birdsbeforethestorm.net.

Phil Smith

Threshold

this is the threshold.

Gaia steps between the trees.
she moves from one to the other
slipping behind a maple
going on to a birch.
she sits on a spruce branch
above the tidal rip
and chatters
(in the form of a small squirrel)
at me.
she stares directly at me
daring me, encouraging me
to go to her.
she bounds
(embodied as a doe)
over the rough field
leaping lightly into the air
and then settling back down
over and over again
until she reaches the treeline.

"We exist

within the context of a language

that is our own invention but which controls us…"

      (Cooper, 1978, p. 19)

it was taken from us

(as was most everything)

by those who think that

animal people

plant   people

soil   people

bird   people

rock   people

tree   people

are not part of us

who do not believe that

"we   *are*   the air,

we   *are*   the water,

we   *are*   the earth,

we   *are*   the Sun."

   (Suzuki, 2007, p.17)

they deny what i know:

"it is impossible to draw lines

that delineate separate categories

of air, water, soil and life.

you and i

don't end

at our fingertips or skin."

    (Suzuki, 2007, p. 192)

rather, "... all life forms

are our relations."

    (Suzuki, 2007, p. 197)

but these foolish others –

the ones who live in the whorled

who spend their days buying and selling –

they think

"...that knowledge obtained by scientists

is the ultimate authority,

that as we accumulate information,

our capacity to understand, control and manage

our surroundings will grow correspondingly."

    (Suzuki, 2007, p. 33)

but "...science would benefit

from acknowledging a way of knowing

about the world that includes intuition."

    (Suzuki, 2007, p. 36)

instead, "...we must find a new story,

a narrative that includes us

in the continuum of Earth's time and space,

restoring purpose and meaning to human existence."

    (Suzuki, 2007, p. 46)

we must "...listen

to the language of animal, vegetable, *and* mineral."

    (Cooper, 1973, p. 83)

in the middle of a nor'easter
i walk down to the edge of the tidal pond.
waves pile up against the shore.
the air tumbles
and roars.
ravens dodge driven rain
circling and calling everlasting
as they always have.
the earth is thin here;
the bones of the world
push up through what passes for soil.
the ocean gnaws at the edge
seeking to pull back more
to smash the rocks
pull them down into the mud.
i look out to the far side
of the tidal pond
through the rain
and see Gaia walking
lonely, eyes downcast
on the opposite shore.

i exist
in the place between.
not this, not that.
neither these, nor those.
i am not of the whorled

(i am invisible to it);
i am of the whirled,
though i do not yet entirely inhabit it.
i work to return that which
"has been stolen from us,
like the reality of our dreams and our deaths."
     (Cooper, 1978, p. 14)
that which has been stolen,
we call it madness –
though really it is
our place in the world
that has become mad –
remembering that
"...the teutonic origin of 'mad' is 'maimed'."
     (Cooper, 1978, p. 22-23)
we have maimed the world
we have maimed our place in it
we have maimed our connection with ourselves
we have maimed our connection with each other
and continue to do so.
we think that what we do to
and with
the world
ourselves
and each other
is right and good.
we are wrong
mislead by greed
and vanity

and hubris.

we are killing ourselves:

"...there is no correlation between happiness

and social class,

per capita consumption

or personal income."

    (Suzuki, 2007, p. 236)

We have forgotten that

"to live fully, people need

a direct relationship to nature..."

        (Forbes, 2001, p. 70)

and that "any time a people's connection

to land is severed...

the culture is in trouble."

        (Forbes, 2001, p. 13)

we have lost all understanding

of how to be in the world, and

"...because of our total lack of consciousness

we don't know how,

amongst many other things,

to produce a society of minimal technology

which means a society of minimal pollution

(in every sense)

and of maximal free time."

    (Cooper, 1978, p. 28)

i walk out of this whirled
into the other, horrid whored whorled.
surprisingly, the distance
is not all that far: 1.5 miles
along an unmarked trail
up and down
around and about
over sumps and streams.
today, the woods
and the path are covered
with new snow
and the air this mid-November
is colder than it's been in months.
just before i reach the boardwalk
over the old beaver meadow
i stop:
on the ground
in front of me
in the snow
are Gaia's footprints.
i can see by the story they tell
that she walked in
then walked out
turning around at just this place
amongst the birches.
why did she stop?
why didn't she walk all the way in?
i follow the footprints for a while
hoping to meet her.

after perhaps half a mile
of tracking her steps coming and going
i see that they turned south off the trail
into the spruce woods
the prints lost in bare spots
under the trees.
i stop there on the trail and wonder:
did she not want to be seen? touched? noticed?
though she speaks to me –
sometimes in dreams,
sometimes in the voices of
animal people
and tree people
and bird people
in the whirled –
i've never been able to speak to her
ask her the questions that need asking.
perhaps that, in itself, is a kind of answer.

the destruction of the whorled
this destruction of ourselves
this destruction of each other
is violence, pure and simple
a way of not-living based in competition –
"where for one to succeed, another must fail…"
    (Coperthwaite, 2002, p. 4)
the ultimate manifestation of violence

is war, which is itself
"...an inherent, inevitable, and essential element
of the civilization in which we live
because it is the final large-scale flowering
of the domination or violence
which almost all the time
permeates all our human relationships."
 (Gregg, 1944, p. 204)
to create a culture that is rooted in non-violence
means stepping wholly (holy) and completely away
from society as we have come to know it
in the second decade of the twenty-first century.
it means renouncing all parts of that society.
it means creating "nonviolent beauty –
beauty contained in nonmaterial things,
such as a way of life, learning,
relationships with others..."
 (Coperthwaite, 2002, p. 28)
it means stepping away from institutions
as we have constructed them.
take, for example, education:
"Forced learning is violence."
 (Coperthwaite, 2002, p. 54)
this stepping away requires understanding that
"...society is itself largely responsible
for the conditions which create criminals."
 (Gregg, 1944, p. 138)
this stepping away means attending
to love, truth, unity –

practicing a kind of "moral jiu-jitsu."
    (Gregg, 1944, p. 43)
to do these things
means – ensures – that one will be made
perhaps already is
mad.

i wake in the night
and look up through the skylight
at the top of the round, tortured house
in which i stay here in the whirled.
the branches of the red maple
that lean over the place –
bare now of the leaves
that were there when i first arrived –
are decorated with a star at each of their tips.
coyotes howl in the distance
(this is what woke me)
calling to the full moon
speaking to Gaia.
or, perhaps, they are Gaia
and it's me to whom they're speaking.

this madness of which i speak

is a kind of "destructuring-restructuring –"

    (Cooper, 1978, p. 35)

a "...permanent revolution in the life of a person."

            (Cooper, 1978, p. 36)

this "madness is the destructuring

of the alienated structures

of an existence

and the restructuring

of a less alienated way of being."

            (Cooper, 1978, p. 40)

the important work of this madness

is to call madness itself into being:

"One most effective weapon of counter-violence

is our personal-collective poetry,

our creation (poesis)."

    (Cooper, 1978, p. 15)

this is because

 "...madness participates in the poesis,

the general sense of making, creating..."

    (Cooper, 1978, p. 84)

poetry embodies

"...repetitive, echoing forms of speech... [that]

shape meaning out of randomness,

mimic and embody

the cyclic, interdependent processes

that create and maintain life on Earth –

the web we are part of...

poetry... struggles with boundaries

in an effort
to mean more,
include more...
It is the dance of words,
creating more-than-meaning,
reattaching the name, the thing,
to everything around it."
     (Suzuki, 2007, 286-287)

Gaia comes to me in a dream
or in the whirled –
i can't tell if they're different
or the same
or if it matters.
Gaia stands before me,
hands on her hips,
speaks:
"you must step out of the whorled –
the horrid whored whorled world
of laundromats
and grocery stores
and restaurants –
and into the real, living whirled

of	birch	people
and	raven	people
and	stream	people
and	stone	people

and   fish   people.
in doing so, your madness
will be made manifest
and all will be right and good.
do it.
now.
don't wait."
then she is gone, again.

madness, i understand, "is a way of knowing..."
   (Cooper, 1978, p. 155)
it speaks through poetry, these
"crafted words attempt to resolve
the contradictions of consciousness,
catching speech
(as insubstantial as air,
as transitory as breath)
as it comes and goes,
tying it into the eternal."
     (Suzuki, 2007, p. 288)
i also understand that
"...the method of studying the field of madness
must itself be involved in that madness."
     (Cooper, 1978, p. 157)
madness speaks to me
and i, in my turn

speak to it

of it

about it

through it

create it out of whole cloth

(cloth to be worn, cloth to shelter).

it tells me what and how

to know

to do

to be

(do-be-do-be-do):

"What is the meaning of life?

Answer:

life.

Why are we here?

Answer:

to be here

to be-long,

    (Suzuki, 2007, p. 292)

madness has taught me this:

"*Tegsh* in Khalkha Mongolian

means 'level, equal, tranquil, a sense of order...'

Mongols believe that the goal of life is to live tegsh,

in balance with the world.

one stands alone and in power

at the center of the world,

with infinite blue Father above

and Mother Earth supporting and nurturing below.

by living an upright and respectful life,

human beings will keep their world in balance
and maximize their personal power."
 (Kemery, 2006, p. 142)

i leave the whirled
walking one last time
down the trail
carrying everything i own
(it now all smells of woodsmoke)
on my back.
i pass a man's grave
and thank him for his labor.
at the place of leaving the whirled
and entering the horrid whored whorled world
Gaia waits for me, perhaps impatiently.
she looks directly at me
says:
"you will come back."
it is not a question, or a suggestion.
it is a directive
spoken through the words
of generations that have gone before
that continue to go through me now –
the "...spirit-among-us (the sacred, the holy)."
 (Suzuki, 2007, p. 285)
as i climb into my truck
i know that Gaia is right:

i will be back.

really,

i never left.

this is the threshold.

things to which i have referred, brought back from the other whirled

Cooper, D. (1978). *The language of madness.* NY: Penguin Books.

Coperthwaite, W. (2002). *A handmade life: In search of simplicity.* White River Junction, VT:
Chelsea Green Publishing.

Forbes, P. (2001). *The great remembering: Further thoughts on land, soul, and society.* San
Francisco, CA: The Trust for Public Land.

Gregg, R. (1944). *The power of non-violence.* NY: Fellowship Publications.

Kemery, B. (2006). *Yurts: Living in the round.* Layton, UT: Gibbs Smith.

Suzuki, D. (2007). *The sacred balance: Rediscovering our place in nature.* Vancouver, Canada:
Greystone Books.

Acknowledgments

Thanks to the Dickinson's Reach Community for their support and generosity in making my Residency in the fall of 2019 possible, and which allowed for the work and learning re-presented here to become (wo)manifest.

Thanks, too, to j., for letting me take the time: this is your love enacted. and to m., for giving me food and drink, to and from: this, too, is your love, enacted.

Phil Smith is whatever-comes-after-being-a-perfesser, an educator, an activist, an adventurer (in more ways than can be described), neuroqueer, and Mad as fuck. He's published widely, in journals and books, including in AutPress's *Spoon Knife 2* and *4*, and *Writhing Writing: Moving Towards a Mad Poetics*. A poet, playwright, novelist, and visual artist, he's ridden his bicycle around Lake Superior, hiked the Long Trail, and served as President of the Society of Disability Studies. He spends as much time as he can in a very secluded cabin beside Lake Superior, where the neighboring squirrels, wolves, and ravens try valiantly to figure out what the heck he's doing.

Verity Reynolds

Oh, Won't You Take Me With You?

My death was easy, as deaths go.

The body didn't want to die – bodies never do – but I saw my death coming, and I accepted it readily enough. I had signed up for the sort of work that makes death more likely than not, almost as if I'd known, at the tender age of 25, that this incarnation was going to do me very little good. I saw my death coming, and I closed my eyes to await the peace that lies between death and birth.

I died.

Then – I awoke.

I wasn't *reborn*, mind you. I, the ego at the head of my most recent incarnation, *woke up*.

Every human has died and been reborn, whether or not you remember it. Conveying the experience, then, is not difficult; everyone understands it even if they can't say how.

I have yet to meet anyone who understands what it means to awaken from the far side of death into someone else's body.

My first impression is of an acute sense of unease, as if I'd woken from a dead sleep to the sickening discovery that I was in the wrong bed, in the wrong house. This realization is followed at once by a pang of guilt, as if I not only woke up in the wrong house but have always known I have no business being here.

The third is that I'm not alone.

This is when it dawns on me: I'm not in my own body.

As an experiment, I try lifting the body's limbs, opening the eyes. Nothing. The nervous system works; I can feel it, a series of live wires perpetually cognizant of its boundaries. But it won't obey me.

Whoever is in here with me has control over the motor functions. This is, properly speaking, their body, not mine. And they, at the moment, are sound asleep.

I do not exactly welcome our first meeting.

I must have fallen into a doze or reverie without realizing, for my next conscious experience is of the arms-that-are-not-mine stretching above the head-that-is-not-mine, a hollow yawn issuing from the face-that-is-not-mine.

We apprehend one another at precisely the same moment.

It's better than nothing, she says, or rather thinks. I have no words.

I use *she* as a placeholder, the closest pronoun my previous incarnation's language has to describing her gender, which actually has no human analogue. I know this like I know her right foot itches or that her eyes, once opened, are far more sensitive in low-light conditions than any I've previously had. She's no species I recognize. I can read the interiority of this body; I just can't do anything about it.

I'm certain of very little, but I believe she just called me an "it."

I beg your pardon? I manage.

Motor functions continue to elude me – I *wish* she'd scratch at that distracting itch – but at least this exchange tells me I can think at her and she me.

She smiles, an expression that reaches her eyes but not her mouth. *At least you're not dead.*

I can't call that a triumph.

She leans over, fishing two clods of rubbish from beneath the bed. She kicks the ragged blanket away, revealing a pair of stick-thin legs so white they seem to glow in the murky red light. Her movements stir up a cloud of dust and sour body odor.

The rubbish turns out to be most of a pair of boots. She shoves her feet into them as I try to take stock of our surroundings. They are, in a word, *grimy*.

We're in a small compartment of some kind, precisely the length of the bed and only a bit wider: a metal box built around an old mattress upon which lies a torn blanket. A pile of soiled clothing juts out from beneath one end of the bed. At the other, a large wrench lies atop a pile of old magazines. One sputtering yellow lightbulb overhead allows me to pick out certain details: the stains on the mattress, a knot in her boot lace, and the coating of dust and grease that has settled into the creases of her finger joints, dark against her otherwise pale skin.

The tang of stale sweat and the rottensweet smell of food going bad permeate the compartment, underscored by a thick, acrid odor that tugs at my memory. I know I've smelled it before, in some previous life; I cannot, at the moment, recall which.

What I don't see is any evidence of a door or hatch.

Just as I begin to ask, however, she swings her feet round and kicks the wall at the foot of the bed. It falls open with a clang, and she scrambles out.

A harsh orange sunrise makes her blink momentarily, but does not surprise her, and I realize that she thinks of this place as home.

"Home" is on wheels, a four-meter-high behemoth of a vehicle. Sitting forward of the compartment she's launched us from is a glass-fronted cab with a single seat; in front of that is another compartment which, I presume, houses the engine.

This monstrosity is attached to a long tank, more rust than metal and perched on several alarmingly smooth tires. The whole thing is backed into an alcove on the side of a building that stretches into the distance, obscured by the bulk of truck after truck, all of which appear to have been built from different scrap heaps.

A blast of hot exhaust from the neighboring truck hits her in the face as we round the front of her truck, and despite having no control over the body's nervous system I am possessed of a sudden urge to gag. She isn't; this is normal for her, comfortable, expected. She'd have trouble starting her day without a lungful of carbon monoxide.

I remember what that pervasive acridity is. It's diesel exhaust. Petrochemical fuel. Hydrocarbons. It's been several lifetimes since I smelled that.

I'm wondering how to tell her this – I'm wondering how to explain it to myself – when a voice causes her head to whip around.

"Sixteen-jay-en!"

She throws up a skinny arm in something like a salute as a tall man, of the same species or something close to it, stops in front of her vehicle. Her eyes drop downward, avoiding his face, leaving me to contemplate his boots.

They're work boots. They were nice once, and he clearly tries to keep them that way, not like the trash on her feet. But he's out here every day, in the dust and oil and God (if these people even have a God) knows what else. The boots are shiny enough to say he's gunning for a promotion and worn enough to tell me he'll never get it.

He scans her right palm with a handheld device, which lights up green and beeps.

"You're zero point three percent behind schedule," he says to her. "Fix it or you're fired."

Her people, I realize, smile for the same reason apes do: to disarm you before they go for the throat.

"Sir," she says.

He looks at her like he can't decide whether to spit on her or grope her, then moves away. She looks straight ahead as she climbs into the driver's seat.

Before we pull out, she pops the lid off a can of vegetables mashed into a thick paste. She eats it cold, grimy fingers scooping the sludge straight from the can with one hand as she swings the massive truck onto the road with the other.

I wait until we're well underway, on a flat stretch of road with no other vehicles in sight, before I try speaking to her again. *What's your name?*

16JN, she answers, a bitter joke.

Your parents gave you a serial number? I ask.

She groans, nearly audible over the chug and clang of the engine, and pushes her hair out of her face.

Reth, she says. She pronounces it *wraith*.

Reth, I repeat. *That's pretty.*

If she could throw me out the truck window, she would. She's never been called "pretty" except to mock her.

To change the subject, I ask *Where are we going?*

Military installation on the other side of this district, she says. *I empty this tank, I go back, I fill it again. At least until the war gets too close or someone else gets blown up.*

The war? I ask, though I remember.

The war, Reth confirms, in all caps – THE WAR – as if there has only ever been one war. Which, for a shipper in the middle of dust-ass nowhere, may well be true. *The massacre.*

This is Reven, I say, putting the pieces back together. *And you're – Reveni?*

Rehhn, she says, as if I should know the difference. *Though I guess we all look the same to you.*

I've never set foot on Reven, I say.

Reth replies with a sound I would have called a snarl, but I can sense the emotion behind it. Reth is laughing. *That's technically true, flyboy*, she says. *I never did find your legs.*

I remember those legs. I remember my name: Alexander C. Edwards. My rank, junior lieutenant second grade, Gliesen Standby Defense. I am 25 years old. I have a Labrador retriever named Sam and a girlfriend named Lydia. Or is it the other way around?

My fighter went down over Reven. I had just enough time

to register the dull negative of radio silence before a ball of orange fire, more intense than a hundred Reveni sunsets, swallowed me from the bottom upward. I was still thinking about the radio when the windscreen shattered, taking my eardrums and lungs with it.

Deprived of air, the body panics; but I, older than the body, knew what was coming. I met the ground in quiet anticipation of the gentle amnesia that precedes birth.

We all know what happened next.

When this mental image clears, I find Reth waiting for me.

You finished? she asks, and I realize she's seen the whole thing.

I also realize: I do remember her.

Not her face, which I still haven't seen, but her hands, long-fingered, scarred and caked with dirt, the one identifiable *thing* in my field of vision just before I woke up inside the body that wielded them. A sense of *peeling*, as she pulled the part of me that cannot die from the part of me that could no longer live.

I may not have an amygdala – I can't find one in Reth's head – but I still have the capacity for anger.

Is this your way of saving my life? I ask. *Because that wasn't necessary. I don't know how it works for your kind, but humans reincarnate. Instead I'm stuck here.*

Think of this stay as temporary, she says. *A vacation.*

Some vacation, I say.

We ride in silence for a long while after this. I give up trying to remember whether the girlfriend was Lydia and the dog was Sam or vice versa. Instead I stare through Reth's eyes at the scenery, such as it is.

The sun is high now. It reveals nothing in our path worth seeing. Only a colorless sky and a continent of red dust.

This place used to be beautiful, Reth tells me.

I don't have to speak; she picks up on my skepticism at once.

Not the way you're picturing – your weird green planets. But this all had vegetation, once. And rivers. Even the sky had more color than it does now.

I suppose that's the war's fault too, I say. My bitterness surprises me.

Yes, says Reth, though she doesn't need to.

I know why I'm bitter. It's because, even with all my perspective, my coveted lifetimes of experience, I let myself get carried away. Alexander C. Edwards bought the propaganda, the jingoist nonsense about liberating this place from Reynolds' imperialist grip. I murdered civilians, but worse, I believed it was the right thing to do.

I suppose it doesn't help for me to say I'm sorry, I say to her.

Reth reaches for a grimy piece of rope dangling from the dashboard, yanking it to blow two sharp blasts from the horn at a scraggly animal in the road. The creature bolts for exactly six paces, just far enough to reach the shoulder.

No. It doesn't.

Not saying "I'm sorry" leaves me with nothing to say, so I say nothing.

We never did a thing to you, you know. We were living our lives, until your precious corporation decided to use this planet as a weapons testing ground.

That wasn't us, I protest, though I can already tell my objection is futile. Humans all look the same to Reveni, too. *That was Reynolds. We were trying to stop them—*

You were trying to acquire *them,* Reth says. *So you could bomb us yourselves.* There is no mistaking the expression on her face for anything but a sneer.

In all honesty, I knew this. Alexander C. Edwards had been mostly ignorant, but I have been one of those decision-makers in a previous life. I knew that Reth and her people had never registered in those offices and situation rooms. One corporation found a place to test its weapons; another wanted what the first one had.

Yet I couldn't think of my most recent incarnation as a waste. I've lived too many lives to indulge in that sort of self-pity.

There's still time, Reth says. *To play the hero. That's why you're here.*

And that is all she says. For miles. For hours.

As the sun peaks, we come upon another long, low building, the exact image of the one we left this morning. Red dust-caked walls stretch on and on, studded by hundreds of identical docking bays.

Again, Reth seems to know exactly where to go. She backs the truck into one of the bays, then climbs out. She walks up to the wall beside the truck and, with effort, turns a valve nearly as large as she is.

An oily burble issues from inside the tank. Reth climbs back into the cab.

Exactly eighteen minutes later, she climbs out again, turns

the massive valve the other way, and climbs back in.

I realize this is her entire life. Reth repeats this same sequence of steps every day, with little variation and no space to innovate. Drive the truck, empty the tank, drive the truck, fill the tank, drive the truck....

For the first time, I feel sorry for her.

How much do you know about Rehhn? Reth asks, suddenly.

I know I dropped a few dozen bombs on your planet, I say. *And that at least one of you eats cold soup from a can for breakfast.*

Again, that snarl that serves as her laugh. *We're a subspecies of Reveni. Basically extinct at this point. Though that's not the war's fault. Our own cousins have been trying to wipe us out for years.*

Why? I ask. Alexander C. Edwards, dog owner and flyboy, would not have cared. But I need to understand how I got into this situation.

We have a third sex, she says.

Does Reth think this is a bombshell? Species with distinct third sexes are rare, but a spectrum of presentations in the reproductive-bits department is as common as carbon-based life. Perhaps more common.

And? I ask.

Reveni are diploid, she says. *You get the usual variations in structures, but as a rule you need two gametes to make one baby. Baby is made of chromosomes from both gametes. Baby, generally, grows up to be a producer of one gamete or the other.* She says this acerbically, as if it's something children know.

And Rehhn do what? I ask.

Most Rehhn fit the pattern. But once in a great while, they'll get a baby who isn't either. Baby has chromosomes from each

*parent, but Baby doesn't produce one gamete or the other. Baby...
reproduces differently. We don't need someone else's biomass to
kickstart gestation. We need something else.*

I don't want to ask what the *something* is, but I know I
have to.

By dying on this rock, I have become part of Reth's plan.

What else do you need? I ask.

A companion.

Reth's head is a muddle of shame and anger.

To do what? I ask, and the truck's engine chooses precisely
this moment to die.

Reth swears and jerks the wheel, coasting the truck per-
ilously near a roadside ditch as the whole thing rumbles to
a halt. A cloud of oily blue smoke billows out of the engine,
rolling into the cab, triggering a thick cough.

Let's get out of here, I say, but Reth has already grabbed
the door handle. We half climb, half fall out of the cab as the
door gives way.

Reth fetches her tools from the sleeping compartment as
the smoke dissipates across the red road. There are no other
vehicles. There are no animals. There may not be any insects;
if they exist, they do not make their presence known. I ha-
ven't heard silence like this since Alexander's Earth History
class took a VR field trip to the 20th-century Swiss Alps.

If I could give Reth any gift right now, it would be a truck
cab full of snow.

The metal engine cover hisses as Reth touches it. She ig-
nores the pain, throwing the panels back in sequence – one,
two, three, four – to reveal the engine.

It's not a configuration I recognize, of course. *What's wrong with it?* I ask.

It's older than shit and twice as dirty, she says, and extracts a wrench from her bag.

I watch as she works, though I can't begin to guess what she's doing or why. Reth works intently and quickly, lining up parts on the open engine cover as she removes them.

She plunges a hand into the depths of the engine and extracts a fingerful of hot grease. The heat and texture remind me of turning my head to avoid vomiting into a rabbit carcass while my uncles laughed.

Reth, untroubled by memories of bunny slaughter, repeats the procedure several times. She flicks the grease clumps into the dust, where they vanish.

I hope she doesn't step on any of them. The last thing I want to do is endure the sensation of engine guts on her feet.

Finally she reassembles the engine, climbs the open door to the cab, and hits the ignition. The damn engine turns over like nothing happened.

Reth bangs the cover closed and climbs back into the cab, stowing her tools under the seat.

We need to make time, she says. She's still angry, but her earlier shame has been replaced by a fear that has nothing to do with discussions of her reproductive habits.

I see the source of her fear in her thoughts as clearly as I can hear her: The loading dock guard from this morning.

You're afraid of him, I say.

Reason to be. Reth swings the truck onto the road so hard the cab wobbles.

I don't understand, but I don't want to push her, either. She's very close to shutting down, and Reth is the only one of us who can drive this truck.

She straightens the wheel and opens up the engine, filling the cab with diesel fumes and the chug of the pistons.

After a while she says, *If I'm late again, he'll fire me.*

I can't tell which she hates more: this job or the thought of losing it. *Why not just quit?* I ask before I think.

Reth sticks an arm out the side window.

The horizon teems with opportunities, she says with sarcasm I can taste.

It's been so long since I've reincarnated into a life of want that it takes me a moment to remember what it feels like. If Reth loses this job, Reth will starve. And there is nothing I can do about it.

For the first time, I wonder what happens to me if Reth dies. Do I go on to be reincarnated again, as I should have before she came into my life? Do I die with her? Or do I go on living in her body?

Whichever you prefer, I suppose, Reth says.

There's no privacy in Reth's head for either one of us. *What do you mean, 'whichever I prefer'? What happens if you don't die?*

You stick around and help me raise our child, Reth says.

Our child, I repeat.

I told you I needed a companion. To reproduce, she meant.

I want to tell her to back up several steps, but there's no point: I have the same access to her mind as she has to mine, whether I want it or not. I start putting pieces together.

You need a companion in order to reproduce. But not for biological purposes. You need something else. A soul? A consciousness?

Close enough, Reth says.

And how do your people ordinarily get these companions? Who else has been where I am, and how did they get there?

I sense the portent of the answer before Reth says it. *We kill for them.*

I understand now. That's why the Reveni want the Rehhn wiped out. The Rehhn third sex is a race of soul vampires.

Fuck you, says Reth, and I realize I've gone too far. *I didn't want to kill anyone. I was ready to die childless, if I had to. And then you crashed in front of my truck.*

I didn't need you to save me, I remind her.

I didn't want you to go to waste, she says.

If I had control of the lungs, I'd take a deep breath right now for us both. Instead I count to ten before saying, *I'm here now. What do I do?*

You've already done it, she says, and her snarl is almost sly.

I bounce around her nervous system for a bit, trying to figure out what she means. Trying to confirm my suspicions. Before long, I realize I'm looking for the wrong thing. I won't find any foreign chromosomal material in here because there isn't any. That wasn't what she needed me for.

You're pregnant, I say.

Reth smiles.

When-

Pretty much as soon as I picked you up, flyboy, she says. *It doesn't take much more than your presence.*

So you got what you want, I say. *And I'm stuck here?*

Yes, she says, maddeningly nonchalant. *You can make yourself useful, or you can turn us both into terrible parents. It's your call, really.*

Sam was the dog. Lydia was the girlfriend. We'd been trying for a baby.

This is not how I'd wanted to become a parent.

Reth laughs. *Nobody gets to choose how they want to become a parent.*

Well, fine. I may not have a body, a voice, or any privacy, but I do have the combined experience of dozens of previous lives, including several spent as a parent. It can't be that hard to raise a Rehhn child.

The outline of the first building reappears just as a red sun disappears beneath a horizon the color of dried blood. Reth backs us into her usual spot, turns off the engine, and climbs back into her grimy nest.

I let her. Expectant mothers need their sleep.

This time, however, we're awoken not by Reth stretching, but by a violent thump on the sleeping compartment door.

Reth kicks the door open and scrambles out, barefoot.

The same guard from yesterday morning towers over her. I hate the glower on his face at once.

"Zero point *five* percent behind schedule," he says, sounding less angry than triumphant. I feel Reth's veins turn to ice. "You owe me." In the faint pre-dawn light I catch sight of his nametag: *Aqharan.*

"Please," Reth says, and I feel her scrabbling for words. Animal panic fills her throat. "I'll fix it, I swear...."

But the guard grabs her by the throat with one hand, jamming the other down her overalls, and I realize: She never feared losing this job.

She feared what would happen if he found out what she is.

Reth's legs thrust out, catching the guard squarely in the crotch. He collapses, and we're on top of him, fingers tearing, hissing a sibilant chant Reth hasn't heard since her own infancy and that I could not place.

And then I'm in Reth's hands, wrapped around the guard's throat, and I discover that I, too, can *peel.*

I push her off me with one hand and scramble to my feet before Reth realizes I'm gone. "Stop," I cough. "Reth."

She blinks at me from where she's landed, ass-first in a puddle of red mud and engine oil. "You...."

I cough. "I guess this is how it ends."

She shakes her head, slowly. "You were...supposed to stay. I was supposed to carry you forever. That's the sacrifice. That's what it means to be a mother."

I reach down. Reth flinches, then extends a hand, her eyes locked on mine.

I pull her to her feet. "How's the baby?"

Reth shrugs. "Fine, I think."

My mind races, possibilities lighting up before me like streetlights as my mind maps this new body, finds connections, discovers no traces of its previous inhabitant. "I'm Reveni now, right?"

"Right," Reth says, uncertainly.

"I'm a guard. Or something. I can get us both out of here, can't I?"

She laughs, and for the first time I hear it as a laugh, not a snarl. "Good luck."

"I can keep you safe, anyway. We can have a better life."

Reth kicks at the puddle she landed in, most of which now cakes her clothes. "Don't do that."

"Do what?"

"Act like you care about me. I used you. I stole whatever chance you had at a real life because I wanted a baby who will be hunted from the moment he's born."

I want to reach out, to embrace her, but I know she'll push me away. My presence in her head was a necessary inconvenience to her. She doesn't want me the way I want to protect our baby.

I turn away.

We stop sharing a life, but we don't stop speaking to one another. We certainly don't stop arguing.

After about a year, I find a way to have Reth and our son transferred onto an Amalgamated Logistics freighter. I know I'll never see either of them again and I don't care. The planet is dying, and I want them to live.

Reth, somewhat more sentimental post-birth, gives our son two names: Mine, and a variant of her own. I don't tell her this, but I'm grateful. If I get off this planet before the dust pneumonia kills me, at least I'll know who I'm looking for.

He is my son, and his name is Aqharan Bereth.

S. Verity Reynolds is the author of the Non-Compliant Space series, including *Nantais* and *Nahara*. She's currently working on the third book, *The Ambassador*, between stops on a tedious interplanetary flight. See also: http://danialexis.net.

Tito Rajarshi Mukhopadhyay

Caterpillar

That thing in his mind
Caterpillar like
crawled all over - front, behind -

determined to find
his focus; strike
chords of cacophony in that mind

of his. A dissipating time
choked reminders of a very important world outside.
But that thing moved - front, behind,

hammered a din, clamoring an unrefined
stimulation. Just like a termite
it bored through his mind.

Eyes turned blind
to visual details. Black and white
dissolved his front and behind

Like a chrysalis he resigned -
signing out from the world letting that thing thrive
caterpillar like, feeding out of his mind
everywhere - front and behind.

Moon

You've seen the distance,
seen how shapes clarify,
defined darkness at a random instance,

Your vision had no defense
from outbursts of headlights
vanishing at a backward distance.

The moon - a gibbous presence
looked complex, amplified
the definitions of sky. At every instance

time condensed,
capsuled you, multiplied
your impatience at any random distance.

Radio jabbered. You dreaded silence!
You even tried
changing channels at some instance

Quivering shapes lurked at horizons,
distracted you to intensify
your humming. The escaping distance
kept defining a flickering instance.

Tito Rajarshi Mukhopadhyay: My bio is simple. I love to write, I have autism that adorns my reality like the jewel in the crown.

Scott Nicolay

The Thing (*in the Hole [in the Tree]*)

My mother still lives in the house where I grew up, but I can barely recognize the place in the occasional photos she sends me. Aluminum siding has replaced the old wooden shingles, the landscaping is different in every regard, and she never replaced the fences on the sides of the yard, which is why she sees deer in her flowerbeds now. Given the way wildlife has bounced back in that area since I lived there, it might not be long before she gets a bear. When I visited several summers ago there had just been bear sightings around where the train tracks cross Marlborough Avenue, which is not so far away from her house (this location appears in my story "The Green Eye"). Half a mile away at most. Where there are deer, bears will follow soon enough. "When you see him 'quid...then you quick see him 'parm whale," as Queequeg says. Cause and effect still conjoin in at least some circumstances, but the house of my childhood and the house I sometimes visit no longer align.

One of the most important steps in a child's cognitive growth is the development of object permanence, which according to Piaget usually occurs by the age of two. Object permanence refers to the ability to recognize that an object continues to exist even when it is no longer visible. The first step toward this is visual tracking. Hold up your finger in front of a baby's face. Move it from side to side. Do the baby's eyes follow it? If so, then that child has met one of their first developmental milestones. Now when the child is perhaps a year old, take their favorite toy and put it under a box or behind your back. How does the child respond? Try hiding their mother. Does the child understand that she still exists?

I have come to believe that something went very wrong with my sense of object permanence from early on.

My mother still lives in the house where I grew up, but the large and gnarled apple tree that stood in the northeast corner of the backyard is gone. Memory says it blew down in one of the hurricanes that sweep through New Jersey every decade or so as if for exactly that purpose. I could ask my mother to look up the date the tree fell in one of her diaries but I won't. The tree is secondary to our purpose here. Tertiary, really. In the tree there was a hole and in the hole there was a...thing. The thing and the hole and the tree inhabit my oldest memories, but the tree and the hole are gone.

In my memory the tree is always tall, and vast in its expanse. As we were the first family to live in our house, like all our neighbors on that little street, it must have already been old when I was a child, a relic of the farmland or forest that lot had been before our home, before I was born. Decades later I can call up images of that trunk's gray expanse with ease, of its eczematous flesh, how it felt against my palms, the way its pliable branches broke green beneath their bark when bent too far or made to bear overmuch weight. It bifurcated so low I could climb into its crotch before I was old enough to go to school.

Standing in that tree as a child of perhaps three, I could just barely see into the hole. Not a knothole but a real hole, a deep hole, as wide as my face and filled with ants and spiders and stagnant water and…wait. We will get there.

A thick limb must have broken off from that spot, on the inner face of the half of the trunk that leaned out over Mr. Jones' yard. Mr. Jones was our backdoor neighbor, living behind us on Locust Avenue where Venice Avenue bent round in an oxbow. His next door neighbor cattycorner to us on the north was another Mr. Jones. On cool summer evenings both Mr. Joneses often held court from lawn chairs in the open doorways of their respective garages, and I sometimes rode my bike up their driveways to chat with one or the other or each in turn. I remember them both as friendly and wise, but the first Mr. Jones was also the first on our block to fence his backyard, so his tolerance for us neighborhood kids must have had its limits. After that, no more taking refuge during sudden summer thunderstorms under the green corrugated awning of his redwood picnic table.

Neither is the hole itself my subject here, but we are closing in. Like Mr. Jones, that hole was one of two. As was the tree itself. The other old apple tree was in my grandparents' yard, maternal not paternal, their side yard not the back. They lived about a mile away and are both gone, my grandfather in 1977 and my grandmother in 2001. It was their house I used as the setting of my story that won an award. Their tree was also ancient and gray, forked just as low and spreading even wider, its secondary trunks probably bowed far out, perhaps by the childhood climbing escapades of my uncles and aunts and maybe my mom. My grandparents' home was my second home, so I grew up thinking an ancient apple tree in one's yard was the norm. Nothing in my memory tells me how long that other tree has been gone or why, and I doubt my mother would remember either. She doesn't seem to care about such things. My brother and his family live in my grandparents' house now, and a smooth unbroken lawn covers the space where that other tree once stood. My brother has two kids, just as we are two.

The hole in our tree was also one of two and the other hole was higher and on the back of that half of the trunk that hung out over Mr. Jones' yard. I don't think I knew about the second hole till I was a little older and Mr. Jones put up his fence because the only way to see it was to climb up and stand on the flat top rail of that fence. Mr. Jones' fence was the kind they call basketweave, with thin red boards woven together in rectangular sections and fitted into grooved posts. I never see that kind of fence anymore. My parents put up matching fence on both sides of our backyard not long after, and most of the neighbors put up their own fences soon after that, every fence a different kind. I never thought about it then but looking back it was around the time a Black family moved in cattycorner to us on the other side of the first Mr. Jones that everyone started putting up fences. Except the second Mr. Jones. He never put up a fence. The Black family did not live there long and all the original fences on the block have been replaced with new and different fences.

Whoever lives in the second Mr. Jones' house now has the highest fence on the block.

The second hole connected to the first which means that section of the tree was already rotted out and hollow through when I was little. It's surprising that back half of the tree did not fall long before it did, given the periodic hurricanes. Camille hit in '69, which cannot have been too long after the time I am describing.

The two holes were therefore the openings of a single tube or tunnel running through several feet of one half of the trunk. After whatever original accidents snapped off the large limbs that must have once stuck out in those spots, whether gale-force winds or careless climbing kids, and beyond any fungal infection that presumably entered thereby, much of this passage was likely the work of carpenter ants. The ants were a special feature of that tree.

Carpenter ants, if you have never seen them, are jet-black and big, at least half an inch long. Truly formidable when you are a kid. Supposedly they bite but I don't recall them biting me or anyone else even though they were always filing along the fence and streaming up the tree, and we often climbed both, even though Mr. Jones would yell at us when we climbed on or over his fence. The ants go back as far as my memories of the tree go back which means they go back as far as my memories go. Like termites they chew through dead wood but unlike termites they cannot actually eat wood. They don't have the gut bacteria to digest it. Not that I knew that then, although I knew a lot about all kinds of insects well before I started kindergarten.

Carpenter ants are still a concern for homeowners however, and by the time I was in high school they had infiltrated our garage, probably because hurricanes had flooded the basement and garage and begun to rot the wood. I think my parents hired an exterminator at some point after I moved to New Mexico in 1989. Until I visited my mom this past summer I hadn't seen a carpenter ant in decades, but on that visit I saw them in her house three separate places and times. They looked even bigger than I remember from when I was a kid--which tells you something because I've since spent time in the jungle and seen some pretty damn big ants. I'm afraid they're coming back, which is bad for my mom, bad for that house. I told her about them but she didn't seem to care.

I'm not sure I ever saw carpenter ants in the hole before I found out it was just one end of a tunnel. I can definitely remember them funneling through it on a regular basis later. What matters is the ants must have made that hole and they made it more foreboding just by their presence in the tree. Although the hole was unpleasant enough without being full of giant ants.

Besides the ants and spiders and whatever else might have been hiding there, the hole was filled to its in-curved lip with foul inky water. I can still smell that water. Barely, but I can. I have a pretty good memory for smells from my youth--I can also call up the smell of my grandparents' front porch, dank rhododendrons and moldering concrete. In my memory that hole's small swamp smells of sulfur, of methane, of things ripe with death. Not that I knew much of sulfur or methane or death at the time, but I can make those associations now.

Here we are then, at the hole. Something floated in the water in that hole. Some thing. A thing. Round and pale, as things that float in dark waters ought to be. Like an eyeball or a boiled egg. That thing retains a kind of iconicity for me, which is to say not only is it fixed in my memory but also that I remember it as already a fixture of the tree the first time I climbed its divided crotch. I can recall someone showing the thing to me. In a way that may have been a warning. My mother, maybe, or one of the older kids, Debbie Curbow or either of the Sanders girls next door. I think it even had its own name but if it did the name itself does not remain in my memory. There is just the memory that the thing maybe had a name. If it did, it was probably just "The Thing" or "The Thing in the Hole."

What I describe as iconicity is my memory that the thing in the hole in the tree in my yard was already established as a presence from the first moment I ever stood in that tree. The thing in the hole commanded my attention, controlled how I moved in the tree, perhaps even called me to ascend and regard it. I can remember looking into the hole to check the thing was still there each time I climbed the tree. Routinely. A ritual. Before I climbed higher or did anything else. No one touched the thing or even tried to but it was a focus of the tree and the tree was a focus of our yard and even our neighborhood because all the kids came to climb it back when none of the houses on our block had fences. Consider that the thing was already well enough known that someone made a point to show it to me once I was old enough to see it. An initiation. And all that while it just floated in its hole.

In my memory the thing looks most like a turnip, though that has to be among the least likely things it might have actually been. It might have been an old rubber ball, maybe one that belonged to the Sanders' dog, the dog that tried to bite me once but bit my mother instead when she got between it and me. Maybe that thing was a wild onion. Usually wild onions were small, at least in my hometown, but every now and then some kid would pull up one the size of my fist, like an onion from the store but dirty and purple with little dangling roots. Whatever the thing was, someone probably put it in the hole on purpose, but what their purpose might have been I never knew and never will know, and if anyone else knew it I never knew they knew. Now that I'm writing about it the obvious thought occurs that it was probably an apple. It's possible an apple could have fallen from the branches right into that hole all on its own. Or some kid might've stuck an apple in there. You have an apple in your hand and there's a hole in the apple tree, so why not?

I don't recall the thing looking like an apple though, and I think I would've recognized it as an apple if that's what it was. Apples get darker as they rot, not white. Once that tree got going in the summer it dropped apples the way I drop f-bombs today. By fall its side of the yard became a minefield of fallen apples in every degree of rottenness, from hard and fresh to mushy brown. Mostly wormy too, just like the cartoons, though the worms never had human faces or tiny hats. I can't say whether those apples were edible because no one ever ate them. Like touching the thing in the hole, eating those apples seemed an unspoken prohibition. From time to time I asked my mother why we never ate them but she just scrunched up her face and shook her head. We called them crabapples but I don't think that name is right, as crabapples are small and these were a decent size, if not as large as apples from the store. The only thing we ever used them for was chucking at each other or at cars. We had some epic apple fights in those days. The point is I knew early on what apples from that tree looked like so I would've known if the thing in the hole in the tree was an apple. Although all these years that thing has been in my mind and I never considered till now it might have been an apple. Not until I wrote about it.

How long the thing in the hole was physically present in my life I can't recall. In my memory that period feels like an entire summer, but maybe it only took a few days. Childhood memories distort that way. That period has an end however, or a climax at least, if no denouement. To the best of my memory, this is how it went.

At some point my fixation on the thing took a more active turn, and I decided I wanted to see it out of its hole. Whether this happened days, weeks, or months after the first time I saw it, I cannot recall. Neither are my original motivations for wanting to move it clear to me now. It may be the thing's presence had begun to bother me, or that my curiosity grew till I felt the need to see it out in the light. I have a vague sense that at some point the thing's aura diminished to the point where it intimidated me less, and that may be why I made my move. Or perhaps I just got bored. I have always gotten bored easily. A few years after the events I am describing I was diagnosed with what is now known as ADHD.

Our doctor prescribed Ritalin and I had to take that until junior high. That came with a stigma.

Neither can I recall exactly how I got the thing out. I probably used a stick or two to move it. What I do remember is how it popped out of the hole with unexpected suddenness and ease. I must have flinched reflexively and shut my eyes out of fear it might touch me or get some of that muck on my face or clothes. I recall a glimpse of the thing tumbling to the ground on my right, my right as facing Mr. Jones' house, Mr. Jones the first Mr. Jones. That was the last time I saw it. It being the thing, not the house.

Although I only closed my eyes for a moment, when I opened them again and hopped down from the tree, the thing had disappeared. It should have been right there on the ground. I looked all over and called the other kids to help, but no one could find it. If it really was an apple it might have gotten mixed in among all the other apples lying around. Except I think I would remember if it had been an apple. I can't remember how I flipped the thing out of its hole or why, but I can remember vividly how I searched all around the tree, and my memory shows me only thin grass and packed dirt. Maybe it was spring and there weren't any apples down yet. I don't think that thing was an apple, and I don't think any apples were on the ground at that time, meaning it was either too early or someone had raked them up.

All of that happened half a century ago. After that the thing disappeared as a tangible, visible thing, to be followed in time by the tree and the hole, all the old fences, and both Mister Joneses. Disappearing is not the same as being gone.

All those other people and things are gone, but I know where they went, or at least the general how and why of their leave-taking. The thing disappeared forever a second after I flipped it out of its hole. But it is not gone.

I never once climbed into the apple tree afterward without checking in the hole to see if the thing had returned, or if another thing like it had appeared. How I would have distinguished a second thing from the first I do not know, but I swore if a second one showed up I would not repeat my mistake. I knew if I could examine a second thing, I could solve the mystery of the first. No second thing ever appeared however. Not there and not in any of the similar holes in the other tree in my grandparents' yard, because I began to check those as well.

I didn't just look for that thing in the holes in the trees though. For as long as I lived in that house I never went near that corner of the yard without thinking of the thing and searching for it, if only for a moment. Pushing the lawnmower years later I looked for it on every circuit of the yard. Even though I don't live there anymore, that weird little sphere has never left my thoughts. Somehow I still expect to find it.

I moved west after I graduated college in 1989, first to New Mexico then several years ago on to California. My father died in 1995. For the last ten years or so I've gone back to visit my mother once or twice a year, sometimes with my own kids, sometimes without. At some point during my visits I always walk out in the backyard, usually because my mom wants to show me her flowers. And I always look for that thing. Not only does my mind tell me it is somehow still there, it tells me exactly where to look.

The corner of the yard where the thing disappeared has changed over the years. The apple tree is gone, as I already said, along with the pit beside it where my father, and later I myself, would dump the grass clippings from our mower. All the other trees that used to occupy the yard are also gone. The gingko I planted when I was seven went down during Sandy. My mother sent me photos of that when it happened. Mr. Jones' fence is gone but whoever lives there now put up a new one. It's tall and white and looks like plastic.

We are left then with a Latourian litany of vanished pairs: two houses, two yards, two trees, two holes. Two Mr. Joneses. Two brothers still here, but this is not about two brothers. All those other things are gone, but the singular thing in the hole in the tree is not. I realize now it will never go. In whatever way it still exists, it will always exist. Perhaps somehow it caused me to free it from its prison in the tree, just as it compels me now to tell its story. This story belongs to thing, after all, not to me.

Blah blah blah blah rational explanation, I know. Probably whatever that thing really was, rotten apple or rubber ball, it bounced or rolled away in the grass, or into Mr. Jones' yard or somewhere else I think I looked but didn't. It must have dissolved into dust, into molecules long ago. I know. That's not the thing I'm talking about now. The thing under discussion exists in my cognitive framework, the part of my mind that insists this pale orb, eyeball or turnip or onion or egg, still occupies some space in the corner of my mother's backyard. Somehow when I popped the thing out of its socket in the tree, I popped it out of normal space. It became inaccessible and so it remains, remote and at some strange remove, yet with me always. It left its imprint like some long ago lump of Ediacaran mystery meat, not in mudstone but in my brain.

Samuel R. Delany once proposed a "modular calculus," i.e. a semiotic mathematics whereby given a set of *signs* in System B corresponding to a set of *things* in System A, an observer in System C could calculate the contents of System A in their entirety. Or at least the operational rules of System A. In Delany's words, such a calculus would consist of "a set of equations that will take any description of an event, however partial, and elaborate it into a reasonable, accurate, and complete explanation of that event." If System A = "the world," and System B = "my memory," does System B contain enough information to recover Thing X from Hole Y in System A? Because that is my struggle here.

My undergrad courses in educational psychology suggest one interpretation, possible though purely hypothetical. I estimated my age at the time of that encounter with the thing in the hole in the tree as three or four years old, but I am only really certain it all happened before I started school. I may have been as young as two. Or younger. In that case my grasp of object permanence may not yet have become permanently fixed in my cognitive architecture. Perhaps that experience marks a liminal moment, a watershed in my wiring when my nascent sense of object permanence was operating in an ecstatic hyper-excited state. Perhaps the module of my brain responsible for recognizing the continued existence of that object when it was no longer in sight flipped some irreversible switch. Which would explain why for me that slimy lost orb became fixed in space and mind while forever removed and receding in time.

Like Philip K. Dick's great *Exegesis*, this written meditation could sprawl on as long as I live and can write. Could I eventually thus construct a full System B, a mirror of the universe in System A? Or can I only approach my goal asymptotically, never quite reaching close enough to slit the thin film between the past and now enough for me to reach through and pull that thing back over into System A. That I cannot feels like a failure of my memory, and my ability as a writer, though such a system would be an abomination of particularism, like that produced by Borges' Funes the Memorious.

The day is not so far off when the house I grew up in will leave my family and I will no longer have access to it or that unremarkable corner of its backyard. Even then that bulbous thing will remain in place, somewhere within a few square feet of a point only I can identify, but removed from my access that much more.

Someday I myself will die, but even that will not destroy the thing. I fear I made it eternal the day I popped it out of its hole in the tree, that it will continue to exist in its shadow world, constrained to a limited set of coordinates, but permanently untethered from our world by my demise, an object-ghost with no one left to haunt.

Or perhaps it was I who trapped it all these years, with my hyperactive sense of its existence, in which case my death will free it from that final anchor in its strange other space.

Where will it wander when it is finally free? What will hatch from that unwholesome egg?

Scott Nicolay: Father, author, translator, cave archaeologist. Loves trees and birds.

Jessica Goody

Certain Doorways

Behind each wooden portal,
between brass digits and flowerpots,
lives occur. Auras of lamplight illuminate
domestic scenes like something in a play.

Every house is a box filled with heartbeats,
footsteps, history, a potpourri of voices.
The old trees lining the street bear witness
to their gossip, their comings and goings.

As I pass, I consider the geometry of every door:
Narrow windowpanes, light glowing through stained glass,
the mouth-flap of the mail slot, the gleam of knob and
    hinge,
the relationships that shift and evolve with every entrance
    and exit.

It is human nature, when one encounters a box,
an eagerness to look inside and discover its secrets.
The most basic desire is the one to open the door,
to step inside, secure in the knowledge of arriving home.

Jessica Goody is the award-winning author of *Defense Mechanisms: Poems on Life, Love, and Loss* (Phosphene Publishing, 2016) and *Phoenix: Transformation Poems* (CW Books, 2019). The winner of the 2016 Magnets and Ladders Poetry Prize, Goody's writing has appeared in numerous publications, including The Wallace Stevens Journal, Reader's Digest, Third Wednesday, and The Maine Review.

Orrin Grey

New and Strangely Bodied

The first of the bodies that washed up on the beach crawled three feet before it stopped and lay still. Sheriff Perkins said that it was the tide, pushing the body around, but I was there with my camera, and the tide was way out, never came up that far at all, and there were little round holes in the sand, all in a curving line, where fingertips had dug in and pulled it along.

The body itself reminded me of movies I had seen in the past—the special effects that are supposed to be bad, unrealistic, not what a body actually looks like. The Claymation transformations at the end of *Evil Dead*; what a film school friend once called "a lamb chop with an eyeball stapled on it" in Fulci films. It didn't really look like anything that had once been human, except for the bones. It looked like something made out of the sea, and the things that live in the sea. Anemones, jellyfish, corals, seaweed. All built around the framework of a human skeleton, one arm outstretched, calcified fingers digging into the sand.

Next morning's paper confirmed the former humanity of the corpse with the headline, "Body Found Near Hodgson Cove." One of my photos was underneath. Not of the body, just the sheriff's cruiser parked in the sand, red and blue lights washed to grayscale because the Bridgeport paper wasn't big enough to print in color. The article itself was mostly day one journalism stuff; who, what, when, where, but not any why. The reporter had asked the coroner about cause of death, at least, and had gotten the noncommittal response, "Seems like it's been down there a long time."

When the second body washed up, I was sound asleep in the back room of Cargo Cult Video. The Cargo Cult had a couple of back rooms, connected to the store by a long, narrow hallway paneled in fake wood. One was used for storage, and the other was where I lived.

It looked a lot like it had when it had been Rob's instead of mine—an old futon in the corner piled with random blankets, a TV stacked on top of an old entertainment center and hooked to a couple of different VCRs and DVD players. I hadn't added much in the way of feminine touches; I wasn't really a feminine touches kind of girl. There was a bathroom with a stand-up-only shower, and for food I used the kitchenette and the fridge in what had been the employee break room, back when the Cult had any such thing as employees.

The phone was on the wall in the hallway, one of those yellowy plastic jobs with a long corkscrew cord. I had put in a cordless phone up front that rang a different number, so I could switch it to voicemail when the store was closed.

While the back room was mostly dark, the blinds let in light from the alley that ran between the back of the store and a wooded gully where water from the hills drained down into the bay. I stumbled out of bed and knocked the phone off the wall before fumbling around in the dark to pick it up. "How soon can you get down to Hodgson Cove?" a familiar voice asked from the other end. "They found another one."

I had a friend at the coroner's office, Rudy. He told me that the bodies were filled with things that he had never seen before. Not really bodies at all; just skeletons, eaten away by fish and other sea creatures, all the cracks and crevices, all the chambers and compartments filled up now with slugs and jellies and anemones and corals. Strange living things caught halfway between plant and animal, all of them thriving inside these corpses. "Almost like they're trying to find some sort of equilibrium," he said. "A symbiosis. To make something more than the sum of their parts."

Rudy was a smart kid, working at the coroner's office during the summer to help pay his way through med school down the coast the rest of the year, but he also read a lot of science fiction magazines. I'd met him when he came down to the Cargo Cult, where he always wanted the weirdest foreign stuff I could rent him. Pornographic anime, cheapie college movies about alien abductions or demons that knew kung fu.

The official story that the sheriff's office eventually came up with involved the *Seagrass*. It had gone down off the coast a couple of months ago, with all hands on board. A big blow had come up unexpectedly and turned the fishing trawler over in the water, sending her straight down to the bottom. The bodies had never been recovered, and they'd lain down there, trapped in the wreckage, where they'd undergone a sea change into something rich and strange. Now, a deep-sea current was carrying them up to the shore, one by one, and the transformations that time and tide had wreaked on them were just the result of their being down so long.

Of course, that didn't do much to explain why each one was making it farther and farther inland. After the third body was found on the side of the coastal highway, its mushy fingertips like gelatin on the edge of the asphalt, I had a dream.

Like a lot of my dreams, it started with me at work. I was closing down the Cargo Cult for the night, shutting off the neon signs and the lights, checking the back porno room to make sure that no extra perverts were stowing away back there, when I saw someone standing outside the front door.

They were little more than a shadow in the dark, a silhouette against the light of the streetlamp. Even so, they looked somehow wrong. As though they tapered from the bottom to the top, like someone dressed in ecclesiastical robes. "We're closed," I shouted from where I stood, but the shadow didn't budge.

There was a gun in the back room, under the bed, that I had fired maybe three times in my life—another bequest from Rob—and I kept an old, scarred-up baseball bat leaning behind the counter, just in case, but I didn't move toward either of them. Instead, I walked to the front door.

The door was glass from top to bottom, and the figure stood just off our front step, on the old boardwalk, giving me an unobstructed view, had I switched the porch light back on. Something made me stop, though, and instead I opted to flick on the neon OPEN sign, painting the porch in reds and blues that made a purple light.

When I did so, I expected to see one of the crew of the *Seagrass*, a nautical zombie with its face eaten away and wriggling with worms or the fronds of anemones. Instead, it was someone I almost recognized. Dressed, as I had thought, in the robes of the clergy. Starfish clung to his vestments, fish swam around him in the night air, and an octopus wound its thin tendrils about his feet.

In his hands he held a bell, and on it was carved a face at once humanoid and monstrous, its mouth an open circle, its eyes filled with wrath. Its beard was made of sea foam, its crown a bed of coral. The figure rang the bell, and I heard it echo from somewhere out over the water, or out under it. Ding-dong, bell.

While I wasn't sure what the dream meant when I woke up, I remembered where I knew the figure from. It had reminded me of old archival photos that I had seen at the newspaper office, and it had also reminded me of Rob, even though the two looked nothing alike.

What is there to tell about Rob? He was in the army for a while, but he never deployed overseas. He was driving a jeep on a base someplace down in Oklahoma, and there was a head-on collision. The guy driving the other truck had been drinking. Everybody walked away, except for Rob.

His seatbelt, of all things, cut him almost completely in two; paralyzed him from the waist down. "Can't feel a fucking thing down there," he'd say, demonstrating by poking himself in the thigh with a pen or a letter opener or whatever pointy object he happened to have on hand. "Not even a twitch. Doesn't mean I don't still suck a mean cock, though, when the opportunity presents itself."

And that was Rob. He used the disability pension that he got from the army to open up the Cargo Cult Video store in Bridgeport, and live out of the rooms in the back. The store was the only rental place in town, besides a few mainstream movies in a corner of the local Golden Apple Grocery and a spinner rack at the Rapid Stop on the corner of Langdon and Market.

But rentals weren't the Cult's main source of revenue, not even in those early days. Rob sold videos through the mail—VHS back then, DVDs later—of stuff that was hard to find, stuff that he had to order from overseas or drive down to LA or other, more distant places to pick up.

Cargo Cult carried things like *Traces of Death* and Stanislaw Gauvin's *Demogorgon* and *Tribesmen*, the movie where the cast and crew famously went crazy on some island and actually filmed killing each other. The back storeroom was where Rob kept movies that were too outré for the regular clientele, or that he was preparing to ship.

That was all before I knew him. Rob gave me my first job when I was fresh out of film school down in Eugene, back when I still thought I was going to head down the coast to La La Land and become a DOP.

I worked on a couple of no-budget local horror flicks with guys that I knew from film school; all guerilla filmmaking, *Evil Dead*-style. I remember one special effects guy who had come up with this sort of stop-motion way to make the corpses decompose using sculpey and melting wax, with these bright, almost phosphorescent fungi sprouting up from the bodies. I helped him figure out how to get the timing of the exposures right to make the process work. "When you think about it," he said once, "rotting isn't really going away, like we think it is. It's just getting a new body."

Later I would think about that in relation to my own mom, embalmed and lying in the ground back in Phoenix, and Rob, who had been cremated, as per his wishes, his ashes scattered in the bay, so there was probably no new body for him. Which maybe that would be the way he wanted it; he'd never been that fond of his old body, anyway. "Too short, too fat, too hairy," he'd say. "It's a good thing I'm a sex machine, or I'd never get any action at all."

Back then, I was just a chubby girl leaning toward goth with nothing but a camera that seemed expensive as hell at the time and would be shitty now, and a lot of big dreams that never happened. Rob gave me a job working the counter at the Cargo Cult while he prepared movies to ship out in the back room, or traveled around to pick up more stock. It was just the two of us, and back then he was pretty much the only friend I really had. He always told me I was going on to bigger and better things, and I always wondered how he could believe in anything, given what had happened to him.

"What happened?" he asked me one night when we were closing up and I made the faux pas of saying something about it. "I had something shitty happen to me. Who hasn't? And in return I got something great. I fucking love this place," he said, gesturing around at the Cargo Cult, with its low ceilings and musty carpeting and dim rows of weird-ass movies. "What do I have to be unhappy about?"

In those days I thought I had a lot to be unhappy about. I hated my figure and while I had finally come out as a lesbian while I was in film school, there wasn't exactly a big dating pool in Bridgeport, even if I had been hotter. Now, I dunno... I think maybe trying so hard to be happy is what makes everybody so damned unhappy.

Even while I thought of myself as pretty pissed off, I liked working at the Cult, and I liked Rob. We screened all kinds of crazy shit up on the monitors in the store, not too concerned with what the folks who came in might think. I remember watching *Hausu*, and wondering if Rob had slipped me some mushrooms without telling me.

It took me six years of standing behind that counter, popping bubblegum at the customers and watching weird-ass movies before I realized that I was never going to California, was never going to be behind the camera of anything with a budget that you couldn't scrape together with a stay at one of those clinical research trials. So, I quit the Cult and went back to school, this time majoring in photography. I got pretty good at it, and found that I liked shooting still photos better than I had ever liked working in the movies.

I don't know what would have happened then, if things had gone different, but the week after I received my diploma I got word that my mom had died back in Phoenix. I flew down there for two weeks to settle up her shit, and by the time I got back home I heard that Rob was gone, too. Complications from some surgery. I hadn't talked to him in a couple of years, had just fucking abandoned him when I went back to school, didn't even call, and yet he had left the store to me, the whole business, and the building, which he apparently owned outright.

Of course, right before graduation, I had also broken up with Lynne. Not knowing what else to do with myself, I drove back to Bridgeport with everything I owned piled in what had been my mom's station wagon. With nowhere else to go, I moved into Rob's old rooms at the back of the Cargo Cult. I think that I expected to just clean the place up and get it sold, but it didn't work that way, and four years later, I still lived there, in those same back rooms, running that same weird video store, though by then our selection was a lot more DVDs than VHS tapes.

Back in the old days, Rob used to put out this catalog. Black-and-white pages on newsprint with grainy photos of video covers and creased posters, and two-or-three sentence descriptions of the movies, the more lurid the better. That's how he found customers in the days before the Internet. Now, I sold almost everything online, through a catalog on the poorly-pieced-together Cargo Cult website, and through listings on places like eBay.

Rob's disability pension had always been what allowed Cargo Cult to stay afloat, though, and I didn't have that, so I supplemented my income by taking pictures for the Bridgeport Journal Gazette, a local newspaper that seemed like it had gotten its name by pulling a handful of options out of a particularly large hat.

They didn't ever put me on the payroll—they only had one full-time photographer, a girl in her twenties who had mostly taken wedding photos before landing this gig and always did the puff pictures of store openings and city council meetings. Instead, I got freelancer pay to take the occasional more newsworthy story that required me to drag my ass out of bed at three in the morning, or close the store down unexpectedly for forty minutes while I drove to the other side of town for pictures of a fender bender along the coast highway.

After my weird dream, I was pretty sure that the bodies we had been finding didn't have anything to do with the wrecked *Seagrass*. I didn't open up the Cult that day, and instead drove around to the offices of the Journal Gazette, which occupied one floor of a narrow, three-story stone building across the street from the wharf, where I dug through the archives until I found what the dream had reminded me of.

Up on top of the cliff, near where the bridge that gave the town its name crossed the bay, there was an old clapboard church. It stood back off the road now, a rutted gravel path grown up with weeds the only way to get even a Jeep up to it. I'd never been up there myself, but it was the genius loci of a lot of urban legends around town. Word had it that the church had originally been some stripe of Baptist, and that another kind of preacher had taken up residence there when the Baptists cleared out. A cult leader who called himself Obediah Blum, he preached that a new race of man was coming to replace humanity, whose time was rapidly drawing to a close.

"They will come up from the sea," he'd said. "And they will be like men, but new and strangely bodied. And though we will not know them at first, they will be our successors, and it will be for them to inherit the earth that we leave behind."

The story went that he re-christened the church to Neptune and Poseidon, named it the Esoteric Order, without any further preamble or clarification, and attracted quite a little following before the locals got tired of him. A lynching party came one night in the middle of one of Blum's sermons, dragged him out of his church in front of his whole congregation, and hanged him from the bridge. Local ghost stories said that he could still be seen dangling there on some foggy nights, though now his body was encrusted with barnacles and grown through with coral. Another version said that a giant hand—or maybe it was a tentacle, or the claw of some huge crab—had reached up and plucked Blum's body from the bridge, dragging it down into the depths.

After that, Blum's entire congregation went and drowned themselves. Just walked out into the ocean with stones in their pockets. Nothing about any of this was contained directly in the archives of the Bridgeport Journal Gazette—the paper didn't go back that far, having been founded back in '82—just references to it in other stories. These events weren't exactly ancient history in Bridgeport, though. Not something from before Oregon was a state, like some of the tall tales that floated around up and down the coast. This had happened just a few years ago, in the early Seventies. There were still people around who could remember it.

Blum was who I had recognized in my dream, his round, bald face immortalized in some blurry black-and-white archival photo. The Bridgeport Journal Gazette didn't have whatever I was after, though, so I got into my range rover—which had replaced mom's old station wagon a few years back—and drove across the bridge and up to the rutted track that led to the old church, the weeds brushing the underside of the chassis.

I'm not sure exactly what I went up there looking for. The Gazette wasn't running my pictures of the bodies themselves—too graphic, my editor told me—but I thought maybe if I could tie them into the old story about Blum and his cult, I could sell them somewhere else; a bigger magazine, or at least some kind of *Fortean Times* or *Weekly World News* sort of operation.

The church wasn't immediately visible from the main road, and even once it was, coming out from behind the trees as the track took a slight bend, it just looked like any other church. White clapboards turned gray by time and the wind from the ocean, a steeple that stood up above the front door. The only difference was the sign out front, hand painted, that said "Esoteric Order" above a symbol that looked a little bit like those Jesus fish that some people had plastered on the backs of their cars, though also somehow different in a way that I couldn't pin down.

I parked and walked up to the front of the church. Graffiti marred the front door, everything from "Jack Loves Miranda" to "Blum had it right" to pentagrams and drawings of penises. The only thing that seemed worth documenting was something kind of like an octopus or a jellyfish, spray painted in black, its tendrils dragging down through all of the other tags like mascara being streaked by tears. I raised my camera to my eye and took a picture.

Although the door had been chained shut once, rust had

taken care of the need for me to break an entrance, and the chain hung defunct, the door already standing partly open.

The church's windows had been broken out and boarded up, and there was a hole in the ceiling that let in cloud-filtered light to catch what should have been the dust motes that hung in the air, but the inside of the church didn't seem dry. It seemed damp and cold, like the inside of a cave down by the shore. While the pews were still there, the rest of the church had been transformed, the walls hung with all manner of ephemera from the sea. Shells and dried out starfish and the jaws of sharks.

The far wall was dark, cast in shadow, and I raised my camera and popped off the flash. There was a cross, complete with life-size suffering Jesus of the emaciated Catholic variety, that had been broken from its pedestal and leaned against the back wall of the church. There was something wrong with it, though, and I walked closer, raising my camera for another flash.

In place of thorns, Christ now wore a crown of coral on his head, and the body of a giant eel had been wound carefully around his body, secured with the kind of rope that they used to make fishing nets down in the harbor. While the other nautical-themed decorations seemed like they had been out of the sea for a long time, the eel still looked fresh and wet, and smelled like the fish market. I put out my hand, expecting it to suddenly lash and flop at any moment, and when I put my palm against its body it was cold as deep water.

Once I was close enough for my eyes to adjust to the dimness, I could see that there was another bit of graffiti on the wall behind the cross, this one much better than anything that had occupied the door. In it, a dark shape with glowing eyes seemed to be crawling up from somewhere. It was humanoid but somehow half-formed, soft and overly rounded and damp. Stylized fishes swam around its head, making a halo, or a crown.

I took a bunch of pictures inside the church, making sure to get plenty of shots of the graffiti and the Jesus wrapped in the eel, wondering as I did if whoever put it there had ever seen Ken Russell's *Lair of the White Worm*; if I was looking at some sort of bizarre homage.

Then I just went back outside, got in the range rover, and left. I drove back to the Cargo Cult, where I had converted a broom closet into a makeshift darkroom. I developed the photos there, but I didn't take them to the sheriff or the paper. What was I going to tell them? That someone had vandalized the old church that nobody but punk kids who went there on dares even cared about anymore? This didn't have anything to do with the bodies that were washing up. At least, not to the naked eye.

But I couldn't stop thinking about Blum's congregation, the way that they had marched down into the sea with their pockets full of stones. They were true believers, and I had to wonder if now they were finally coming back. Was this Blum's new race of man? Or at least, the first stage in its evolution?

So I waited for more bodies, more rings of the phone in the middle of the night, though by now I was getting calls from Rudy at the coroner's office more often that the paper, which had decided that my photos were not what they were looking for in this instance and assigned the regular photographer to the job. Still, I went out when I could.

I took to driving up and down the coast road at night, and so I was the first to find the fifth body. Collapsed in an alleyway between the shops that ran along the seawall, not five blocks from the Cargo Cult. It was grown through with coral, and the jellied bodies that filled the caverns of its bones were already starting to decay. "These are the pearls that were his eyes," and all that jazz.

When Sheriff Perkins showed up, he asked me what I was doing out there, and I told him, "Just out for a drive."

It took them six tries before they reached as far as my door. I heard it before I saw it. The wet squeal of damp rubber on glass, a squeegee across your windshield. I was sitting on the couch at the back of the store, not even in my bedroom, and when I looked up, I could see the shape in the doorway. It wasn't like the shape from my dream, not at all, but it was familiar. I had seen it painted on the wall of that old church, behind the defaced statue of Christ.

Sort of like a man, but low and oozing. A dark shape that nonetheless glowed. Slime the color of the ocean bed covered it, though within that darkness luminous shadows moved. Its skeleton glowed through, the ribcage, the face, the phalanges of the big, wet hand pressed against the glass. It was as if its bones had been hollowed out, replaced with something bioluminescent from the bottom of the sea. And who knows, perhaps they had?

I stood up from the couch, frozen between stepping forward and running away. There was a back door to the Cargo

Cult, an alley and, beyond that, the wooded gulley. But how far would I have to run next time? They had made it farther inland with each excursion, and I didn't think they would be stopping anytime soon.

I don't know now if I really heard the voice, or only imagined it. Dreamed it, standing there in the dark at the back of the store. A wet sound, of course, the squishing of feet in full galoshes. And yet, there was a familiarity in the voice. It was Rob's voice, it was my mother's voice, and it said my name from the other side of the door.

That's what made me walk forward instead of back, what made me throw the bolt on the front door and pull it open. And what collapsed at my feet was nothing more than a pool of black water and old bones, dead and dying sea creatures spilling out across the threadbare carpet in a tidal wave. I stood there for a long time, waiting to see if something else would come, before I went to the phone and called the sheriff.

I don't know why it came to the Cargo Cult. Was it simply because I was close to the water—I traced a map later, and found that the video store was smack in the middle of a beeline course from the beach to the old church up on the cliff—or was it something more?

After my nocturnal visitor, I dug through Rob's piles of old VHS tapes, the ones with hand-written labels, until I found one that said "Blum, 73" and below that the words "New Man." I left it sitting on top of one of the VCRs for three days while I thought about Rob, about his ashes spread across the bay. If Blum's congregation had come to the Cargo Cult after all these years, it had to be for him, not for me, and he was gone.

The body that came to my door was the last one that was ever found, though people continued to report strange things around the town. Odd noises in the night, pets that went missing, wet footprints on days when there had been no rain. Kids in town started claiming that they saw Blum's body hanging from the bridge, and then even adults were seeing it, though it was never there whenever they brought anyone back to look.

The other bodies, the ones that had been taken to the coroner's office, were dumped into a pauper's grave in the cemetery out east of the bay, but they didn't stay there. The graves were found dug up, the dirt around them churned into mud, the bodies gone. Eventually, the sheriff went up to the church on top of the cliff, on an "unrelated vandalism complaint," and found that it had been cleaned out. Nothing from the old congregation remained behind, no nautical decorations, no desecrated crucifix. Not even the old sign out front. A short time later, the church burned down.

All the while, I stared at that tape sitting on top of the VCR. More than once I went to pick it up, let my fingers rest on it, imagined that it felt cold, like the bottom of the sea. Once I even held it, pushed it against the mouth of the VCR for I don't know how long.

It was something Rob had left behind. Maybe if I put it in, pressed play, it would explain something, or at least let me see him again. But if I watched whatever was on the video, if he had something to do with what was happening, I might judge him, and I had already let him down too completely for that. So, I took it out back, pulled all the tape out, dumped it into a metal garbage can in the alley and set it on fire. My memories of Rob were good; I wanted them to stay that way. I owed him that much, at least.

With the bodies now all gone and the video too, all that was left were my pictures. I sold some of them; not to the *News of the Weird* or anyplace like that, but to a gallery down in Point Reyes, where I haven't ever gone to see them. I can't bear to look at them myself, not anymore. I wonder, in a few dozen years, when the new race of man is ascendant, if I will be seen as a prophet or a traitor to my species. I'm not sure I care too much either way.

Orrin Grey is a skeleton who likes monsters and also the author of lots of spooky books. His stories about monsters, ghosts, and sometimes the ghosts of monsters have appeared in dozens of anthologies, including Ellen Datlow's *Best Horror of the Year*. You can find him online at orringrey.com.

David Robinson

Intertidal

A wrinkle in the earths crust,
a tiny piece of shield
the size of a dump truck
– a rugged black island in a swamp of green

It's polished, gouged, fractured by the sea of ice that rose
here not long ago
and fell back
rose before that
and fell back

We have built on a beach
boundary between earth and water
ice and stone
between ages
and I, like a hermit crab when the sea pulls back
barely see across the nearest ripple in the sands of time
barely remember the last great tide
never think about the next.

David Robinson lives near the centre of the North American Craton, where the continent's most ancient rock is exposed. At dinner in the spring and fall he watches the sun set behind the headframes of two nickel mines. He has been a climate activist, a candidate for the Green Party, and for many years, a teaching economist.

Craig Laurance Gidney

Coalrose

She looks at you, imprisoned in a poster: a creamy sepia photo artfully blurred until the edges merge with the white borders. A cloud of frizzy hair shaped in a bun with her trademark 'do: two elegant, snaky strands to frame her high forehead. Her full lips are slightly parted, and her dark eyes glisten sensually. She's wearing a black velvet blouse embroidered with an Oriental design. A white lace skirt covers her booted feet in foam. At first glance it is simply a romantic '30s style photograph. But she changes, ever so slightly, like she's watching you. Sometimes, there's a tear in the corner of her eye, a tiny diamond of vulnerability. Other times, she is brutal and mocking: a sliver of tongue shows between the too-white teeth. And sometimes she is enticing – her blouse open slightly and you can see, nesting in her cleavage, the start of the legendary tattoo.

Here's a picture of Zoë Coalrose nude. Hands hide her eyes. The fuzzy, out-of-focus room is bare. Skeletal. (The negative is in such bad shape...) All you see of her face is her lips, which are twisted. Is she crying? Or laughing? But she makes it clear that she is responding to the photographer.

I: Etta (1930)

Mama warned her of juke joints, with their zoot-suited criminals, peddling prostitution and cocaine. So she managed to steer clear of Harlem, somehow. This fear made her miss Lena Horne at the Apollo and Cab Calloway at the Cotton Club. But he stood in front of her now, in spite of her caution, a cigarette dangling from his teeth. His conked hair shone in the weak winter sunlight. His suit was ostentatiously white, his fedora arrogantly perched on his head. A hot pink handkerchief obscenely peeked out of his suit's pocket.

"Hey, gal," he said. His eyes slowly swept up and down her body, deliberately stopping at her breasts. "How you doin'."

Etta pulled her coat close against her as she decided how to deal with him. It was daytime, in the middle of a very busy 6th Avenue. Maybe she had nothing to worry about. She would play it straight.

"I am doing fine; and yourself, sir?"

Zoot Suit smiled widely. Lots of gold sparkled in his mouth. He would have been good-looking without it. But with it he was positively irresistible. "You from the South, huh? Whereabouts?"

"Just outside of Atlanta," Etta said. She started sweating, in spite of the cold. She could practically see into his mind. She saw a small, dirty fleabag room, with a green dresser-drawer. She saw herself and this man (Dewey was his name) snorting a trail of white powder he'd arranged on her nude body, then having his way with her. Violently. Etta gasped. The image was so real.

"Why you so jumpy?" Dewey asked her. (How did she know his name?)

"Because I've got to be on my way." And she made to move.

He grabbed her by the arm. "Where you got to be so fast, darlin'?"

She smelled his desire, rank beneath his supersweet perfume. Perfume stronger than her own (she wore vanilla extract, a cheap, country fragrance substitute).

"Please, sir." Etta looked around frantically. Throngs of indifferent New Yorkers wove through the sidewalks. None of them gave a damn about a colored girl. They probably thought Dewey – *how do I know his name?* – was her pimp. She suddenly wanted to be back in her home just outside of Atlanta, with its pastures, sweet water and hundreds of kind, loving faces.

"You ain't got nowhere to go, gal." Dewey was leering at her. She jerked herself out of his grasp. He grabbed her again.

Then he jumped back, and doubled over in pain. "Damn, gal! What the fuck you got in your purse? A lightning rod?..."

His voice was fading and distant, because Etta was walking away quickly. She was shaking, from all the violence she'd seen in his mind. Mama was right. New York *was* a far cry from Atlanta. In Atlanta she was safe, the people in her neighborhood were friendly, completely unlike the folks in her tenement. Some were nice, but many of them had developed that callous rudeness that seemed so prevalent in the North.

Etta stopped in the middle of the street. She felt a little faint. She checked her watch: she still had time to spare.

Enough for a cup of coffee, to get herself together. She entered Café Robincheau, and ordered a cup and a madeleine. Some of the patrons stared at her. She ignored them. *I have to develop a thicker skin, if I'm to make it here.* This was true. There was no self-contained community to support her like there was back home. The theater scene here was so insular. She had no desire to join the route of the tawdry showgirls that populated the Harlem stage. She wanted to be a serious actress. Last year, before she got the scholarship to Barnard, she had been the star of the Negro Dramatic Arts production of A Midsummer Night's Dream. She'd attracted the attention of several county newspapers. Etta sipped her sweet and bitter brew. She nibbled her cookie, gently flavored with a hint of lemon. The people in the café looked like extras in a Dickens novel, with bloodshot eyes and ruddy noses. A few glared at her. *Let them stare.* It was still a novelty, being able to go where you wanted to, even after all these months. Jim Crow was a presence in her, but he was slowly dying. She closed her eyes, erasing Dewey, his name, his face from her mind. Her mother's voice came up instead: "If you'd gone to Spellman, you wouldn't have had this problem…"

She laughed. The cruelty and the danger were all worth it to her. This city (*the* City) was fascinating, with its tempos, languages, smells and different kinds of people. Home was nice, but a little boring. She saw herself getting married to her first boyfriend, Terrence, and putting her dreams on a shelf somewhere, to collect dust. Living her mortal existence in an endless flurry of children, cooking, cleaning, and church. Beginning each conversation with, "I used to be an actress..." Etta wanted to be an immortal, forever on black vinyl, or on the Silver Screen. Not that she had any illusions about the roles available for colored actresses. Acting was her passion. She felt she could tap into other people's souls, and weave their feelings together. She gave them back to the people watching. Puck had been easy. Androgynous and ageless, s/he seemed to exist in a corner of everyone's mind. So Etta wove the rural haints, shades, and spirits of the audience into the English woodland fairy. It was like echoing people's dreams and souls. She couldn't *not* do it, even if she tried. How she managed, she didn't question. It was a gift.

She had been Puck, lived his ephemerality. That had to count for something –

She glanced at the ornate clock on the café wall. Realizing the time, she finished her coffee and brought the rest of the cookie with her. It wouldn't do to be late for her first meeting with Harold.

Etta had met him when she posed for a Columbia University art class. The pay was terrible and the work boring. But it did give her some exposure to the art crowd. She figured that since she couldn't get a toehold in the theater community, she'd try the next best thing. (Maybe some casting director would be looking for a *type*)...

Harold looked like a weasel with dark, close eyes and sharp, rodent-like features. A few wisps of hair were on his chin, and angry red acne. He looked suspicious, but Etta didn't feel anything bad about him. She only saw his art. For some reason, images of brown women clad in bright, solid colors, in a lush tropical setting, danced around in his mind. A few weeks ago, Etta had gone to the Metropolitan Museum of Art and seen these very images for real. They got to talking, after the session, about Gauguin and other artists. Etta knew next to nothing about art. But she somehow knew what pieces he was talking about. They floated in the air. They became friends, of a sort. He took her out to dark, salon-like cafes, where she was introduced to espresso and biscotti. Places she could never go in Georgia. (If they had places like these in Georgia). The names he dropped – Cocteau, his chance encounter with Gertrude Stein when he lived in Paris – she wasn't familiar with. After a conversation with him, however, she found that she knew the plot of *Les Enfants Terrible*, or knew of the burgeoning artist's community on the Left Bank. She put it down to his passion. When Harold spoke, spit charmingly flew everywhere, his eyes had a far away glimmer, like beetles' wings. And his acne – they were blood anemone decorations for his face. When he invited her to be a model in his new project, she'd been more than delighted.

Etta reached the building and rang the buzzer. It was a dilapidated building, the color of cigarette ash. He buzzed her in. Cat piss and broken marble. Grimy stairwells and squalling children. But there was something arty and mysterious about it. A romantic ruin. She came to a scraped door that had loud music blaring out of it. Count Basie.

Etta knocked demurely. She got no response. Her knocking became louder. Harold opened the door, disheveled. He was unshaven and smelled of beer. His acne seemed to ooze.

"Come in," he said indecorously. He motioned for her to

sit in a chair littered with old clothes. He offered her a dirty glass of water before he went to his bedroom to get ready. Etta glanced around the exposed pipes, the greasy accordion radiator and the pock-marked floor. There was something not right about this. *Maybe I'm still shaken up about what happened earlier,* she thought.

Harold came back with a dirty, paint-spattered shirt and pants. "I'm ready," he grunted. "You sit there."

She meekly complied. This was deeply ingrained in her. Where she was from, if you looked at a white person the wrong way, it could mean death. But she was disturbed by his gruffness. She moved over to the makeshift throne he'd made of a wooden chair. Holey cushions, hard wood. An off-white tarp was draped behind her. She became acutely aware of the coldness of the room.

"Take off your clothes," said Harold.

She did as she was told. This was nothing new; she'd posed nude before. She gathered herself up in a proud pose. And she was proud: no matter what the outside world said, she thought her brown, glossy, muscled body was beautiful. For the next twenty minutes, she posed and preened. These were tasteful, arty photographs. Her religious mother might not understand, but that didn't matter. For most of the time she was able to shut out the dark thoughts that darted in Harold's mind. Then they changed. Etta could trace the change of the session to a glare in Harold's eye. The blood dots on his skin seemed to pulse.

"Spread your legs," he whispered. His urbanity, his education slipped from him. He was a pornographer. Somehow, she knew this: that he made and sold pornography to pay for his other art projects.

A shred of something made her say no.

He made her regret it.

"Now come on! Don't be like that." He'd raised his voice immediately. "Just relax," he softened his voice, "let the camera capture your – *essence*. No. No. If you think you're getting out of here without me getting what I want – "

She'd stood up. He approached her now, menacingly. She sat down. Jim Crow stirred and rose within her.

"Yes, that's right. Now spread those thighs. You're so pretty. Now come on! Put your hands down. *Relax.*"

She had started crying. She wanted home, now. Fried chicken, lazy summer days, Mama's bosom warm and soft. Then she heard Harold's voice, his hidden voice: *Stupid nigger bitch, she's more trouble than she's worth. Who'd want to buy these pictures anyway? Who'd want to fuck a thing like that?*

That shred of something that she'd felt before stirred. It grew, like a fire. Rage. She took her face out of her hands, and looked at him, dead on, through her tears.

Harold was saying something; she'd better stop crying or else.

That acne on his face shone an unwholesome red color. Not like blood anemones at all. Nor like the comforting red clay of Georgia riverbeds that she'd played in when she was little. No. They were like ants, fire ants. A red swarm of fire ants on his face. His skin was pale, white like lime powder. Lime, that you sprinkle down an outhouse, to stop the stink and decompose the fecal matter. If you got lime on your hands, you'd better run to your Mama, before it starts burning. Fire ants, swarming over hills of white lime and dried river beds of red clay. Fire ants, devouring the red, red blood of anemones. Harold had been talking. Etta barely noticed when he stopped. She couldn't, however, miss him screaming. Or him clawing at his face, at his acne. Count Basie's trumpeter drowned out the screams. They stopped before the record was over.

Etta stood up, looking at his body. It was still, even though his eyes were opened. There was no blood. No ants. What had she done?

I killed him. I wanted him dead, and now he is. She didn't need to feel his pulse. No thoughtforms swirled in his mind; that was knowledge enough. She gathered her things and began to dress. She did this mechanically. She felt – this emotion was new, and nameless. She felt soulless. *I know that I am evil now. The Lord can't help me. Dewey and Harold just recognized the evil within me. Dirt attracts dirt. Just 'cause I drew them, and their evil to me, does that mean that I should've killed them?* When she was dressed, she went to the Victrola and plunked the needle back down onto the phonograph recording. She did this listlessly, as if she were in some other's employ. Etta passed by Harold's inert form, ruined by her evil, and left. When she reached the outside, she glanced back. The building wavered and darkened. It whispered, *Who would want to fuck a thing like that?* Dewey's unctuous mind and flea-bitten bed. Harold's Paris and Gauguin, never to live again. His skin, bursting with pornographic flowers, ants writhing on their petals...

Etta turned and ran.

Another poster shows Zoë Coalrose as Venus, with whispery fabric gracefully dropping to the feather-strewn floor. Clamshells mask her forbidden parts, hair extensions cascade down her back as she leans against a pillar. She is not beautiful. She is much too dark, her nose is too wide and flared, her breasts and buttocks too voluptuous. Yet, if she is not a classical Venus, she is some darker aspect of Her. Love gone wrong, or unquenchable desire. Maybe closer to the earthy, pagan vision of the goddess.

II: Vivian (1931)

It was such an obvious pseudonym, Vivian had to laugh. It smacked of pretension and stood out on a roster full of Marys and Alices. He had to give it to the dancer, though. Anything to stand out.

He kept his voice neutral as he called out, "Zoë Coalrose." Maury, the show's producer sitting to his left, briefly glanced up from the pile of account books spread out before him. His assistant, Miss Clementine, was the very model of engagement.

A short, dark girl walked on stage. She was darker than a brown bag, and had wide hips. Coalrose, indeed. Her nose was flat, her lips too full. She wore an unflattering shade of pink. Poor thing—she probably didn't know the unspoken requirements for Negro performers. It would be a rude awakening. Viv looked over at Maury; there was a frown on his face. Maury hated auditions, and at the same time, he insisted on attending them. The Negro Follies was his show, and Maury felt he had to oversee every aspect of it.

"You can begin at anytime," he informed the dark girl. She nodded to George, who plonked out a workman-like version of "Some of These Days." Viv settled in for a minute or two of a middling performance. He thought of a children's book he'd once seen, with a female hippo in a pink tutu, gracelessly pirouetting over a stage...

The stage got brighter, the light intensifying. White light, Viv knew, was made up of an arcane combination of the color spectrum. Somehow, he could see how each strand of color, a ribbon of yellow, a slash of red, a flow of blue all come together, in illumination. They made and unmade the strand of light that came from no spotlight on the dancing girl. The dark girl who whirled in pink, like an azalea blossom caught in honey...

Viv sat up, shook his head. It was too early to fall asleep. Sure, auditions were tedious affairs. But he prided himself on not drifting off, for having a strong focus. Viv looked at the stage, at the pathetic girl moving on the stage...

She is no longer a girl in a pink dress. She's no longer a she. She is darkness devouring pink, pink swallowing darkness. An evolving statue, form and formlessness coming together. The shapes she makes with her body are repulsive and mesmerizing. Snake and stone; sylph and sinner;

air and angel. Evershifting...

Viv turned away from the stage. To focus on the Coalrose girl was to be nauseous. The things she did with rhythm and her body were...wrong. Instead, he watched Maury, anticipating his signal to end the audition. He was transfixed, his eyes glassy, his mouth slightly open. Mouthbreathing. Viv looked at Miss Clementine—the same look was frozen on her face. Viv turned to the stage, to the spinning form in front of him. He intended to pause the audition, and suggest that she try one of signature dances of the show, the Can Can. Before he could open his mouth, the music changed to boogie-woogie, and Coalrose was swiveling her hips and buttocks like Josephine Baker. The light divided into gay and merry colors, swirls of lemon and cobalt. Viv couldn't look away—he was ensnared. The dark, heavy girl danced the universe into creation on the stage. Viv knew the universe would stop when she stopped dancing.

III: Bertram (1933)

I was closing up shop when the colored woman came in. She was short, not more than five feet if an inch, but for all that, she was uppity. She strutted in my store like a prize rooster.

"Ma'am," I said as nice I as could, "We're closing. And 'sides, we don't tend to your sort."

I indicated the sign on the wall: MUST WEAR SHOES. NO DRUNKS. NO WOMEN. NO COLOREDS. I didn't want no trouble, but she didn't move an inch. Maybe she couldn't read. She didn't look drunk, but she was certainly a woman and a nigra. She said, in a high falutin voice, "I would like a tattoo, and I understand that you are the best."

"Why thank you. Much obliged. But as I said...I can't help you. Maybe there's a colored tattoo artist somewhere. I don't know. But I can. Not. Help. You." I moved toward her, put my hand on her arm, with the intention of steering her toward the door. But she wouldn't budge. She was a statue, a complete dead weight. It was like she weighed a thousand pounds. And she smiled at me. It was like – I swear – almost a pitying look, as if she was sorry about something. Now, I know from experience that ladies can fight something fierce. Neath their dresses, makeup and high heels many a woman is a wild cat, just waiting to come to life.

She said, soft and dangerous, "Please."

I said, firm and threatening, "No." I could get in trouble for working on a nigger. Word gets around fast, and I'm not saying I agree with it, but some folks won't patronize an establishment that works on their kind.

Now, I don't have the words to describe what happened next, but I'll try. I have my beliefs. I never saw a ghost or a flying saucer or anything like that, but I can't say they don't exist, cause who knows? I've seen good buddies, real sensible ones who could face death and disease and famine reduced to tears because they saw something they couldn't explain, the face of a long dead relative in a window, or the Blessed Virgin speaking to them while they were ill. I believe in Good, and I believe in Evil. Angels and demons, that sort of thing. (You can't travel around the world like I have and not believe in it; there are things in the East that will convince you of deviltry). I also believe that there are things that can't really be explained in those two categories. Forces of nature...

I'm not an artist. At least, I don't think what I do is art. Mother's names, crosses, skulls, dancing mermaids, the occasional more elaborate thing, like the Chinese dragon I once inked on a young man's skin. But sometimes, I get inspired. I've had a couple of fellas come in here, and told me to draw whatever I wanted. And once I was certain they wasn't drunk, I've done it. Mostly abstract stuff, patterns and the like. So when the colored gal sat down on the chair, and brought out her breast, I got one of those inspirations. It was immediate. I didn't have no choice. That curve of brown flesh told me what it wanted on it. The vision came silently, slithering. Vines, thorns and the curled blossoms of burnt roses. I knew that I'd do the job, or it would bother me, somehow. Like those dark roses would carve themselves into my brain like medieval woodcut. I don't remember getting my instruments. They just appeared, plucked from the bright darkness in my shop. I don't remember tracing the design on her brown flesh. Black ink flowed under her skin, while a thin trickle of blood rose from her, like an exchange of fluids. I was worried that the detailed work I was doing would fade, because her skin was so dark. But each rose, each thorn, each vine was defined, with a living blackness that I've spent many an hour trying to recreate. Black is all colors, right? Even when I mixed my most vivid inks together, it only looks gray beneath lily-white skin. How was I able to get that color on Negro skin?

When I was finished, there was a spray of black roses on her breast, hiding in a thicket of thorns.

As I put the gauze over the new tattoo, she said, "Now, was that so bad?"

She rose from the chair like she was a queen. She left a wad of bills on seat, and floated out into the predawn light.

I closed up and walked to Eli's Diner to get a cup of joe. And I saw her again, her face staring at me from a poster. THE NEGRO FOLLIES AT THE CHTHONIAN, the poster said in bright red lettering. Beneath the arc of words, ('One Week Only!') there were drawings of spooks dancing, and at the center, there was a great, fat lady spook with feathers coming from her hair. Though it was a caricature, I'd recognize that face anywhere. In smaller, black letters, the poster read, 'Featuring the Exotic Zoë Coalrose.' Don't know why, but I shivered, remembering the lost hours, filled with black roses and prickly vines. I swear, I thought I saw 'em begin to spill out of the poster, like tiny black ants.

Zoë made her appearance at the Panther Club in Chicago. See the publicity still from one of her acts. Her hair is short and in a Marcel wave. She stares at the camera and not even the ghost of weakness is there. She wears a translucent gown; more of a robe, really. On her breast, there peeks out the tattoo: a rose, its thorny vine begins to trail down into her cleavage. A rose that's a threat. Zoë eventually became a headliner at the Panther Club. She was called the Josephine Baker of the Midwest. I've got a picture of it. Even in black and white, it's a glittering ornament. Colson's book *Erotomania* describes the Panther Club like this:

The front of the Panther Club was shaped like the onion part of a minaret, done in black marble. A flight of black marble stairs led to the circular doorway, guarded by two stone panthers. A large, neon pink sign flashed in front, in Arabic stylized letters. Inside was a scene from the 1001 Nights. The waiters were dressed in turbans with costume jewelry and fiery garments. Palm trees lined the walls, and instead of seats, there were cushions. Men would sit down, order exotic drinks, and the show would begin... It could be Angel, the blonde child-woman dressed as her namesake that they were looking for...or Jasmine, the bellydancer. Or it could be Zoë, the smoldering, dancing temptress...

Her dancing became legendary. She didn't do striptease like her colleagues. She refused. She put her heart into her movements. Against bright jazz, she would whirl and high-kick herself into a frenzy. By all accounts, it was spellbinding. Much more meaningful than the bump-and-grind such establishments were known for. But this was not mere entertainment for those who saw her. Her power to weave and shape the stuff in minds was still there.

IV: Lenora (1935)

The junk in her veins didn't send her anymore. So when they came inside her mouth or her vagina, she felt it, and heard their grunting. But sometimes, if Lenora closed her eyes as they were kissing or fondling her, she could see something else. Or someone else. As rough and unshaven as their faces could be, as stinking with whisky and gin as their breath was, if she worked hard enough, Lenora could see *her*. That dancer's soft mouth, pressed against hers. The dancer's hands, exploring her body. But this never lasted. For one thing, johns were always crude. They couldn't help that. And for another, males were invasive.

The junk didn't work.

This man grunted. Through her hurt, she was cool. Pressed against his chest, she didn't know or care if he was black or white, married or not. (So, in one way, the junk *did* work). She merely noticed that he was being transported. She wasn't. After he finished, he slapped money down on her dresser, and went into the bathroom. Lenora showed him out of the door. As she walked to her bed, she passed the mirror. She looked at herself analytically. How old was she now? She forgot sometimes. She was nineteen. Her breasts sagged, her neck was covered in bites from overexcited men, her arms with track marks. She looked like she was forty. Good. Maybe she wouldn't have to do this work anymore. She'd have a real reason to quit. Except how could she afford her need?

Lenora didn't really care much. She would find a way. And if she died of hunger for this stuff, so be it. Some hungers are better to die of than others.

She walked over to her dresser, collected the money, still greasy with his essence, and put it in her purse. She set about getting dressed. She rifled through her closet, throwing on the first dress that she touched. She was on her way out when the mirror caught her attention again. The dress. Royal blue, with tiny white daisies printed on it. Camilla's dress. She couldn't wear it.

Before she knew it, Lenora was fighting with the dress, wrestling to get it off. It seemed to take a while. Finally, it was a blue ball of daisies in a corner of the room. Lenora went to her closet again with a vengeance. Finding a pair of slacks and a blouse, she forced herself into them. Which wasn't hard to do, considering that there wasn't much of her to shove into anything.

As she left her tiny room, she kicked at the balled up dress. At Camilla.

It really is all her fault, Lenora thought as she bolted down three flights of stairs. She wouldn't be like this, living like this, if it weren't for Camilla. Dusk was settling in on the streets as she made her way to the grocery store. She would buy some food. The leftover money would buy her junk and some needles from Brand.

Three years ago she had lived a pretty good life in Hickory, North Carolina. Papa was a preacher, Mama was a seamstress. The white house with green shingles had always been filled with love, God, and the congregation's gifts of food. Collard greens and chitterlings perfumed the place, seemed to emanate from the very wallpaper. The living room was mostly full of Mama's sewing things: headless female torsos and wooden body frames draped with fabrics, or stuck with pins. It was the mannequins that first tipped her off, that she might be different. There was something about their forms. The gentle slopes, curves and swells of their bodies spoke of grace. It wasn't that men's bodies were bad – she didn't feel that *then*, at least – it was just that they didn't call to her in the same way. Nothing echoed there. But Lenora ignored this feeling. God was a god of brimstone, judgment, and distance. Eventually she would marry a man and bear children.

But the feeling, this difference, didn't go away. When she played spin-the-bottle with the boys at birthday parties, she felt their wet lips on her skin, her mouth. But no connection. Maybe that would change in time. Lenora immersed herself into sports. She became something of a star on the girls' softball team. In the ninth grade she'd even won a trophy. But the accolades of her school, the rigors of the game, the trips to Greensboro, Gastonia, and Durham, these did nothing to fill the hollow space inside of her. There was nothing to cool the hot space she felt inside when she saw the girls' sweaty bodies, their muscles and breasts straining against grimy uniforms. After games, in the showers, taking furtive glances at slick forms underneath the water sprays. One girl from an away team caught her looking once. She smiled back.

Her name was Joanna. They became friends. They talked about softball, college and future plans. But not boys. This went on for about a week. At the end of the week, underneath Joanna's school's bleachers, they kissed. Lenora thought at first that she was going to Hell. But the feeling she felt when they kissed, it was how she imagined people felt when they were filled with the Lord. In Papa's congregation, when someone felt the Holy Ghost's presence, they would flop around like fishes, or slither like serpents on the church's floor. In Joanna's arms, she'd gasp for air and slither over her body. Surely this was just another way to get the Spirit, wasn't it? And if it wasn't, did God want her to feel hollow and empty the rest of her life?

One day, when she was sure that Mama and Papa would both be out of the house on various business, she invited Joanna over. They were pretty far along when Mama opened the door to Lenora's room. It seemed that she'd left something or other in there, maybe her good shearing scissors. It happened so fast.

With junk clouding her mind, Lenora could only remember bits and pieces. Mama fainting, Joanna leaving. Shivering and naked on the bed. Mama and Papa conferring. Papa, his black skin purpled from the rage coloring his face, quoting Bible verses: Corinthians 6: 9-10. No, not quoting; *screaming*.

Lenora shook her head. Junk could do that sometimes, cloud the brain. That, or the need of junk. She passed by a wall plastered with posters of *her*. Zoë Coalrose. Her bright smile shone from her dark face. Lenora found it irresistible. A few weeks ago she'd even stole one of the posters from this wall. It lay on her closet floor. There was something enchanting about the features. Something she couldn't place. She wasn't beautiful. But she was. The tawdry showgirl dress showed her cleavage. The black rose tattoo hid there. Lenora loved the name, too. It was poetic, and it was also funny. That ugly girl with a weird, hypnotic quality was something this Coalrose character had in common with Camilla, her only real lover.

For someone sixteen and just recently kicked out of her house, Lenora showed a remarkable resilience. For two nights she slept in the park near her home. On the third day, she watched and waited for her folks to leave the white house with green shingles. When they had, she broke in, smashing a window and went to the coffee can where the emergency money was kept. With two hundred dollars in hand and a suitcase of clothes (including some of the clothes that Mama intended to give to paying customers), Lenora walked to the bus station and bought herself a ticket North, to Chicago. After two days of cramped quarters and bad greasy spoons she arrived in the Windy City, exhausted. Somehow she found a women's hotel for that night. A few days later she found a job at Madsen's Funeral Parlor.

It was a stroke of luck. She walked in amidst the wax flowers, polished coffins, thinking that she was going to see an embalmed corpse and lose what little lunch she'd eaten before. It turned out that Mr. Madsen was from North Carolina, too. He'd migrated to the North years ago after finishing his mortician's degree.

"There's good money in death," he'd told her.

He was an elegant and dour man, without the slightest trace of a Southern accent. With an uncharacteristic wink he said, "Of course I'll help a hometown girl out. Even if you aren't from my hometown proper." She became his receptionist.

Madsen's Funeral Parlor was a family-owned and run business. Mrs. Madsen handled the books. She, like her husband, was serious, her "good" hair always wound up in tight, severe bun. And like her husband, she had a warm streak like a vein of gold hidden within rock. Their daughter Camilla arranged the presentation of the funeral services. Flower and candle arrangements were her domain. That was about all she could handle.

Where her parents were stern and serious, Camilla was blushingly silly. Where they were warm and genuine, she was sweet and distracted. She was the color of caramel candy with soft, brown hair and large, shining dark eyes. Her plumpness and thick, lustrous lashes added to her charm. Camilla took to Lenora like a bee to honey.

At first, Lenora thought that this was merely annoying. She was cloying, both in her personality and the toilet water she drenched herself in. She would talk to Lenora as if she were a character in those awful girlie novels that she hated. One day after Friday dinner at the Madsen's, the two of them had gone to Camilla's bedroom – a nightmare of dollies, doilies and chintz – ostensibly to check out dress patterns. Lenora had sat on the frilly, frou-frou bedspread, plotting her escape when Camilla shyly clutched her hand. Lenora thought that she was going to go into one of her "we're the best of friends, ever" speeches. It was a shock when Lenora learned of her true intentions. For a year and a half the two became secret lovers. Eventually they moved in together in an apartment subsidized by the oblivious Madsens.For that time Lenora was her life-sized dress-up dolly, cook and maid. Lenora was reasonably happy; what more could a black lesbian without a diploma ask for? It wasn't her lot to question things. Then Camilla decided to get married. The not-so-oblivious Madsens found a suitable beau from one of Chicago's burgeoning black bourgeois families. Camilla didn't protest; maybe she couldn't. The ever warm-hearted Madsens told her that she could still live in the nice, dollhouse apartment, for a low rent. Lenora refused. She had her pride...

The grocery was coming up quickly. She shook the fog out of her head and tried to concentrate on what she needed. Some kind of fruit, apples maybe. Some kind of meat... She teetered a bit. She almost bumped into the flower stall in front of the store. The little Asian man who ran the cart looked perturbed.

"Look, man, I'm sorry; I ain't mean to do that..." She was unsure if she'd spoken aloud or not.

Flowers. Girlie things. Camilla loved them. They looked like candy-colored lace skirts to her. Except – there, on one of the shelves, there was a bouquet of black roses. She'd never seen any roses that color before. The color of ink. *Coalroses.* Something, she didn't know what, made her buy six of them. The Asian man called them Midnight roses. She blew her food money; so what? She walked further on, not knowing what to do with the roses. *Maybe I'll build some sort of shrine or something, with the poster and the roses... I wonder if she's seen them, these coal-roses. I bet she has —* Lenora had an idea. It was crazy, but she couldn't stop herself. Before she knew it she was on a bus headed for the Westside.

It was only until she got to the door the club that she recognized that absurdity of what she was about to do. They probably wouldn't let her in. She could hear them now: *Fuckin' bulldagger wants to see the Panther Club...* No, this was a bad idea. The junk's idea. A waste of money, another hungry night. She held the midnight roses and began to walk away from the gaudy, ornamented club. Just then a shiny black Cadillac pulled up. A liveried driver got out and opened the back door. Zoë Coalrose stepped out.

Her ebony flesh was encased in a spangled, brilliant strapless dress. She seemed to drift. She floated to the stairs of the club.

"Miss Coalrose – "

They tried to stop Lenora, a group of men.

But, "It's alright, fellas," came the dusky contralto. Dusky and dulcet at once. They parted to let the little junkie girl who could've been forty hand her a bunch of black roses. Coalrose smiled, and her smile was brighter than her dress. It reminded Lenora of diamonds, even though she knew that this was impossible. It was a smile of welcome.

"What you got for me, sugar?" Zoë asked her.

Lenora felt as silly as Camilla as she gave her the bouquet.

"Ain't you sweet," said the dancer, accepting them, "coal-roses."

Lenora caught a glimpse of the tattoo, the thorny vines winding down her cleavage.

Zoë handed the flowers to an attendant bodyguard. "Would you like my autograph?" she asked her. The two coils on her forehead seemed to move. Being wrapped in their tendrils wouldn't be so bad...

"I don't have anything for you to sign, Miss Coalrose; I just wanted..." *Stupid fool*, she thought, *I'm crying...*

"Come here, sugar," said Coalrose. She embraced her. She kissed her forehead, and knew. Her father, God, the mannequins, Camilla, her first hit of heroin, hooking, everything. And in turn Lenora knew about her: a frightened girl named Etta, running and hiding from herself and the evil that was lurking in her mind. The evil subsuming the Southern girl, and the birth of Zoë. The coils on Coalrose's head were rose vines. The thorns pierced her. Something soothing and cold spread throughout her body. This contact which seemed to last for a long time was over.

"See you later, darlin'," said Coalrose. She began ascend the steps. "Take care of yourself, sweet thing." She disappeared behind the doors of club.

The sweet chill in her body rejuvenated her. The whispering of the stuff in her veins died down. She didn't feel quite so old. But Lenora *was* hungry. She found a diner not far from the Panther Club, and ate a large breakfast. Pancakes, bacon, coffee and orange juice – it never tasted so good. It gave her energy. It was night when she emerged from the diner. She took the L back to her dingy little apartment. It would be all right, somehow. *For Christsakes, I'm running!* Her veins sang. They were free. The gaunt, ugly men would never touch her body again.

"Nora!" Someone called her name. She was underneath the clattering platform of the L. She saw Brand, her dealer, not far from where she was. He was walking quickly towards her.

"Nora, let's you and me have conversation. I got something you're gonna like..."

"No, I'm busy right now."

"Some fella can wait a few minutes to get off. Lemme

show you something – ”

"No!" He'd been guiding her to an alley near the elevated tracks. "Let me go!"

He stopped. In the darkness, she could sense him sizing her up. She moved toward the streetlights. He followed.

"Well," he said slowly, "what have we here? What's gotten into you?"

"I don't need your stuff anymore. I don't need it."

"The hell you don't." He laughed.

And Lenora looked at him. Looked at him. Brand looked straight back at her. The thorns that had pierced her grew, and slithered. She could feel them rising behind her eyes. Roses. They rustled, kind of making her eyes itch a little. The vein-vines glowed with darkness. Her own darkness.

Brand backed down. He must've seen them, a silent garden of coalroses in her eyes, daring him. His voice cracked as he said, "Don't know what the fuck's gotten into you... but you'll be back..." He backed away, uncertainly.

When she got to her apartment, Lenora turned on the light. It was just a hunch, as she walked to the mirror. Her face was the face of a nineteen year old. Her skin was new. It glowed.

V: Victor (1962)

The Vine was run down. The red vinyl of the banquettes were more maroon, and the flocked wallpaper held cigarette smoke and stains. An old Chinese waiter, his face as pebbled as a beach, led me to my table, to the left of the stage. A candle flickered in a red fishbowl, illuminated nothing. Since I really didn't drink, I ordered Simon's favorite—a gimlet. The drink appeared before me—it was too dark too see beyond the gloom of the club—and I sipped the harsh lime infused concoction. "For you," I whispered, and toasted the empty seat.

I looked at the dingy stage. A double bass rested against a stand, and a piano was angled to the side. A microphone, a silver plant with a mechanical flower at its top, stood between the two instruments. So, she was going to sing. Not surprising—she was a bit long in the tooth to be dancing. I didn't like her voice. In fact, I didn't think she could really sing. Hers was a quivering contralto, full of drama. There were times when she didn't sing at all—she just spoke the words. The only thing I did like about her 'music' was that the repertoire was a little unorthodox. She eschewed the standards, your Basies and Gershwins, opting, instead, for things like lieder, chanson or folksongs along with the expected show tunes and gospel. "Too bad she has no talent," I'd say. Her records were dreary things, perfect for fog bound days in this damned city. Simon loved it, though. He was a complete devotee of Zoë Coalrose.

Her face stared down at us from the framed poster he had in our living room. Her eyes followed you everywhere. And that odd tattoo that poked above from her cleavage... It was downright scandalous. I could only imagine what Mother would say if she saw it. (As if she ever would travel across country to visit her homophile son). Yes, there was something sinister about the poster. But it had been his prized possession. I couldn't bear to remove it, after he passed away.

"She gives me strength," he told me once, during one of our fights. When he was bedridden, I moved the poster into our bedroom so that she could look down on him as he slept. When I did that, I could swear his nightmares disappeared, and the fevers were no longer as fierce. Nevertheless, the poster creeped me out. I remember one vivid nightmare: her nude body with pendulous breasts, writhed in black roses. She was winged and vampiristic, as she drained the fever from sleeping Simon. The black roses got engorged, and burst, like boils.   She was a comfort to Simon, yes. But ultimately, she couldn't save him. Maybe she leeched his life away....

That was a silly thought. I focused on the gimlet, its acidic sourness, the astringency of the gin.

"You're such a good boy," he'd say, when he drank and I stuck to Coca Cola or juice.

"Mama raised me right."

"Maybe I would've been raised right, if I had a Mama."

"What's the use of having a Mama," I'd say back, "if she won't talk to you?"

I knew that Simon had a past that he didn't talk much about. He'd been raised in various state institutions and by reluctant relatives. He drank too much, so his morning breath had that faint stink. He didn't age well at all—crows feet, washed out blond hair with a receding hair line, not-blue, not-green eyes caught in a web of burst capillaries. He was too loud and loved 'queening it up,' something that caused more than its fair share of trouble in public. But for all that, I missed him. I would give anything just to fight with him once more. Maybe that was why I was here.

Zoë Coalrose was a piece of Simon. Since he was gone, she would have to do.

The lights dimmed, with a single spotlight focusing on the mic. A pianist and a bassist walked out in the gloaming, while a man in a tailored tux stood in front of the microphone. He uttered some introductory words about the "legendary songstress and dancer" Coalrose as the duo played soft contemplative music. This theme continued until she took the stage herself.

She was shorter than I imagined, and had a matronly girth. But her hairstyle hadn't changed at all, the two snaky tendrils plastered to her forehead. A black velvet blouse with an Oriental design, the seafoam of lace swirled about her in a skirt. The black rose vine growing from her skin.

Coalrose started singing, and the room dropped into darkness. Her voice sounded ancient. Cigarettes, booze, years of screeching couldn't create that sound. It was the voice of a dying woman, scratchy and ravaged. She croaked out a tune, some piece from an old Broadway show long forgotten, and a song by Edith Piaf. The band played beautifully, deep bass tones, silvery piano notes that floated in the air. I still didn't like her voice, but it had a certain—charm? Gravitas? I couldn't place the word. She didn't really sing, per se. She *incanted* the words, gave them reverence, like a poetess. She made sure each break and quiver in her voice had a musical resonance. I was thrown back to when I first met Simon. Both of us were hayseeds from the sticks, and had joined the Navy. Neither of us had been further west than the Mississippi. He was tall, dashing and blond. I was small and black. Both of us were freaks. When we figured out the feelings between us, there had been hell to pay. But it was worth it. Both of us chose this fogbound city, far away from anyone we knew, at the edge of the world. Listening to Coalrose took me back to those endless Sunday nights, when mist walked the hills of the city and we were safe inside, listening to a dark voice as it curled through the night and Simon's cigarette rings...The flow of a white skirt. And I remembered as Zoë Coalrose watched over us. Her eyes following us everywhere. Black Madonna or vampire woman? As each song ended, the audience clapped thoughtfully. I was surprised that the room had filled up, and the number of folks in the audience. Mostly colored, a few whites scattered here and there. Her audience grew in darkness.

At the end of the set, Coalrose stopped to introduce her band in that deep, crackly voice. After that, she said, "I was born Etta Mae. Naïve, callow Etta, afraid of her own power. When she found what she could do, she died, and Zoë rose in her place. This song is dedicated to Etta."

I recognized the song within the first few notes played by the pianist. Everyone else did, as well—there was the gasp of recognition. This was Simon's favorite song. And Coalrose actually *sang* this one.

Years dropped off her vocal cords, and spoken words soared. But I don't remember anything else about the performance. Because, I saw Etta, gingham dress, church hat and all, standing on the stage. Or—superimposed over the aged woman. But she faded as the song changed. She moved her hands and I swear, the spotlights and the shadow obeyed her.

It's masterful, isn't it?

I turned, and there was Simon. Or some part of him. Made of shadow and light, slithering with tendrils. His eyes were petals. I glanced around the room, to see if other people saw him. But everyone else had a flowered shadow around them. I glanced at my gimlet.

You aren't drunk. His shape rustled in time to the bass, the piano and voice. *I hear her everyday. In heaven.*

"Then you must be in the other place," I whispered to my man of shadow.

He laughed. Or rustled. And faded, as the song ended.

She didn't come out for an encore.

A stylish sister, dressed in a man's suit, quietly put a rose on the stage where Coalrose had stood.

Of course, it was black.

It took me years, but I found their stories, those touched by Zoë Coalrose. I'm sure that there are many others. I wasn't a fan, but I became one.

What she was, I don't know. There are words, but they are inadequate. But I think the clue is in her name. It's a work of genius, really. Zoë: an ancient name, evocative, resonant with power and nobility. It also sounds modern, as well. A tinge of the masculine in its pronunciation. And Coalrose. Coal is a nascent, unborn diamond, pure black that transforms into something that's clear, beautiful and unbreakable. A rose made of coal: intricate, kissed with the memory of fire.

Craig Laurance Gidney writes both contemporary and genre fiction. He is the author of the collections *Sea, Swallow Me & Other Stories* (Lethe Press, 2008), *Skin Deep Magic* (Rebel Satori Press, 2014), *Bereft* (Tiny Satchel Press, 2013) and *A Spectral Hue* (Word Horde, 2019).

Awards

Susan C. Petrey Scholarship to attend Clarion West Writing Workshop (1996)

Gaylactic Spectrum Finalist for "A Bird of Ice" (2008)

Lambda Literary Finalist: *Sea, Swallow Me & Other Stories* (2008), *Skin Deep Magic: Short Fiction* (2014) *and A Spectral Hue* (2019)

Bronze Moonbeam Medal (2014) and Silver IPPY Medal (2014) for *Bereft*

Amara George Parker

a moment's peace

let me float, suspended
in thrumming cosmic ink –
it pools at life's edges,
still,
unspilled,
inert,
innocuous –

both I and it filled with the potential
for a million different colours and lies and feats,
all safely unwritten,
undone

let me rest here for a while
restore
so that when that snap
of a catalyst comes
I am ready
to give

Amara George Parker is a poet and novelist. Her works have been published in literary magazines Voice of Eve, Aeva, Sufi Journal, She Who Knows, i n k s p a c e, and Earthpathways Diary. Connect with her at: amara.g.parker@gmail.com or https://www.instagram.com/a_g_parker/

Something Nice

Junior Special Agent Meilin Chen sat on the couch in Bianca's office with her arms wrapped around herself. "I'm sorry. I know I'm supposed to talk about it. I know that's how counseling works. But I just can't."

Bianca, cross-legged in her armchair, let Meilin's words linger in the air a moment while she savored the young woman's anguish. "It's all right. You don't have to say anything. I see it in your mind. I can see everything that happened to you."

The shock on Meilin's face, and in her mind, was priceless. Meilin had known Bianca was a telepath, of course—everyone on Denebola Base knew that much—but like most of Bianca's patients, she hadn't suspected her memories could be laid bare with such ease. Shouldn't she have noticed the intrusion? Shouldn't it at least have required Bianca to exert some visible effort?

Bianca hid her amusement behind a practiced mask of sympathy as she watched Meilin's alarm turn to mortification—and then to a dawning recognition of the gift Bianca was offering her. If Bianca could know her mind so deeply, Meilin no longer had to carry her pain alone. Someone finally understood, without the need for Meilin to speak the unspeakable.

"Shh," Bianca said. "It's all right. I know. I'm here with you."

Bianca got up and went over to the couch and held Meilin while she cried. Skimming through the young agent's memories of early childhood, Bianca saw how Meilin's mother used to comfort her by stroking her back and whispering in her ear. She stroked Meilin's back in the same way, whispered in the same tone, and Meilin lay in Bianca's lap and sobbed so hard it felt to Bianca like she might shake herself to pieces.

Bianca looked down at Meilin and thought about how delicious it would be to manipulate the tender little thing into mentally reliving each agonizing minute of her trauma, over and over. How easy it would be to help Meilin convince herself that what had happened to her was her own fault. So sweet. So tempting. But no, she didn't dare.

It was the nature of her kind to feed upon the suffering of others, and the Commander of Denebola Base was well aware that Bianca drew sustenance from the emotional pain of her patients. He was willing to tolerate this state of affairs as long as patients continued to make near-miraculous recoveries under her care, and as long as she confined herself to feeding only on the pain they already carried within them. But he'd made it clear that if he ever had cause to suspect her of intentionally worsening anyone's suffering in order to more fully indulge her appetites, she'd get no second chances.

Her success with the first patients assigned to her had surpassed all expectations. Now, two decades later, her skill as a counselor was legendary. She was permitted to roam freely within the base's extensive recreation areas, and most of the personnel stationed here these days had no idea she was officially classified as a prisoner.

Bianca had no illusions about her position, though. Maybe, after all this time, she could get away with occasionally toying with a patient to increase the pleasure of her feeding—or maybe she couldn't. Sometimes, with a particularly tasty treat like Meilin, the temptation was excruciating. But nothing was worth the risk of being handed over to the interrogators again. Few of the traumas she saw in the memories of her patients could compare with the things that had been done to Bianca during the first year of her captivity. She had her scars to remind her of that, and her nightmares and claustrophobia, and the tiny rounded stumps where two of her fingers had been.

So she kept her appetite under control, and continued idly exploring the private recesses of Meilin's memories as she waited for the tempting little morsel to cry herself out. Afterward, she sat side-by-side on the couch with Meilin and held her hand while they talked. Bianca's access to her patients' minds made it easy to find the most helpful things to say, to plant the seeds of healing. She could already tell that Meilin would be another success. Another damaged agent salvaged, another boost to Bianca's good standing with her captors.

When the session was over, she walked Meilin to the office door. "Until tomorrow, then," she said.

Meilin paused in the doorway and ventured a shy, tearful smile, the first one Bianca had seen from her. "You're so kind. Honestly, I was a little scared when they sent me to you. Everyone says you're amazing, but some people say…" Bianca could taste Meilin's sudden embarrassment, the flash of fear that she might offend the one person she'd been able to feel safe with. "They say you're, um..."

"Some sort of horrible spooky vampire?" Bianca suggested, with a little smile of her own.

Meilin blushed, still embarrassed, but her anxiety turned instantly to relief. "Oh my God," she said. "It sounds so *silly* now. But I was so nervous, I just..." She shook her head, smiling again.

Meilin was adorable, Bianca decided. The kind of human she might once have kept as a pet.

Bianca had figured out early on that the best way to deal with the vampire rumor was to make a joke of it. The frost-white color of her skin and hair, and the fact she'd been on Denebola Base almost a quarter of a century and still had the face of a woman in her twenties, marked her as other-than-human and inevitably gave rise to speculation. Agents had to have a fairly high security clearance before they were allowed to know the Reality Patrol had a lloigor in captivity; a lot of younger agents like Meilin hadn't even heard of lloigor, or assumed they were mythical. Everyone had heard of vampires, though, and the Reality Patrol recruited such an interesting assortment of personnel that the idea they'd employ the undead wasn't entirely implausible.

"I give you my solemn word," Bianca said, "that I have no intention of drinking your blood or anyone else's." This was true; she'd tried human blood ages ago, out of curiosity, and found it thoroughly disgusting. "Now off you go," she said. "I wish to turn into a bat for a while. Oh, and one more thing.

Serious this time. Schedule something lovely for yourself, my dear. A spa day? A favorite virtual reality scenario? Spoil yourself a little. At least twice a week, as long as you're on leave. Doctor's orders. It's so important to have something nice to look forward to."

She closed the door behind Meilin and returned to her armchair, pausing at her desk to grab the folder containing the details on her final patient of the day. This one was a last-minute addition; the folder had been delivered this morning along with a note from Dr. Madaki. She hadn't been pleased to have another appointment tacked onto the end of her shift, but her lack of choice in such matters was one of the realities of life in captivity.

She had no memory of the catastrophic event that had led to her capture, or of the weeks leading up to it. She'd been running a slave-trafficking ring in the largest city of a declining empire, and enjoying herself immensely; the feeding was excellent and the cutthroat world of illicit commerce kept her entertained. And then one day she'd woken up strapped naked to a hospital bed, in a bright sterile room she'd never seen before.

She'd experienced a brief surge of alarm, but quickly recovered herself. There was someone in the room with her, a human woman in a lab coat, busy with some task at a computer terminal. Like any lloigor, Bianca could telepathically control the minds of humans as easily as she controlled her own limbs. Bianca had explored the woman's consciousness and discovered she was a medical doctor who worked for the Reality Patrol.

The first thing Bianca wanted to know was how she'd ended up here, and it was easy to find the answers in the doctor's mind. It turned out that some sort of massive telepathic shockwave had killed every single human in the city where Bianca had been running her trafficking business. The shockwave had echoed across dozens of parallel universes, drawing the attention of the Reality Patrol. The agents who arrived to investigate had found Bianca unconscious in the ruins of a collapsed building, at the shockwave's apparent point of origin.

Bianca learned that she'd been in a coma for three weeks, and the doctors on Denebola Base had spent the first half of that time just trying to determine what she was. When they figured it out, it had caused quite a stir. There were only about thirty lloigor in all the known universes combined. Their origins were a mystery; they didn't mate or reproduce, and were so territorial that there was no record of two lloigor ever peacefully coexisting on the same planet. Ancient and immortal, they were the apex predators of the multiverse; they spread cruelty and ruin wherever they went, and feasted on the suffering they caused. Even the Reality Patrol, with its vast reach and resources, had never captured one alive—and certainly hadn't expected to do so by accident.

By the time she woke up, the Reality Patrol had concluded that the telepathic shockwave had been triggered by a psychic battle between Bianca and another lloigor who'd intruded on her territory for reasons unknown. Bianca may have ended up in a coma, but she'd won the fight; the reason the investigating agents hadn't spotted the other lloigor at first was that there was nothing left of it but an oily residue which had to be scraped off of various surfaces and sent to Denebola Base in a jar.

Bianca had also learned from the doctor's mind that Denebola Base was a manmade structure the size of a small city, floating in deep space. This would be interesting, she'd thought. She'd never taken over a Reality Patrol base before. She'd thrust an impulse into the doctor's mind: *Come over here and undo these straps.*

And nothing had happened.

Her duel with that other lloigor had left Bianca damaged on some level that neither she nor the Reality Patrol scientists understood. She'd lost access to most of the powers that enabled lloigor to prey with ease upon humanity. She couldn't shapeshift or regenerate her physical form anymore, or traverse the void between universes—and although she could see into the minds of others as clearly as ever, she no longer had the ability to bend those minds to her will. In the months that followed, she could read the thoughts of her interrogators and see each new way they were going to hurt her, but she couldn't make them stop.

Devastating as it was to have lost her mind control powers, the loss of her shapeshifting and regenerative abilities was worse. She couldn't properly repair her body. She still healed from physical injury far faster and more effectively than a human, but that healing had its limits now. She learned those limits all too well when her interrogators set out to catalogue them. She learned exactly how severe a burn had to be in order to mar the whiteness of her skin with blue-grey scar tissue that never went away. She learned she could re-grow her fingernails and toenails in a few weeks, no matter how many times they were pulled out, while teeth took months to grow back and a severed finger wouldn't grow back at all. And although she remained impervious to the effects of aging, the unanimous opinion of the doctors was that she was now as vulnerable as any human to being killed by violence or mishap.

Something was wrong with her memory, too. The disastrous battle with the other lloigor, and the weeks leading up to it, weren't the only things she was unable to recall. The interrogators wanted a timeline of her existence, and she tried her utmost to satisfy them; anything to buy herself the slightest mercy. But there were vast stretches of her history she simply couldn't remember. Entire centuries that were lost to her. One gap that spanned a full millennium.

Most frustrating to her interrogators, who made sure she felt their displeasure, was that she had no recollection of her origins. Her oldest memories went back at least ten thousand years, but there seemed to be little difference between the Bianca of ten thousand years ago and the Bianca of thirty years ago. Age held no meaning for her; she didn't feel old and didn't remember ever being young. She could shed no light on how she and the rest of her kind had come to be as they were. She couldn't even be certain whether these were things she'd forgotten or things she'd never known.

The Reality Patrol assumed her memory loss was another symptom of the psychic damage she'd sustained, but Bianca wasn't so sure. One of the things she couldn't clearly remember was what her memory used to be like. What if she'd been losing track of her history all along, through all those centuries, and simply hadn't noticed it until her interrogators had pressed her to give an accounting of the time? What if the gaps in her recollection were normal for lloigor? Perhaps it was an inevitable consequence of immortality; perhaps it just wasn't possible for any being to retain ten thousand years of memories. Perhaps *all* lloigor had forgotten their origins. How would they know, when their instinctual animosity toward one another kept them from discussing such matters among themselves?

She pulled herself out of her reverie. Her new patient would be here soon, and she hadn't even opened the folder and looked at his file. Had she always been so prone to letting her mind wander? That was another thing about herself she couldn't remember.

The file identified her patient as Special Agent Stanford Brock, a forty-three-year-old human male with a record of distinguished service and a preference for direct action over subtlety. His latest mission had gone sideways: he and his team had been caught in a chaos storm and flung randomly through space and time. Brock had somehow found his way back; when the storm passed, a search party discovered him wandering alone and haggard in more or less the same spot from which he'd vanished. From his perspective, he'd been gone for months.

Brock's superiors were eager to debrief him, but he wasn't ready to talk about what he'd been through. He'd requested counseling to help psychologically prepare him for the debriefing, and specifically asked for Bianca. A telepathic counselor was the obvious solution for a patient who was having a hard time speaking about his traumatic experiences; even so, the hard-nosed man described in this file would only have volunteered to allow a stranger into his mind if he were truly desperate.

Twice a week, Bianca was permitted to spend a few hours immersed in a virtual reality scenario of her choosing. She chose to be a hawk, usually; to soar through vast open skies, free from the claustrophobia that had plagued her since the first time the interrogators had tortured her with suffocation. Anticipating those hours of blissful flight helped to get her through each day. Like she'd told Meilin, it was important to have something nice to look forward to. The addition of Brock to today's schedule meant she'd have to postpone tonight's virtual reality session—but if he was as desperate as it sounded, his trauma might prove rich and tasty enough to make the postponement worthwhile.

She'd find out soon enough; he should be arriving any minute. She reached out with her mind to see if he was nearing her office yet. Physical barriers like walls and floors posed no obstacle to her telepathy, and she liked to surreptitiously tune into her patients' thoughts and feelings while they were still en route. Knowing patients' mental states in advance of their arrival helped her to greet each one in whatever way would inspire the most trust.

She located Brock right away. He'd already left the elevator and was striding down the corridor toward her office door. She should have guessed from his file that he'd be punctual. At this pace, he'd be there in seconds. Still, a lloigor could read a great deal about a person in a very short time.

She extended a psychic tendril into his mind...

And recoiled.

Special Agent Stanford Brock intended to kill her.

His hatred blazed white-hot as he imagined driving his fist into her face, wrapping his hands around her neck, staring into her eyes and watching her die as he squeezed and squeezed...

No time to look deeper. No time to find the reason for his fury.

Seconds. He'd be there in seconds.

If only she could still shapeshift. She didn't stand a chance in this frail and vulnerable body.

She fought her rising panic, tried to think.

No use locking the door. Any agent's thumbprint would open it, including Brock's.

Any furniture big enough to barricade the door was too heavy for her to move.

She could sense other people in nearby rooms, but what good was that when she no longer had the ability to control their minds and make them come help?

There were other ways to summon help, though. Human ways.

She ran to the door and flung it open, and she was face to face with Brock.

He'd been about to open the door himself, and for the briefest instant he was caught by surprise. In that instant, Bianca screamed as hard as she could, shrill and piercing, a raw animal sound that had only ever come out of her before under torture.

Her scream froze him in his tracks for the space of a heartbeat. Then he launched himself at her, bellowing. She saw his intention in his mind and scrambled to the side just in time, and the force of his attack carried him past her.

She lunged for the open doorway. If she could make it out into the corridor, run and scream until help came...

Brock pivoted and grabbed her by the hair, so fast that knowing what was in his mind did her no good this time. Her head was jerked backward with such force that her feet went out from under her. He hurled her across the room like a rag doll, and she crashed sideways into the back of the couch and felt her ribs break.

Then he was on top of her, choking her, too strong, broken ribs shrieking under his weight, massive hands crushing her throat, and she couldn't breathe, couldn't make it stop, couldn't breathe, couldn't think, couldn't make it stop, couldn't breathe. And then a terrible blackness, and then nothing.

Pain in her ribs, bright light against her eyelids. Something around her neck, human minds nearby. She opened one eye, carefully, just a little. A hospital room. She was in a hospital bed, human figures looming over her. She couldn't turn her head. A memory of terrifying suffocation.

She must have blacked out while the interrogators were suffocating her, smothering or mock-drowning her, and now they would start again...

Panic seized her. She pulled frantically against the restraints—and her arms and legs flailed freely, not meeting the expected resistance, the sudden motion sending spears of agony through her ribs and neck.

There were no restraints. She was clothed, and partially covered in a blanket that had been thrown askew by her thrashing limbs. The minds and faces of the three humans around her reflected not leering cruelty, but concern for her well-being. The restraints and tortures were more than twenty years in the past.

Her heart wouldn't stop pounding. She tried to calm her breathing. She was safe, and surrounded by people who meant her no harm: Jackson, Denebola Base's Chief of Security, who'd rescued her from the hands of the interrogators all those years ago. Dr. Madaki, the Chief Medical Officer, who'd overseen her long recovery from what they'd done to her. And Meilin was here, too. The sight of Meilin's worried face brought back the memory of what had happened: waiting for Brock after Meilin's counseling session, the murderous intent in his mind, his hands on her throat...

"Please stop moving," Dr. Madaki said. "On top of some

truly impressive bruising, you have two cracked ribs and a mild case of whiplash. And stop trying to turn your head. You're wearing that neck brace for a reason."

She opened her mouth to speak and found her throat was so painfully swollen she couldn't even whisper. Fortunately, while she couldn't control the minds of others anymore, she could still psychically communicate her thoughts to them. It wasn't something she did often; ordinary speech suited her perfectly well most of the time, and many humans found it disconcerting to hear her talking inside their heads. Jackson and Madaki had always been comfortable with her telepathic voice, though, and she suspected Meilin would be fine with it under the circumstances.

She sent her question into their minds: *How did I survive?*

Meilin gave a little gasp of surprise, then recovered her composure—and then lost it again when she realized that Jackson and Madaki, who both outranked her, were looking at her and waiting for her to speak first. She blushed and took a deep breath.

"Right after our appointment," Meilin said, "I was walking down the hall, and you'd been so comforting, I was feeling such relief, and I just started crying all over again. In a good way, but I really didn't want to run into anyone in the state I was in, so I ducked into the restroom near the elevator and just bawled my eyes out. I was at the sink cleaning myself up when I heard you scream. I mean, I didn't know it was you at first. I wasn't even sure it was a scream, I was all the way down the hall, and the water was running... but I went to check, and your door was open, and..."

She paused, searching for the words to describe what came next, but Bianca could already see it all in the young agent's memory: Meilin approaching the open doorway and peering inside. Brock, his back to Meilin, kneeling astride Bianca on the floor. Meilin reacting without thinking, her Reality Patrol combat training momentarily overriding the trauma-induced sense of helplessness for which she'd been sent to counseling. Moving swift and silent, coming up behind Brock and putting her full power into a single strike, the blade-edge of her hand landing in just the right spot at the back of his neck...

Bianca's eyes met Meilin's. *It's all right,* she said in Meilin's mind. *I can see it. You don't have to say anything.*

Brock had been knocked out but was still alive. By now he'd probably been revived and questioned by Jackson's security force, so Jackson might already have the answer Bianca wanted most: *Why did he attack me?*

Jackson turned to Madaki. "Doctor, now that that Agent Chen has seen for herself that Bianca's going to be okay, maybe you could give her something to help her sleep?"

Meilin turned to look at Bianca again as she followed Madaki out of the room, and Bianca sent a parting thought into her head: *Thank you.*

Meilin managed a smile. "Actually," she said, "saving you was kind of therapeutic."

Bianca's interrogation in the first year of her captivity had been overseen by an old-school torturer named Eskagon, who'd circumvented the Reality Patrol's policies regarding humane treatment of prisoners by having Bianca classified as a research specimen. Back then, Jackson was a young agent serving under Inspector Shiota of Internal Affairs, whose job was to make sure the Reality Patrol's myriad research facilities weren't misused. On a surprise visit to Denebola Base, Shiota and Jackson had discovered Bianca, broken and emaciated, cowering in a cage in a research lab that Eskagon had turned into a makeshift chamber of horrors. They'd had words with the Commander, who'd ordered Eskagon to terminate the interrogation. Eskagon chose to interpret this order creatively; when Jackson had returned to the lab to check on the situation, she'd caught him preparing to inject Bianca with a massive dose of poison. Jackson had taken the syringe away from him, breaking his wrist in the process, then picked up Bianca in her arms and carried her to the base's hospital.

Bianca was glad Jackson's career had eventually brought her back to Denebola Base to stay—although she always felt shy around Jackson, a strange, awkward feeling she was only able to name because she'd observed it in humans. There was a time when Bianca would have said that the desire for friendship was every bit as foreign to a lloigor's nature as remorse. But in recent years, to her great discomfort and confusion, she'd found herself wanting Jackson to like her.

She never looked into Jackson's mind. Jackson had asked her not to, long ago. Bianca had agreed, and had kept her word; although her telepathic incursions were generally undetectable, she'd always suspected that if she broke her promise to respect Jackson's privacy, Jackson would somehow know. With the shape Bianca's throat was in right now, it was a good thing Jackson didn't have a problem with Bianca speaking to her telepathically as long as the telepathy stayed strictly one-way.

"How are you holding up?" Jackson asked, after Meilin and Madaki had left the room.

Well enough to hear why Stanford Brock wanted to kill me.

Jackson sighed. "I guess you saw in his file that Brock and his recon team got caught in a chaos storm out on the Plateau of Leng. Well, they got displaced in time, and they ran into a past version of you."

Me?

"You, in the past. Before Denebola Base. Before you lost your powers."

Ah. I imagine that wouldn't have been pleasant for them.

"Far as we can piece together from Brock's ranting, you were in some theocratic city-state, running the local version of the Inquisition. A reign of terror. Must've been a real feast for you."

Bianca cringed at the hard edge in Jackson's voice. *I know my past disgusts you,* she said. *But I'm different now.*

"I know you are." Jackson was silent for a few seconds, then she took a deep breath and said, "Look, this is hard for me. I believe in second chances. I see how much good you do these days, for people like Agent Chen. But you were a mass murderer. Jesus Christ, you were a fucking *slaver*. I mean, I know what you've been through. You've suffered enough, as far as I'm concerned. But I can't pretend the shit you've done is okay with me."

That's fair, Bianca said. *I'm sorry.* She felt a tightness in her heart that wasn't just from her injuries. Why did she have to care so much what Jackson thought of her?

Jackson gave another sigh. "It's fine. Forget it. Anyway, about Brock: your Inquisition arrested his whole team. They were in no shape to put up a fight after going through that chaos storm. Brock evaded capture, but couldn't rescue the rest of the team. He was watching from a rooftop when you had them publicly tortured to death for witchcraft. Couldn't do anything to stop it. And you were right there, personally overseeing the whole thing."

Ah. I see. And he wouldn't have stood a chance against me, back in the past when I still had my full powers. But he knew that if he could get back to the present, he could find me powerless on Denebola Base. He couldn't save his team, but he could avenge them.

"Yep. And don't get me wrong, I'm glad he didn't kill you, but I honestly can't blame him for trying."

I understand.

"Yeah, so, look, we want to get as clear a picture of what happened as we can. The Reality Mapping and Time-Tracking divisions would love to know what universe Brock's team met you in, and at what point in the timeline. Brock has no idea. So much of his tech was destroyed in the chaos storm that to get back to the present he basically had to jump into any interdimensional portal or wormhole he could find, and then into the next one he could find, and so on, hoping he'd end up somewhere he could identify before he ended up somewhere he couldn't survive. Which he did, eventually, but it's not the kind of path we can retrace. So our only chance of figuring out where he was is if *you* remember it. I know your memory's got some serious holes in it, but does Brock's story ring a bell?"

I don't know. I've been involved in so many Inquisitions. History repeats itself a lot in ten thousand years. And even the parts of my past I still remember tend to blur together. Maybe if I could see him?

"Seeing you again is the last thing Brock needs."

He doesn't have to know I'm there. I just need to be close enough to look into his memories. Maybe if I could see that city in his mind, it would help me access my own memory of that time.

"Guess it's worth a try," Jackson said. "Let's see if Madaki will let you out of bed yet."

Dr. Madaki agreed to let her leave the hospital under Jackson's supervision for a couple of hours, if she promised not to exert herself. A short time later, after a journey through the corridors of Denebola Base in a wheelchair pushed by a member of Jackson's security force, Bianca was ensconced in a darkened observation room with Jackson beside her. A window of one-way glass offered a view of the brightly-lit interrogation cell where Stanford Brock sat in a chair in front of a metal table, restrained by cuffs built into the armrests. The chair across the table from him was empty; Jackson had instructed her people to leave him alone for a while.

Brock stared straight ahead, stoic and immobile, but his mind raged and boiled and tore at itself. In granting clemency to a monster like Bianca—the very embodiment of the chaos from which they claimed to protect the multiverse—the Reality Patrol had made a mockery of his lifetime of service. The career to which he'd given everything had ended in ignominious betrayal: they'd locked him up like a criminal for doing what should have been done from the start. And they wouldn't even tell him whether his attack had succeeded. After all this, the monster might still not be dead.

His suffering was exquisite. Bianca gave a sigh of pleasure as she drank in the delicious warmth of it, so dark and nourishing and alive.

"You okay?" Jackson asked.

Oh, yes, I'm fine, she said inside Jackson's head. *Just preparing myself. Here I go now.* She closed her eyes, took one more refreshing sip of Brock's pain, and plunged her psychic tendrils into his memory.

There was the city: looming spires of elaborate grey stonework against a dull reddish sky; grim-faced citizens in somber clothes eyeing each other with suspicion as they went fearfully about their business in the shadows of high stone walls and forbidding cathedrals; crowds in the marketplaces parting to make way for priests and officials with jeweled rings on every finger and eyes bloodshot from secret debaucheries; the branded and mutilated bodies of the Inquisition's victims hung on display everywhere, an inescapable spectacle, some still alive and writhing in their slow death-agonies, lips sewn shut to mute their screams.

She couldn't recall this particular city. Her tenure among these bleak stone walls and spires was one of the countless pieces of her history that was lost to her, and seeing the place in Brock's mind did nothing to awaken her own memories of it. She couldn't even guess what universe it was in, much less where it fit into that universe's timeline or her own. It could have been anywhere, in any of those long missing centuries that mocked her with their unyielding blankness.

She found the moment in Brock's memory where he'd watched her past self preside over the torture and execution of the four captured members of his team. The execution was held on a stone stage in front of a towering citadel, at one end of a crowded public square. Brock's rooftop hiding place was too far from the square for him to hear Bianca's voice as she addressed the crowd and directed the masked executioners, but a pair of high-powered binoculars let him see every detail of the proceedings.

The physical form she wore in Brock's memory, with its delicate features and frost-white skin, was the same one she still wore today. It occurred to her that if she'd worn a different form back then, Brock wouldn't have recognized her and wouldn't have tried to kill her on his return to the present. But lloigor were creatures of habit; she'd kept this face and body for more than sixty centuries, as best she could recall, shedding it only for those relatively brief periods when her feeding was better served by impersonating some particular individual or assuming a shape that was much further from human.

The version of herself she saw in Brock's memory still had all her fingers, of course, and when she raised a hand to salute the crowd the sleeve of her black robe slid down to reveal a forearm free of scars. But what Bianca hadn't been prepared for was the way her past self moved. Had her bearing truly been so regal, her stride so bold? The features, magnified by Brock's binoculars, were unmistakably her own—and yet the majestic figure that commanded the stage was impossible to reconcile with the fragile, stoop-shouldered creature whose haunted eyes gazed back at Bianca from the mirror each morning on Denebola Base.

She'd forgotten the grace and confidence with which she'd once carried herself, the raw joyous vitality with which she'd lived for over ten thousand years. She'd mourned her lost powers, her freedom, the violence done to her body—but the grief that twisted inside her now was something new. Until this moment, until she'd looked into Brock's mind and seen herself as she used to be, she hadn't fully understood what her torturers had taken from her.

The solid touch of a hand on her shoulder brought her back to the present. "Are you okay?" Jackson asked.

Bianca felt something wet on her face and realized she was crying. *I'm sorry,* she said in Jackson's head. *Seeing his memory of that city didn't help me remember it myself. I still don't know where it was, or how long ago. I'm sorry I couldn't help you. I'm tired now. Can we go back to the hospital?*

The recreation areas of Denebola Base were home to a wide assortment of bars, clubs, cafes, and restaurants, but the only one Bianca frequented was the Blackstar Lounge, a large quiet establishment lit in dim violet. One entire wall of the Blackstar was transparent from floor to ceiling, a window looking out on a breathtaking starscape. Outside of virtual reality, it was the one place she could go where she didn't feel the weight of claustrophobia pressing in on her.

Two days after Brock's attempt on her life, she sat sipping tea in one of the small semicircular booths that faced directly onto the Blackstar's invisible wall and the grand vista beyond. As always, her body was healing faster than a human's; her throat was still a riot of pale blue bruising, hidden beneath a loosely-wrapped silk scarf, but her voice was working again and her neck and ribs didn't hurt too much as long as she moved carefully.

The virtual reality session she'd missed because of Brock's attack had been rescheduled for later this evening. Soon, for a little while, she could be a hawk again. It had been a hard couple of days, and she was glad to have something nice to look forward to. Starting tomorrow morning she'd be back in her office seeing Meilin and her other patients again, and she was looking forward to that, too.

She sensed someone approaching, and when she turned around she saw it was Jackson.

"Mind if I join you?"

"Please do."

Jackson slid into the booth. "How are you feeling?"

"Much better, thank you."

There was a pause. Jackson seemed to be struggling with something. "You cried," she said. "When you looked into

Brock's memory, you cried."

"Yes." Bianca wondered where this was going.

"Was that remorse? Were you feeling remorse over the things you did back then?"

She'd cried over her own loss, not anything she'd done to anyone else. Remorse wasn't an emotion lloigor were even capable of, as far as she knew. But if Jackson thought Bianca felt bad enough about her past, if she believed Bianca was tormented by guilt over all the suffering she'd caused, maybe Jackson would finally be able to put aside her own feelings about Bianca's history. Maybe they could be friends.

She looked down at the surface of the table. "Yes," she said. "I was a monster. You have every right to hate me." It was ironic, she reflected, that if she actually could feel remorse she might have more qualms about faking it.

She could sense Jackson watching her. She kept her eyes on the table and fought the urge to look into Jackson's mind.

"You really *are* different now, aren't you," Jackson said at last.

"Yes."

"I'm glad. Tears of remorse are a good sign. Can't be easy to face all the stuff you've done, but keep at it. Feel it. That's how to not be a monster."

"You're right," Bianca said. "Thank you."

They sat in silence, looking out into space. After a minute or so, Jackson said, "What would you do if you got all your powers back?"

Bianca thought about the version of herself she'd seen in Brock's memory; the regal beauty she'd had before her captivity, before the interrogators got their hands on her. "I'd reclaim my body," she said. "I'd erase every mark of what was done to me. I'd get rid of every scar. I'd grow back the fingers they took from me, and all the other pieces they took. My vitality, my sense of ease. My dignity. I'd learn to live in this body with grace and confidence and joy again. I'd make it my own again."

She was crying again, just a little. She hadn't meant to speak so frankly, to reveal so much of herself. It had just come spilling out.

Jackson was looking at her in a new way now, her face softer than Bianca had ever seen it. "Wow. That's... not what I expected."

Bianca dabbed at her eyes with a corner of her scarf. Crying always made her throat feel clogged; some tea would help. She was just lifting the cup when a thought came to her.

As far as she knew, and as far as the Reality Patrol knew, her situation was unique. There were no other known instances of lloigor losing their powers as she had. Neither she nor the scientists understood precisely how it had happened. Which meant that there was no way of knowing whether the loss was permanent.

And what she had just told Jackson was true: if she ever did recover her powers, she'd reshape this physical form to make it her own again. She'd make herself look exactly the way she used to. The way she'd looked in Brock's memory.

And people who got swept up in chaos storms were flung through the multiverse and through the timeline at random. Her execution of Brock's team could have happened anywhere, at any point in time.

And yes, there were vast holes in her memory. That was probably why she didn't remember that city where Brock's team had run afoul of her. But there was another possible explanation.

Maybe she didn't remember it because it hadn't happened to her yet.

"Bianca," Jackson said. "Are you okay?"

"What? Oh, yes. Sorry. Just lost in thought."

"Must've been quite the thought. You had the strangest look on your face for a moment."

Bianca took a sip of tea, gazed out at the stars, and smiled. "Oh, it was nothing especially deep," she said. "I was just thinking about how important it is to have something nice to look forward to."

Nick Walker is a queer autistic author, scholar, and educator. When she's not writing disturbing speculative fiction, she's a professor at California Institute of Integral Studies, where she teaches students who are preparing for careers as psychotherapists. Bianca and Jackson previously appeared in Walker's story "Bianca and the Wu-Hernandez," which was published in Spoon Knife 2 and takes place several years before "Something Nice."